DISCOVERED MEMORIES

DISCOVERED MEMORIES

THE DISCOVERED TRUTH SERIES ROMANTIC SUSPENSE
BOOK TWO

JULIE BAWDEN-DAVIS

Roses
ARE
RED
PUBLISHING

Cover by Judy Bullard (customebookcovers.com)

Book design by Jeremy Davis

Palm logo design by Kayla Curry

Roses are Red logo design by Kyle Kane

This is a work of fiction. Characters and incidents are the product of the author's imagination. Any perceived likenesses are coincidental.

ISBN-13: 978-1-7337505-8-5

ISBN-10: 1-7337505-8-4

Distributed by Roses Are Red Publishing

rosesareredpublishing.com

❀ Created with Vellum

ACKNOWLEDGMENTS

As they say, it takes a village. Here's my village. I'm supremely grateful to each of these fabulous people!

ARC Reading Gems
Julie Schlueter
Mandy Stanley
Pros
Judy Bullard, cover design
Kayla Curry, logo design
Kyle Kane, logo design
Sharon Whatley, editing
Sabrina Wildermuth, design consultation
Jeremy Davis, book design

To Sharon and our shared observations, experiences, and obsessions; writing being the greatest obsession of all.

1

Getting hit by a car in La Paz, Mexico would definitely screw up her scoop. After a dented Hyundai careened around the corner, slammed on its brakes and spat gravel in her face, Alexa Kent reluctantly stepped out of oncoming traffic and resumed her post on the edge of the dirt sidewalk. This vantage point didn't give her what she had hoped for. A view of pedestrians heading her way from downtown. More specifically, a view of her informant, who was one minute late and counting.

Humidity clamped down on the nape of her neck, plastering hair to her skin. Grabbing her mane in both hands, she braided a ponytail and let it flop down her back. Stop freaking out, he'll be here, she chided herself. They had worked together for weeks now, and Rodolfo hadn't let her down yet. Tonight, he promised to lead her straight to the traffickers. Good thing, too. In their last phone conversation, her editor had made things clear. Produce a Pulitzer-worthy story yesterday or the newspaper would pull her off investigative reporting and kick her back to the equivalent of journalistic preschool—general features. The thought jerked her anxiety up another notch. Alexa loved being a foreign correspondent. Loved lifting rocks, exposing slimeballs and helping innocent victims. Finding what she expected tonight would cement her status as a foreign correspondent worth noticing.

Finally, Alexa spied Rodolfo Flores approaching and let out a sigh of relief.

Pulling a handkerchief from his pocket as he walked up, her informant mopped his face and neck. "Sorry, *Señorita* Alexa. I was in church lighting a candle."

"Praying about tonight?" Alexa said, immediately sorry when he scowled at her. Truth was, they needed all the help they could get. If Rodolfo's trip to church meant they would finally locate the human sex traffickers she'd been trying to pin down for weeks, why should she complain?

"Let's go," he motioned for her to follow. Together they crossed through the traffic, moving with emerging shadows along a side street of the seaside town. She stayed close to Rodolfo as they passed the familiar aroma of fried tortillas wafting from paper-thin walls of apartment houses and the echoes of doors shutting and locking as dusk draped its gray shawl onto the narrow streets. When they reached an abandoned building, Rodolfo spoke. "My source promises this is the alley where they meet. We'll hide in there." He jerked his head toward a splintered door.

Alexa followed him inside and together they worked the door shut behind them. Flipping open her cell phone and momentarily lighting up the dank passageway, she double-checked the ring status. *Silent.*

"What do you think we'll find?" Alexa whispered.

Rodolfo shrugged his wiry shoulders. "*Señoritas* who know no better? Women thinking they will find riches in America?"

Alexa studied her informant's face in the peppering light coming through the door. How much did she know about this man who she relied on in such a basic way? Why did he so willingly immerse himself in this vile story with her? Money, she decided. The fellow journalist who recommended him said he had a disabled child. Having his family depend on him must anchor him and give him a certain fatalistic calm. Alexa would love some of that, she thought as anxiety at missing out on the scoop thrummed in her head again.

"It's almost eight o'clock," she informed him, pressing her face against the door and peering through a slit that gave her a narrow view of the street.

"They'll be here," Rodolfo replied.

The sentence still hung in the air when a man stopped directly in front of the door and lifted his arm to lean against it. The door crackled under his weight and a wave of sweaty stench reached Alexa's nostrils. Apparently, if you spent your days trafficking women, you didn't have time for niceties like bathing.

Another man arrived seconds later and barked in Spanish, "The boss lady wants a report. She got new ones but wants to know what you found in the barrios."

"I rounded up enough to make her happy. Got 'em cheap."

Scuffling ensued, followed by what sounded like a punch and groan of agony. "You better not be lying like last time, or it will be a knife in your throat, *estúpido*. C'mon, she needs help moving them." Alexa watched the man shove the other toward the curb and tracked them as they slipped into the crowd. She and Rodolfo pushed the door open.

At first, Alexa worried they'd lose them, but one man, his middle bulging from what looked like too many beers and enchiladas, lagged behind the other Mexican. Once the men arrived at the farthest edge of town, they quickly disappeared into a warehouse that teetered on the water's edge near the wharf.

Alexa and Rodolfo ducked into a cantina across the street.

"*Qué pasa?*" asked the owner of the cantina, who smelled of cheap whiskey.

"Keep your mouth shut, *amigo*," said Rodolfo, pulling out twenty *pesos* and waving it at him.

"I see and hear nothing," the old man vowed, lifting gnarled hands before grabbing the money and disappearing into the back of the bar.

The corner of Rodolfo's right eye twitched as he watched the warehouse. Sensing the tension in his body, Alexa knew they would move soon, so she stood ready to run.

"Let's go. Stay low," he instructed.

No time to think, Alexa shadowed Rodolfo as they approached the warehouse. The smell of days old fish weighted the air and loose gravel crunched under her tennis shoes. As a yellow glimmer of light coming from the warehouse window slid across Rodolfo, he halted and jutted his arm out to stop her.

"Quietly," he whispered, moving forward with the padded silence of a cat until they stood just inches from the building. Alexa heard whimpering of what sounded like a young child. "*Quiero mi mamá! Quiero mi mamá!*" the voice quavered in Spanish. Where was the child's mother? Alexa puzzled.

Rodolfo crossed himself. "*Ay, Dios mío!*"

"What is it?" Alexa asked, watching him grip the ledge and pull himself up to peer through the window.

Seconds later, he dropped down to rest on his haunches, eyes wide.

"The women?" she mouthed.

Rodolfo only shook his head and spat in the dirt at his feet.

Turning to stand beneath the dirty panes of glass, she heard another child's cry and a woman yell, "Shut up!"

Alexa searched out Rodolfo's face in the dim light. Something shifted inside her as she probed his eyes, which held a warning. Standing on tiptoe, she looked into the warehouse and gasped when she saw a group of little girls, who looked to be between eight to ten years old, huddled in the center of the drafty, old building clinging to one another. The warehouse doors stood open on the opposite wall, exposing the waterfront and a waiting van. Alexa dropped to her heels and stumbled against the wall for support, the damp stucco crumbling under her palms. Hearing several more children whimper, she bit down on her lip to keep from crying out and slid to the ground next to Rodolfo.

"I—I—don't understand. I expected to see young women."

"The babies make more on the black market." Rodolfo passed his handkerchief over his face with a weary gesture.

"You mean?" she croaked, unsure if the words actually came out.

"*Sí.*"

Pressing her head between her hands, Alexa felt tentacles of helplessness slither over her. "It wasn't supposed to be like this, Rodolfo. Not innocent little children!" Her eyes searched the street. "Surely, there's something we can do."

"You will find no help here."

"We can't let them take those girls away!" she cried.

"What are you going to do *Señorita* Alexa? They have guns, no?"

Alexa struggled to breathe evenly, finally standing up to peer in the dirty window again. Most of the children cried quietly, except for a sobbing girl in a rumpled pink dress, whose hair had been braided with ribbons. Nearby stood a burly man with a goatee and a short, heavyset woman dressed in black polyester pants and an orange blouse. She held a shotgun in her hands and barked orders at several men, who struggled to calm their hostages. The pleas of the girl in the pink dress continued unabated until the woman marched over and slapped her so hard that she fell to the ground several feet away. The violent strike quieted the girl, who curled into a fetal position and hid her face in the folds of her dress.

Alexa clutched her heart. "I can't believe anyone—especially a woman —could be so inhuman," she hissed.

"*Animales,*" Rodolfo replied.

The Mexican woman moved to the doorway next to the wharf and shouted, "Put them in quickly."

Yanked to her feet by one of the men, the little girl in the pink dress stood shaking, her fist pressed into her mouth. When the woman saw her standing there unmoving, she shoved her at the van and ordered, "Watch that one. She's going to be trouble!"

The man with the goatee grumbled and started for the van, but not before glancing back at the window where Alexa stood. For a split second, she looked into his eyes and then ducked, sucked in her breath and waited.

As if on cue, Rodolfo pointed to the cantina. They dashed across the street, slipping inside the bar as two men came around to the front of the building to the spot they had just vacated. Then she heard one of them shout—"Clear!"

Rodolfo's blood coursed with street-smarts invaluable to Alexa. Other foreign correspondents scoffed at how much she paid him—said he wasn't worth what she shelled out. They told Alexa that since she was half-Mexican herself and spoke Spanish that she could blend in and get by on her own. That much was true, but Rodolfo had gotten her out of tight jams many times, and, Alexa felt certain, prevented others from happening in the first place. She knew of reporters caught, tortured, or worse—they disappeared altogether.

"Do you know who they are?" Alexa asked Rodolfo as they made their way back to her hotel.

"I think you got a better look than I did, no?"

"That's true. I saw their faces. I bet they have priors. I'll go into the police station first thing tomorrow and look at mug shots when my contact is there. With all of the corruption, I can't chance telling anyone else."

"Yes, best to be careful about who you talk to," agreed Rodolfo.

They walked on in silence. Alexa wanted to ask about Rodolfo's wife and children, but small talk seemed inappropriate at the moment. Pulsating with cart vendors pushing tacos and paper cups of jicama spears doused with lime and chili powder by day, these same streets had cleared except for rats scrabbling in the shadows, sniffing out trash.

When they arrived at her hotel, she handed him a hundred-dollar bill.

"Thanks, Rodolfo, for once again saving my ass. I mean, butt," she caught herself as he reddened at her choice of words.

"It's my job, *Señorita* Alexa." He motioned to leave, but then hesitated.

Panic zinged through Alexa. Was Rodolfo having a change of heart? Were things getting too dangerous or just downright revolting? She'd never make it without him.

"There is a man who can help. His contacts reach much farther than mine."

Alexa chafed with suspicion. "What man? We can handle this Rodolfo. You haven't let me down yet."

"His name is Macaw," Rodolfo replied.

"Where did this Macaw come from? The trees? Why haven't I heard of him before? And what kind of name is that?"

"Macaw is not his real name."

"Okay, Rodolfo, explain to me why I want to work with a man who is, what? A fugitive? When I'm trying to bring down a ring of vermin traffickers?"

"He is not *Mexicano*. He's Panamanian."

"Once again, why do I care?"

"He is highly thought of and has many connections. Jesse McMillan knows him."

Jesse was the fellow journalist who had turned Alexa on to Rodolfo. He must have worked with Macaw when he wrote his award-winning stories on Panama several years before.

"I trust your and Jesse's judgment," said Alexa, appeasing him. "If you think I should meet Macaw, I'll meet him." She'd only agreed to meet Macaw—not take him on board.

After saying goodbye, Alexa pulled open the doors of *La Cantina Cantata*, the "hotel" she called home when in Mexico. It was actually a combination of five individual rooms for rent atop a restaurant/bar. She walked through the now quiet restaurant and upstairs to what they considered the best room, because it had a telephone and bathroom, the latter of which consisted of a toilet and sink in a narrow closet. She put her keys down on a wooden bureau pockmarked with cigarette burns and pulled open the mini-refrigerator, whose motor whirred steadily in the warm room. Removing a water bottle, she uncapped it and chugged half of it down; then screwed the lid back on and rolled the cool bottle along her neck. She willed herself unsuccessfully to think of anything but those poor little girls. At thirty-three, Alexa was years from girlhood, but not far enough away to forget about her vulnerability at that age.

Once she stripped off her jeans and top and donned her pajamas, Alexa climbed into the narrow bed and grabbed her notebook, making a few cryptic notes on what she and Rodolfo had discovered. Then she lay back and closed her eyes, after a while falling into a restless sleep.

All night long, the kidnapped girls' cries filled Alexa's dreams. The child in the pink dress pulled on Alexa's sleeve, pleading for her mother. Then suddenly, the little girl became Alexa, staring in the mirror in her childhood bedroom. "I want my mama. I want my mama," Alexa said to her own reflection, her heart freezing when a door creaked, and a shadowy outline of a man appeared behind her.

Alexa awoke with a start, sitting up shivering, despite the warm August morning. She pulled her knees to her chest and clasped her hands, assuring herself that the moment would eventually pass and she'd regain control. Inhaling deeply, she exhaled slowly, mentally counting to ten.

When her world seemed steady again, she glanced at the clock. Six o'clock. By the time she sponge-bathed and ate breakfast, it would be after seven and the perfect time to go to the police station. Thank goodness Mexicans were early risers. She couldn't wait to get back to the story.

An hour later, she climbed the steps to the police station, pushed open the black glass doors, and found herself surrounded by the harried atmosphere of cops and complaints, coffee and criminals, citations and warrants. Her editor back home in California had contacts everywhere, and the La Paz Police Station was no exception. Considering the corruption here in Mexico, she needed to know exactly who she could trust.

At the front desk, she asked for Captain Hidalgo, a thin, somber man, who guided her to his corner office, where she explained what she'd seen the night before.

"*Ay, Dios mío,*" he said and shook his head. "You were right to come to me about this. You remember their faces well enough to look through some mug-books?"

"Yes," said Alexa. "I got a good look."

He left the room and returned with mug-books. Two hours, three cups of coffee and twenty mug-books later, she came to the sullen face of the man with the goatee, whom she'd seen the night before. Fernando Gomez. She showed Hidalgo. He nodded and replied, "Wanted for gun and drug smuggling."

"Does he work with a woman?"

"His wife, Imelda Gomez." He pulled out another book and flipped to a page.

Alexa glared at the woman's hard face. Her penetrating eyes held Alexa's gaze for a moment.

"That's them."

"I will have my men look for them and the little girls, but our resources are limited, and the Gomezes are known for eluding capture," he told Alexa. "You find them. We will lock them up. And the chief will be very happy."

"I'll find them."

The officer hesitated, as if sizing her up. She must have passed, because he closed the door. "There is an *hombre* who can help you. His name is Macaw. He owns the Miramar Bar."

"This Macaw must be some guy. That's the second time in twenty-four hours I've heard the name."

"You will be glad if you talk to him," said Hidalgo.

After getting a printout on the two criminals, Alexa made her way to the Miramar, putting in a quick call to Jesse McMillan as she walked. On assignment, he couldn't talk long, but assured her that a visit to Macaw would be worth it. "We grew up together," said Jesse. "His real name is Sam Elvia, but that's just between you and me."

The bar sat on the waterfront in a tourist area. An intoxicating aroma of beef, onion, and garlic floated on the ocean breeze and greeted her at the door. Wrought iron cocktail tables and chairs were crammed into the room, and a red and royal blue mosaic tile bar held center stage. The place was empty except for a bartender, who stood drying beer mugs. Alexa took another whiff of the tempting delicacy and felt her stomach rumble, realizing that it'd been awhile since breakfast.

"What smells so good?" she asked the bartender.

"The best damn *empanadas* you'll ever eat," said a male voice behind her.

Alexa swung around. Her eyes fell on a brawny guy in a tank top. Was this Macaw? Black hair, creamy brown skin. Not Mexican. Too tall and muscular, and he sounded American. Her heart sped up.

"I'll try one," she said.

He cruised behind the bar and pulled a steaming *empanada* from a warmer and plopped it onto a paper plate. Sliding it toward her, he swept over her body with his dark brown eyes and then kept them glued to hers as he motioned toward the salsa to her left with his head. She spied the macaw tattoo on his upper arm, suddenly feeling tongue-tied.

"So what's an attractive babe like you doing here?"

"Looking for Macaw," she managed to get out, while leaning for the hot sauce.

His jaw visibly tightened. "Who's looking?"

"Me," she said, dashing red peppery liquid onto her plate.

"Does Macaw know you?"

"He knows Rodolfo Flores, my *compadre*." Her mouth watered as she reached for the *empanada*.

"Good friends are hard to come by."

"I have another friend, Jesse McMillan."

Before she could take the first bite, he grabbed her wrist. "Follow me. Now."

He led her into a small office. On top of a wooden desk sat a calculator and miniature palm tree. Prominently displayed on the wall hung a framed *mola* that read Panama.

Macaw let go of her wrist and closed the door. "You know Jesse McMillan?" he said, propping his large frame on the edge of the desk and pushing a folding chair her way with his foot.

Alexa remained standing. "He told me about you. Said I should look you up, if I could."

"That asshole is the reason I'm in this shit-hole."

"I didn't know," Alexa answered, wondering if he meant Mexico or this bar in particular. "He did say that you might be pissed off at him."

"That's an understatement. So, how is he?"

"He's a star reporter now."

"Thanks to me," said Macaw wryly, gripping the edge of the desk.

As she watched his forearms bulge with tension, Alexa felt a rush of warmth and forced herself to look away. This story was much more important than some guy's beefy arms, no matter how well toned.

"You were involved in Jesse's story, weren't you?" she asked.

"You could say so."

"You helped take down Gonzales."

"Don't say that name around here," Macaw growled, jumping up, his face just inches from hers. Alexa stood her ground as he demanded, "What's really going on here? You've got thirty seconds to tell me who you are and what you want—and I better believe it."

Alexa bristled. "My name is Alexa Kent. I'm a foreign correspondent from San Diego, and I'm working on a story that involves children."

"Kids on drugs? Old story." He backed away.

"Smuggling little girls for prostitution."

"Shit," Macaw said in disgust, sitting back down on the edge of his desk. "Only the worst kinds get into that."

"Then help me find them and stop them."

"Who you looking for?"

"Fernando and Imelda Gomez."

The names seemed to stop him in his tracks for a second.

"So those assholes have switched products," said Macaw. "No surprise, I guess. Too many players in arms and drug smuggling. I always wondered if Fernando was a pervert, and Imelda is a full-fledged greedy bitch."

"You know them?"

"We moved merchandise together for a nanosecond when I first got here, until I figured Imelda out. I told her to take a hike, and this was her answer," said Macaw, running his hand along a scar from his cheekbone to his chin. "She's psycho."

Alexa felt a crazy urge to trace the scar with her fingertip. Had run-ins with danger made her *loco*? She struggled to refocus and asked, "Do you know where they are now? I tracked them to a warehouse on the southeast side of town last night, but they cleared out of there quick."

Macaw raised his eyebrows. "The southeast side? You have a death wish or something?"

"Or something."

"Give me a couple of days, and I'll see what I can find out."

"Thanks. I can use all of the help I can get," Alexa said. "By the way, Jesse says hi."

Macaw snorted. "What else he have to say?"

"That you're a cool guy, but you think you're hot stuff."

Macaw smiled for the first time and a guttural laugh lit up his face, almost hiding the scar. "What are you, anyway? American? Mexican?" Macaw asked.

"Mexican and American."

"I'm a mutt, too. Panamanian and Italian, but I grew up with a bunch of Americans in the Canal Zone."

"It sucks sometimes, not knowing where you belong." Her last sentence surprised her as it slipped out.

He nodded and put an end to their meeting. "I'll be in touch. Where you staying?"

"*La Cantina Cantata.*"

"I'll get back to you soon," he told her as she walked out of his office. "Don't forget your *empanada.* And the next time you talk to Jesse McMillan, tell him he's an asshole." The door shut firmly behind her, and Alexa felt oddly disappointed.

She wasn't his usual type, but damn, she was hot. Not like the booby bimbos who came into the bar clawing at him, or the prim schoolgirl types he considered loosening up. He'd been around the block enough times to know that most women wanted someone to save them from themselves. This chick had something Macaw didn't see much in a woman, and that was a combination of brains and balls. Not that, what was her name again? Alexis? wasn't endowed and had some killer legs. She wanted his help for something good. It'd been awhile since someone wanted him for a good deed—way too long.

Initially, he said he'd look into finding the Gomezes just to shut her up and get her out of his office. Maybe he was getting soft hiding out here in Mexico, but something about her made him rethink. He could easily find those two wackos, and it'd be sheer pleasure to shut them down—especially considering what they were up to now. Picking up the phone, he began contacting his sources.

Alexa walked back to her hotel munching on the *empanada*. The smoldering combination of savory beef, tomato sauce and garlic and onion, offset by just the right amount of sweet currants, lingered in her mouth as Macaw lingered in her mind's eye.

When she made her way upstairs to her room, she heard the phone in her room ringing. Sprinting up the last few steps, she unlocked her door and ran to answer. "This is Alexa Kent."

"Heavy breathing. Caught you at a bad time?" It was Macaw.

"No, it's okay. I just sent my three boyfriends packing."

Macaw laughed. "Quick thinking. I like that. Now down to business. I just talked to someone who knows a family who sent their little girl away to become a movie star five days ago and haven't heard anything since."

Alexa caught her breath. "How old is she? Do you think—"

"She's ten. What else could it be? I'll take you to visit the parents tomorrow morning."

"No offense, and thanks for the lead, but I work alone. Just give me their address."

"I'll pick you up at nine o'clock. You want to make the Garcias comfortable, so wear something conservative, like a skirt," he replied, hanging up the phone.

She put down the phone and realized her heart pounded. Was it racing up the stairs, the scoop or seeing Macaw again?

The *mariachi* band in the cantina below suddenly blasted their horns and *guitarrónes*. Four o'clock. Happy hour. Alexa went to her window and gazed out as the black, red, and white clad band filed into the street, their oversized guitars creating a loud, pulsating beat. One *mariachi* began to sing full-force, belting out a song about love gone awry.

The music conjured up a memory that always left her with an empty ache at the pit of her stomach.

"What are you reading Alexa?"

"A map of the world, Papa. This is where I want to go when I'm grown-up," she said, pointing to Mexico in her geography book. "Where Mama was born. Tell me about her again, please."

"Your mama was beautiful, just like you. She had the same long black hair you do, and the same pretty brown eyes. And boy could she sing."

"What did she sing?"

"I didn't understand the words, but they were beautiful Spanish songs."

"You don't remember just a little bit? Not even a line?"

"I'm sorry, Lexie," her father apologized, patting her head. "I have to check the avocado trees now. They're predicting a frost tonight. Do your homework, little one."

Alexa looked at the map again, her lower lip and chin trembling as she whispered to herself, "I wish I could hear her sing. Just once, I wish I could hear Mama sing."

Alexa opened the hotel window and leaned out for a good view of the *mariachi* band members, who always impressed her with how effortlessly they strummed their instruments while singing with such gusto. When they looked up and spotted her, Carlos, the band's leader, began singing about a beautiful woman.

"*Hola Carlos, Mario, Mateo y Felipe! Arriba Mexico!*" Alexa cried out as she clapped at their serenade.

The phone rang the next morning before breakfast.

"Is this Alexa Kent?" an American woman asked in English.

"Yes, who's calling?"

"This is Nurse Kincaid from Mercy Hospital in San Diego. I'm calling about your father. He's okay, but he had a stroke."

Alarm shot through Alexa. "I talked to him last week. He seemed all right then."

"It came on suddenly, as strokes do. Dr. Smythe will update you on your father's condition."

The nurse put Alexa on hold. How could her father—one of the strongest people she knew—be in the hospital? Certainly, it was a terrible mistake. He should be tending the avocado ranch in Fallbrook, California now, checking irrigation lines and calculating the coming harvest.

Finally, a jovial voice came on the line. "Miss Kent, this is Dr. Smythe. You are one difficult lady to get a hold of!"

Considering his upbeat attitude, things couldn't be all that bad, thought Alexa.

"Sorry about that, Dr. Smythe. I'm on assignment in Mexico, and communication can be difficult. I guess you got my number from my father?"

"Yes. He's really proud of you. A foreign correspondent! Wow."

Her father was talking, so that was a good sign. "He had a stroke?"

"Yes, a mild one. His right arm is paralyzed, but his mind seems to be functioning just fine."

"Is the paralysis permanent?"

"We can't be sure at this point. Only time will tell. My guess is that it won't be permanent—this time."

"This time?"

"Your father should be on high blood pressure medication, Miss Kent. The stroke occurred because of an untreated condition. If he doesn't begin taking medication right away, the next stroke is likely to do much more damage."

"So what's the problem?" Alexa asked the question but knew the answer.

"He's refusing medication."

"I had a feeling you'd say that. He can be so stubborn."

"His stubbornness could cost him his life, or make him an invalid. I'm hoping you might be able to talk some sense into him. He'll be in the hospital for a few more days, during which time I can keep him medicated and monitored. Once he leaves, though, he'll need full-time care for a while."

"I can probably come home for a little while when he's released and get things settled for him," she said.

"Wonderful! Why don't I call you when he's ready to be released? I'm sure your father will be pleased that you're coming home."

Alexa shook her head as she hung up the phone. How could she possibly leave Mexico when those poor little girls' lives hung in the balance? On the other hand, as her father's only child, how could she not go home?

She jumped when the phone rang for the second time that day.

"Alexa Kent speaking."

"Lex? Can you hear me?" It was Peter Landry, Alexa's editor.

"Yes, I can hear you."

"How's it going? I didn't get an email from you yesterday. Everything okay?"

"Sorry, I didn't check in. Everything's moving along great. I got a fantastic lead and uncovered some explosive information. It looks like the victims are much younger than I originally thought—only eight to ten years old."

"Wow! That is big news. And really unsettling. I hate to sound crass, but when can I expect some preliminary copy?"

"Soon. I've got something to check out today."

"Sounds great," said Peter. "So why don't you sound so great? The story wearing you down?"

"Yes, that, and my dad. He had a stroke. They want me to come home for a few days."

"Jeez! I'm sorry, Alexa."

"The timing sucks. I'm not sure what to do."

"What can you do? He's your dad."

"The doctor's supposed to call me when he's ready to be released. I'll let you know."

"In the meantime, do you want me to send Michael?"

"No!" Alexa almost shouted at the thought of her rival marching in and mucking about in her story.

Peter sighed. "Look, Alexa, don't make me pull rank on you. This is the trickiest situation you've ever been in. Considering what these people are doing, I think a male influence would be good at this point. Michael can keep an eye on things when you visit your dad."

"Besides Rodolfo, I have a new source. He came highly recommended by Jesse McMillan at the *Times*," Alexa reassured Peter. "He definitely knows his way around here and even briefly worked with my targets." Alexa pictured Macaw and the excitement of seeing him again rushed through her.

Peter hesitated. "Alexa, are you absolutely sure you're secure there?"

"Totally safe, chief, don't worry. I'm in good hands."

"Okay. I guess it makes more sense to team up with someone who knows the lay of the land. Just keep me posted."

"I always do."

Peter changed the subject, sounding more like a therapist than a boss. "Relax. Have a margarita after work today."

"Is that an order?"

"Definitely. And don't call me chief."

Too bad she only felt friendship for Peter, Alexa thought wistfully as she hung up the telephone. He was the perfect guy. Thoughtful, intelligent, insightful, even good looking, but no electricity flew between them; only a solid friendship, despite his occasional attempts to make it more. Probably better anyway, because she'd have to get a different boss, and Peter was one terrific editor.

Alexa dressed in a skirt and blouse and went downstairs to order her usual scrambled eggs and toast. When she knocked the newspaper she was reading to the floor and leaned over to pick it up, Macaw's tanned feet and leather flip flops appeared before her.

"That's all a bunch of manufactured bullshit," he said of the newspaper. "No point in reading it. But I like the view down your shirt."

"There is a point in reading it if you're also writing a bunch of manufactured bullshit," said Alexa, blushing at his comment about the sneak peek of her chest.

"You're a fast one," he said, taking a seat across from her.

"I guess being fast is a way of life in your line of work."

"What is my line of work? What did Jesse McMillan tell you?" Macaw wore tight-fitting jeans and an emerald green T-shirt that accented his pecs.

Alexa shrugged. "He wasn't clear, but he implied…."

"Implied what?"

"A little extortion here, a little money laundering there, and throw in a drug run or two."

Macaw smiled. "The good old days. You're sexy when you talk like that."

"And when I don't talk like that?"

"Still sexy."

Alexa's faced heated up as Macaw eyed her. She felt him mentally removing her clothing, one piece at a time. She couldn't remember the last time she welcomed a man looking at her that way. Flirting with someone in the underworld wasn't in her job description, though. Time to get down to business.

"Let's eat and go visit the Garcias," she said.

"I already ate."

"Okay, watch me eat, and then we'll go."

"If you insist."

What was it about him? Alexa wondered as she tasted her scrambled eggs. Good looking, absolutely, but that didn't usually faze her. Definitely not the nicest guy in the world. Certainly not successful in the traditional sense. She had to stop thinking about what he looked like without a shirt and concentrate on the matter at hand.

After she ate, they headed out onto the dusty street.

"I presume that's your car?" said Alexa, nodding at a red MG.

"You presume correctly. Hop in."

Alexa reached for the passenger door of the two-seater and pulled with no luck as Macaw stood behind her and laughed.

"The door's stuck."

"Literally—hop in."

Alexa turned to him. "So is this why you wanted me to wear a skirt? Not because the Garcias are traditional."

"The Garcias are traditional. Me, not so much," he said, suppressing a smile.

Two can play this game, Alexa thought as she marched to the driver's side, yanked the door open, and climbed across and into the passenger's side.

Macaw shook his head and got in beside her. "Not as good of a show as it would have been."

"Just drive, will you."

Macaw maneuvered his car into the flow of traffic, heading west on *16 de Septiembre* Road. His MG inched forward on the narrow street that bustled with vendors selling everything from T-shirts and marble chess

19

sets, to cheap costume jewelry that Alexa knew from experience turned your skin green.

When other more direct routes to the Garcia's *pueblo* came to mind, Alexa opened her mouth to speak, but Macaw answered her question when he stopped the car and jumped out. "I'll be right back."

He approached an old man, who flew out reedy arms in greeting, and Alexa gasped when she saw Macaw pull cash from his pocket in exchange for a brown paper bag. He couldn't be doing a drug deal!

Macaw returned to the car and dropped the bag in her lap.

"Do I want to know what this is?" she asked.

"I thought it might be nice to give the other Garcia kids something. They live in a barrio, so there's a real good chance they've never even seen a toy—cheap or otherwise. That was Eduardo, one of my street sources. I like to check in with him."

Relief gave way to a smile when Alexa uncrinkled the paper bag and peered in to find an array of wooden maracas, yo-yos and spinning tops.

Once he drove onto a less crowded street, they made better time getting to the western outskirts of town. A Mexican pop tune broadcasting from tinny radio speakers greeted them as Macaw shut off the MG in the *pueblo's* town square, which consisted of a set of lean-tos made of scrap wood. One looked to be the town's grocery store, while the other offered pharmaceuticals and liquor.

When they stopped, Macaw got out and waited for her to exit on his side.

"I guess you don't worry about somebody doing something to your car?" she asked as they headed down a dirt path.

"Why do you say that?"

"You just leave it there unlocked?"

Macaw laughed. "There's nothing in it to steal. And if they take the car, they won't go far. My worst problem would be if it rained."

"You can bet they'll get in and goof around."

"No, they won't. They know my car."

Soon they came to a row of crude adobe buildings. In the open-air kitchen of one shelter, a pregnant woman molded corn tortillas from *masa.* With quick fingers, she fashioned the dough into near-perfect, flat circles and flung them onto a charred metal rack that hung over a fire-pit.

Around her ran children, laughing and taunting one another.

"*Cuidado!*" she cautioned one small boy when he toddled close to the fire.

As Alexa and Macaw approached, the woman turned to them and frowned. Flinging one long braid over her shoulder, she asked them if they were looking for someone. "*Ustedes buscan a alguien?*"

Macaw replied in Spanish, "We're looking for *Señora* Garcia."

"I am *Señora* Elvita Rodriguez Garcia."

"We've come about your daughter, Liana," Alexa said.

"Liana! You have found my baby?" the woman's eyes lit up.

"No, but we're going to try," said Alexa.

"Who are you?"

Alexa began to introduce herself, but Macaw stopped her. "We're interested friends."

"*Juan! Ven,*" the woman called. "*Rápido!*"

A slight, middle-aged man emerged from the adobe structure, rubbing his eyes.

"My husband harvested corn in the early morning," she apologized. "He came in for lunch and a *siesta.*" She introduced Alexa and Macaw.

"I didn't want to send our Liana to America," he said. "But my wife, she thought it was a good idea."

Tears sprang to Elvita's eyes. "I just wanted something beautiful for Liana, and the money helped so much. The horrible moth worm caused the nopal crops to do poorly for two years."

Juan scowled at his wife. "There are other ways to make money."

"But she promised so many beautiful things for Liana! She said my baby would have a wonderful life." The woman began sobbing.

Alexa covered Elvita's hand with her own. "*Señora* Garcia. Don't blame yourself. You did what you thought was right. I'm here to help. Please tell me everything that happened."

Macaw gave the women some space, walking over to stand next to

Juan, who gazed out at his crops of corn and *Opuntia* cactus used to make nopal.

Elvita's crying subsided. "Thank you, *Señorita*. You are very kind. I will help any way I can."

Alexa pulled the mug-shots out of her purse and handed them to Elvita. "You can start by telling me if you've seen these people before."

"That's her!" Elvita cried, pointing a lean finger at Imelda's head.

"Is that the woman who took your daughter?"

"Yes, she said she would make Liana a big movie star. She showed me pictures of beautiful little girls. And she promised that Liana would come back home to visit."

"I need you to tell me exactly what happened," said Alexa. "Please try to remember everything she said. How did she first approach you?"

"I was here cooking the lunch when she came. Juan was having his *siesta*."

"Was there anyone with her?"

"Yes, a girl in a pretty, bright yellow dress. It looked like the sun."

"How old was the girl?" Alexa asked.

"The same age as Liana. Ten."

"What else did the woman say?"

"She was very kind. She said that it must be hard to be pregnant and to cook outdoors, and wouldn't it be nice if I had a real home like they have in America with an indoor kitchen and heat," remembered Elvita. "I told her I can barely feed my seven children, and with another baby on the way, how would I ever have a better house? She promised she could help me."

Alexa nodded, encouraging Elvita to go on.

"The woman said that the young girl with her was a movie star in the United States—that she had made her one, and that she had come from a poor *pueblo* just like this one."

"Did the little girl say anything?" asked Alexa.

"No. She waited in the car after we met her. She looked so beautiful."

"You send our daughter away, because someone is beautiful,"

commented Juan. He shook his head and continued to look out at his crops.

Elvita started crying again. "The lady had so much money, and we must feed our children. She promised that Liana would get out of this life —that she would live in a real home with her own bed, and she could send us money every month. I didn't want Liana to go, but if it meant a better life for all of us. . . ." she trailed off and wiped her eyes with the hem of her tattered brown skirt.

Alexa patted Elvita's shoulder. "*Señora,* please think. Was there anything else the woman said? Anything that might help us find Liana?"

Elvita concentrated, her deeply tanned forehead wrinkling with remorse. "What did she say? What did she say?" she muttered.

"I remember something," said Juan. "She said that they would go to California—to a place where the movie stars lived. There, she said, Liana would have a better life."

"That helps," said Alexa, more to make them feel better than anything else. Most likely the girls were still in Mexico somewhere. It would be too difficult to get them across the border into the US.

"We are going to try very hard to locate your daughter," Alexa reassured them.

"*Gracias,*" said Elvita. "You are an angel from Heaven. God will bless you."

Before they left, Macaw handed out the toys. As the children played with the trinkets, Alexa took photos of them and their parents to accompany the article when she wrote it.

On their way back to *La Cantina Cantata,* Macaw and Alexa discussed their next move.

"Do you really think you can find the Gomezes?" she asked him.

"No problem. I've got the word out now—should be hearing something any minute."

"You work fast."

He eyed her carefully. "Not always. Sometimes I prefer to take my time."

Alexa blushed for what was probably the fiftieth time since she met him.

"Good to know," she said as he pulled up in front of her hotel.

"Right now," he added, "I'm thinking how we need to stop those sickos."

"How? We can't just walk up and ask them to hand over the girls." Alexa felt stumped for the first time since the investigation started.

"Yeah, we can. If they think we want them for something."

Alexa's stomach churned as she asked, "What do you mean?"

"You know what I mean. Can you come up with a lot of cash fast?"

"Yeah, by tomorrow."

"Perfect," said Macaw as he answered a call on his cell phone. "*Qué pasó?*" After listening intently, he barked out a string of orders in Spanish and then snapped the phone shut.

"I gotta go. Tomorrow?"

"Yes," said Alexa, feeling suddenly let down by Macaw's need to leave so quickly. "I don't know how I can thank you for today."

Macaw went around to her side of the car. With one quick movement, he lifted her out and set her on the sidewalk. "I'll give you step-by-step instructions on how to thank me the next time I see you."

Before she could reply, he jumped in his car and sped off.

As she walked through the doors of *La Cantina Cantata*, Alexa felt a burning sensation where his hands had just been. Absently rubbing her arms, she wearily climbed to her room and kicked off her shoes. Removing an orange juice from the refrigerator, she sat down by the window and thought about her meeting with the Garcias.

There, imprisoned in a barrio, a woman who had unwittingly sacrificed her first-born daughter for a year's worth of groceries felt certain that God would bestow blessings on Alexa. How did someone muster such faith? Did it come from church and knowing God? When Alexa's mother was alive, they attended a Catholic church in San Diego. Once she died, though, her father quit going, and Alexa really missed it. For some time, she coaxed him to take her to church, until he finally relented and agreed to drop her off at a local Presbyterian Church for

Sunday school. Those lessons opened up a whole new world for Alexa, who had only heard about Jesus and God when her mother worked the beads of her rosary or said Alexa's bedtime prayers. During those Sunday school lessons, Alexa felt a comforting connection to her mother.

But one important Sunday morning, her father had to go out of town.

"I'm supposed to get my Bible today, Papa! The teacher is giving them to everyone who learned the names of the New Testament," Alexa had protested. "Can't you go tomorrow?"

"No, little one, I can't, but Uncle Freddy has agreed to take you."

"Uncle Freddy! No, I want you!"

"You either go with Uncle Freddy, or you don't go at all."

Alexa weighed her options. She hated her father's brother and wished he'd never moved in with them when Mama died. If he took her to Sunday school, though, she'd spend less time with him overall. Maybe it would be a good idea.

The next morning Uncle Freddy sulked as he drove her to church. Considering that he stumbled in really late the night before after spending hours in the bar, she counted herself lucky to be going at all.

When he dropped her off and promised to return in an hour, Alexa bounced into the classroom and easily recited all of the names of the books in the New Testament. Her teacher rewarded her with her own little pink Bible. Alexa flipped it open and smiled when she read the inscription on the inside cover: *"Alexa, what a pleasure it has been seeing you blossom in the word of the Lord. Always remember that He is there for you. And never forget to pray."*

She even looked forward to showing Uncle Freddy her reward, but he didn't show up on time. Eventually, all of the children left, and she sat alone with her teacher.

"Do you suppose something has detained your father, dear? He's always so punctual," asked Mrs. Connor.

"My father had to go out of town this morning. My Uncle Freddy is supposed to pick me up."

"I wonder if he might be confused about the time?"

Alexa didn't reply.

"It's okay. My husband and I don't have any plans today," said the teacher. "We'll just wait for him."

Uncle Freddy swaggered into the classroom an hour later. Considering his tardiness, Alexa guessed he'd been drinking, so she thanked her teacher and bolted for the door.

"Hold on there, Missy," he said, grabbing her arm as she attempted to pass him. "I want to have a little talk with your teacher and see how you're doing."

"I'm doing fine, Uncle Freddy. I got my Bible, see," she said, holding it up. "You're late. She doesn't have time to talk right now."

"No time to talk to the likes of me?" he said, turning to Mrs. Connor.

"I'll be happy to answer any questions you might have, Mr. Kent."

"So my little niece here is pretty smart, huh?"

"Yes, she's a very bright girl."

"She takes after my brother, Tom," said Freddy, leaning precariously on the edge of a desk. "He's the book-smart one. Me, I like getting out and experiencing the action." He gave Mrs. Connor a wide grin.

Alexa hated how he became a stupid show-off when he drank. "Uncle Freddy, Mrs. Connor has to go home now. Her husband is waiting for her," said Alexa.

Freddy straightened up at Alexa's remark, pushing the desk back several inches. "Alexa, you didn't tell me your pretty teacher is married."

"I'm afraid I am, and my husband is waiting on lunch for me," said Mrs. Connor. She started to straighten up her desk.

"You're afraid? How come?"

"That's just an expression, Mr. Kent," Mrs. Connor appeared flustered. "I should really lock up now."

But Uncle Freddy didn't move, and Alexa felt the floor swallowing her up.

"I must get going," Mrs. Connor repeated.

Freddy stood there for a few seconds longer and then guffawed. "You have a nice day. Sorry I was late."

"No problem. You have a nice day, too, Mr. Kent," said Mrs. Connor.

On the way home, Freddy brooded, muttering obscenities under his breath, but Alexa barely noticed. Mortified about what happened, she vowed never to go back again, and she didn't. Mrs. Connor called several times and urged her to return, but Alexa just couldn't face her.

Getting up from the chair next to the hotel window, Alexa went to a portion of the wall where she had loosened the wallpaper. Carefully pulling the paper away, she extracted what she wanted. Her mother's rosary beads. Then, for the first time in a long time, Alexa bowed her head and prayed for Liana and all of the little girls.

3

Macaw sat behind the wheel of his MG in a back alley of one of La Paz's meanest streets wondering what the hell he was doing. Here he sat scoping out a building looking for Imelda when he should be setting up deliveries and ordering booze for the bar. All because some chick asked him to. He'd managed to reach thirty-four years old without getting himself seriously mixed up with anyone. Way too many complications. Like now. He ought to drive away and just forget about Alexa. Except he couldn't stop thinking about her. And he hated what Imelda and Fernando were up to.

Someone opened the door of the warehouse he'd been eyeing for the last half hour, and Macaw let out a low whistle. There the bitch emerged, in all her greedy glory, and Fernando stood next to her. After they shook hands with a tall American-looking guy Macaw didn't recognize and the stranger slipped back inside the warehouse, Imelda began yelling at Fernando. Back when they all worked together, Macaw seriously considered getting earplugs. Imelda screamed at the dumb bastard constantly. He almost felt bad for the guy, but was pretty sure Fernando liked the young girls and that made him want to bash the pervert's face in. All the more reason he should stick with this and help Alexa out.

After she finished railing him, Imelda stormed around back of the building and Fernando followed. Only one way out of the rear parking lot —right onto the street. Macaw would watch them exit in whatever car they'd recently stolen, stripped and added fake plates to. And then he'd follow.

Alexa received a green light from Peter for a good-sized lump of cash that he wire transferred to the local bank. As soon as she got word, she ran out the door. The Mexican government sometimes swooped in and cleared out accounts for "tax" purposes, and she didn't want that to happen. Better to get the money before too many authorities had been notified.

As she headed to the bank just blocks from her hotel, the heady, unmistakable aroma of *churros* wafted toward her.

"Only fifty cents, lady," said a young boy, sticking the cinnamon-sugar pastry out at her as she approached.

"They smell wonderful," said Alexa, looking at the boy, who appeared to be just seven or eight years old.

"Only fifty cents. You buy four?"

Obviously, he had a quota of two dollars from Alexa.

"I just want one."

"Two?"

"How about one, and I'll pay you for four?"

That put a wide grin on his face. He placed the *churro* in her hand and held out his other palm for the money.

Continuing on to the bank, Alexa bit into the *churro* and immediately found herself transported back in time to her kitchen in Fallbrook.

Mama made *churros*, kneading the dough that slowly rose all morning long. Alexa, about five at the time, sat at the kitchen island, watching her press and turn the dough.

"Can I try it, Mama? Please!"

"Of course, *mija*," her mother said, using the term of affection that combined my and daughter. "Watch closely and then it will be your turn."

Her mama leaned in and pushed the dough forward, then wrapped the two sides, pushed in again and continued.

"I saw, Mama. I know how," said Alexa, reaching over the counter and grabbing the dough, which flopped in her hand and landed on the island in a loose mound. As she buried her hands in the dough, Alexa giggled. "It feels like fluffy clay!"

Alexa's mama laughed, too, a high-pitched, tinkling sound that warmed Alexa inside and out.

By the time she reached the bank, Alexa finished the *churro*. Brushing the sugar off her fingertips, she pushed open the heavy glass doors and stepped inside. The rush of cool air came as a welcome relief. Now for the matter at hand—get the money quickly, without attracting too much attention. She knew Rodolfo or Macaw should have come with her to withdraw this much money. But there was no changing that now.

At the counter that protected the tellers with bulletproof glass, Alexa slid a written request through the cubbyhole in the window. She found the less said aloud the better. Reviewing the wire order pick-up, the teller, a pert girl in her early twenties, excused herself and walked to the back of the office. For several minutes, she talked with what appeared to be the manager, who glanced up at Alexa several times during their conversation. When he rose and walked toward her, Alexa prepared to recite her cover story.

"*Buenos días, Señorita* Kent. I am Carlos Rollo. Manager of the bank."

"*Buenos días, Señor* Rollo."

"You have a good stay in our country, yes?"

"Yes, it is a beautiful country."

"You do many fun things, yes?"

Out of politeness, Mexicans rarely get to the point. Knowing that she could endure this circular conversation for the next ten minutes, Alexa decided to satisfy the bank manager's curiosity and tell him what she planned to do with the money—or at least her official story.

"*Señor* Rollo, I am a journalist. My work sometimes necessitates that I travel into the countryside, so I was thinking about buying a car."

"Ah," said Rollo. "A *carro*, eh? A very nice car?"

Alexa grew irritated. It was her frigging money, and she wanted it now before anyone else noticed. She remained polite, though, and decided to change tactics.

"Yes, *Señor* Rollo. A very nice car. Perhaps I will take you for a drive sometime?"

Señor Rollo's plump face reddened at her forward comment and he laughed, but his eyes turned to steel at her insolence. "Have a good time with your new *carro, Señorita* Kent. *Hasta Luego*." Rollo bowed slightly, gave a hand signal to the teller to release the money and then returned to his desk where Alexa saw him pick up the phone.

After the teller slowly counted out the money, Alexa grabbed the wad, stuffed it deep in her front pant pocket and headed back to the hotel, checking behind and around her the whole time. No apparent tails, but you never knew. Rollo's phone call made her nervous.

When the hotel loomed in front of her, Alexa gave a sigh of relief, but it appeared to be a little early. As she checked both sides of the street before crossing, a car pulled up next to her, and her nerve endings sounded alarms. Two men sat in the car, and Alexa looked directly at the driver, who glared at her as his passenger moved to get out. Her heart thumping in her ears, Alexa started to bolt when a car tore up behind them. Relief rushed through her whole body as Macaw braked and hopped out. When the driver saw him, he signaled to his companion and pulled away from the curb with the passenger door still open.

"What was that all about? They following you?" Macaw grabbed her arm and directed her inside the hotel.

"I didn't see them until they pulled up right next to me just before you came. They were either going to grab me or the money, or both. I just got back from the bank. And before you tell me I should have waited for you, don't."

"You ever seen them before?" Macaw asked her.

"No, you?"

"I didn't get a good enough look. You'll have to describe them to me, and I'll do a sketch."

"You can sketch?"

Macaw nodded. "It's a hobby of mine. And I'm pretty good at it."

Once in her room, he asked, "Before we talk about your stalkers, did you get a lot of cash?"

"Yeah," said Alexa, who went to the mini-fridge and opened it. "Want a beer?"

"Sure."

She removed the cap and handed him a Tecate. "Will eight grand do?"

"Nicely. I found Imelda and Fernando."

"You did! Great! When can we go?"

"After you agree to something."

"What?"

"Eat dinner with me tonight."

"We can go out whenever you want. Just point me to the Gomezes."

"That the only reason you're agreeing to go out with me?"

"What do you think?" She smiled.

"You're the investigative reporter. You tell me."

"So, when can we go see the Gomezes?"

"Changing the subject now? We can go tomorrow. Today I want to get those sketches done."

Alexa removed a sketch pad from her bureau and handed it to Macaw, along with a pencil. He flipped it open to a drawing of an avocado tree.

"You sketch, too?"

"Only nature. I've never been able to master people. My forte is really writing."

"Yeah, I know. I read a bunch of your stuff."

"Where?"

"I Googled you."

Alexa frowned.

"What's the look?" asked Macaw. "I can read."

"No, it's not that," Alexa said, flustered.

"What is it, then?"

"I just, you...I didn't know you were that interested." She felt exposed.

"I'm interested in everything about you," Macaw said, leaning in close to her. "Writing tells a lot about a person—even if it's writing about other people."

Squirming under his scrutiny, which had sped up her heart, Alexa changed the subject. "Let me tell you about those guys while they're fresh in my mind."

Macaw spent a good thirty minutes drawing the men Alexa described, including the driver's scruffy beard.

"Are they looking like anyone you've seen before?" she asked hopefully.

"Maybe. I'm going to circulate this around and see what I can find out." Macaw motioned to leave and then stopped. "Why don't you give me the cash for safe-keeping?"

Alexa hesitated.

"I'm not going anywhere with it. But if those guys come back, you can bet they'll take it."

He had a point, Alexa thought. What other recourse did she have? Either the goons would rip the money out of her hands, or Macaw would disappear with every last dollar. Best to go out on a limb, hedging her bets with Macaw. Alexa tore off five one-hundred dollar bills and handed the rest of the bundle over.

"I've got a safe in the bar—I'll put it in there until we need it. See you about eight tonight?"

"Sounds good."

After Macaw left, Alexa felt inspired to sit down and write about the Garcia's one-room home and makeshift outdoor kitchen, brimming with children, except for one. It would make a key part of the story when she wrote it—hopefully with a happy reunion to add. A couple of hours later, she downloaded the story to a flash drive, erased from her laptop what she'd written and shut off her computer. She had captured the spirit of the Garcia's rustic home and trusting personalities, including their desperate clinging to hope that their daughter would return.

Even though she didn't have much to choose from, Alexa took her time picking what to wear that night. She finally decided on a dress—a clingy, electric blue number. She rarely wore it—hardly ever had a reason to—not that *this* was a reason. Just a friendly dinner with a source, she told herself. Yeah, a source with a great sense of humor and an incredible body. Slipping her feet into a pair of black sling backs, she reached for her brush and ran it through several times, letting her hair fall free down her back. Silver hoop earrings and a dab of rose scented perfume behind her ears, and she was ready. Examining herself in the mirror, she started rethinking her outfit when someone knocked on the door.

"*Sí?*"

"It's me." Macaw's baritone voice sounded in the hallway.

"You look great," he almost growled when she opened the door, his eyes slowly traveling the length of her body and back up again.

"Thanks," said Alexa as she tried swallowing the lump of excitement in her throat.

"Do you want to come in? I don't have much in the way of refreshments. I think we drank the last of my beer earlier." Alexa suddenly panicked, remembering Macaw's reputation. "Look, this is just a friendly dinner, nothing more. And no drugs, not even weed."

Macaw laughed. "I know you don't do drugs."

"What makes you think that?" Alexa felt oddly offended.

"I can tell these things. And don't worry. I have no intention of being a bad influence on you. Hell, I don't do drugs, either."

"Never?"

"Okay, I smoke weed now and then, but that's it. I've never done meth —that crap gets you hooked quick—and I used to do a little blow, but I had a good friend die from that shit and haven't touched it in fifteen years."

"But you sell it."

"That what McMillan told you?"

"He inferred it."

"I only transport weed. But don't tell anyone. It'll ruin my reputation. Besides, I'm planning on retiring from that soon. I got some money in stocks and shit. I'm getting older and wiser." He grinned.

Alexa felt better about that somehow. Probably because she'd never heard of anyone overdosing on marijuana.

"You ready to go?" he asked. "I got reservations at one of the best places in La Paz."

They walked downtown to *Restaurante Rico,* a restaurant with an outdoor dining area. As the hostess led them to their table, they passed concrete fire pits whose flames made shadows dance across the solid ground, arriving at a table under a tree draped in glittery white lights.

"This is nice," said Alexa as she sat down in a rattan chair. "You bring all of your dates here?"

"All my dates? I'm flattered you think I'm such a playboy."

"Well, aren't you?"

"I go out now and then. Nothing special. How about you?"

"What about me?"

"Lots of boyfriends?"

"I don't have the time or the patience," said Alexa, picking up a home-made tortilla chip from a basket on the table and sticking its edge in salsa. "Work always comes first."

"A girl who loves her work. I like that," said Macaw, leaning back in his chair. "So you grew up in Southern California. Tell me about it."

"On an avocado ranch," Alexa said and smiled, feeling the cool air under the trees even now.

"The ranch still around?"

"My father runs it, along with Enrique, his right-hand man. It's doing well, although my Dad's health is slipping. He recently had a stroke, but I think he's going to be okay. I'm taking a quick trip there soon to get him set up once he's out of the hospital."

"What about your mom?"

"Mama died when I was six."

"That's tough when you're that young."

Alexa nodded.

"So was your mama from Mexico?"

"Yes, and Papa's from California."

"So your dad's the gringo," said Macaw.

"Yeah, anything wrong with that?"

"Nah, some of my best friends have been gringos."

"Like the guy who died from the cocaine overdose?" asked Alexa, remembering the stories Jesse McMillan had written.

Macaw's eyes clouded.

"I'm sorry," said Alexa, regretting her thoughtless comment. "I shouldn't have said that."

"It's cool," said Macaw, picking up a tortilla chip and staring at it. "Randy was my little buddy, and yeah, he was as gringo as you can get. Damn, was he a kick in the pants. Totally nuts."

"It's hard to lose people who mean a lot to you."

"I guess you know, losing your mama like that. How'd it happen?"

"They say a car accident when she was visiting Mexico. But let's change the subject." A *mariachi* band had just entered, playing one of Alexa's favorite salsa tunes. She gestured to the dance floor.

Macaw shook his head. "I don't dance."

"C'mon, it's fun!" Alexa stood up and tugged on his hands. "Who cares what you look like?"

The band saw her urging Macaw to dance and began calling him.

"*Baila* Macaw!" they chanted. Everywhere he went people seemed to know him, marveled Alexa as Macaw stood and followed her onto the dance floor.

He did a fair job moving to the beat. "I don't know why you don't like dancing," cried Alexa over the music. "You have rhythm."

Macaw only grimaced until the band finished and started a slow song. Then he smiled and pulled Alexa close to him as the *mariachis* whistled.

"Now *this* is what I call dancing," he whispered in her ear.

Alexa agreed as she shivered at the electrical charge between them.

After a long dinner and much sharing about their past, including Macaw's childhood in Panama and Alexa's in Fallbrook, they strolled back to her hotel.

When they stopped in front of her room, Macaw touched her hair. "Damn, you're beautiful, and that ain't no line."

"You don't say that to all of your dates?"

"What dates? Until tonight, I've never had a real date."

"I had a fantastic time," she said.

"Me, too."

"Do it."

"What?"

"Kiss me."

Macaw planted a kiss on her cheek.

"That's not what I'm talking about."

He grinned. "I thought you were a lady?"

"A lady who knows what she wants," said Alexa as she encircled his neck with her arms and drew his mouth to hers. The long kiss made her skin burn and her body ache.

He responded by pulling her even closer, and she ran her hands through his hair, grasping the soft curls that lay just above his collar.

When his lips sought the hollow between her breasts, she surprised herself by asking, "Want to come in?"

"You don't have to ask me twice," he breathed, not letting her go as they moved through the doorway.

When the door creaked shut behind them, something jerked inside of Alexa. Despite her intense desire to be with Macaw, anxiety threaded its way through her body.

He picked up on her hesitation and stopped. "Sorry. I guess we got carried away."

"It's not that I don't want to. I do. It's not you," Alexa assured him.

"Hey, it's okay," he said, concern filling his face. "I know it's not me. Someone hurt you. Who is the bastard? An old boyfriend?"

"No, it's nothing like that."

"My old man used to hurt my mama. I know the signs. Tell me. I'll make sure he never hurts anyone again."

"You're really sweet," said Alexa, running her forefinger down the scar on Macaw's cheek. "I didn't think you'd be so nice."

Macaw snorted. "You don't know me that well. I'm not even close to sweet."

"I know the signs."

4

Macaw rapped on her hotel room door the next morning. "Alexa. You there? It's me."

She pulled open the door and smiled. "Hi me."

"Sleep good?"

"Okay. How about you?"

"A little restless," he answered, walking into the room.

Alexa blushed. "About last night—"

Raising a palm to stop her, he interrupted, "There's nothing to worry about. Right now, we've got a job to do, right?"

Alexa nodded.

"You wearing that?" he eyed her jeans and T-shirt.

"Yes, why?"

"The look is completely wrong."

"I didn't know I was going to a fashion show."

"You aren't, but how do you expect Imelda to think your boyfriend is a rich perv when you look like the girl-next-door?"

"Well, what do you want me to wear? I don't have much in the way of wardrobe."

"That's okay. I got a friend who'll fix you right up." He ushered Alexa out the door.

When they pulled onto a tree-lined street of high-end boutiques, Alexa followed Macaw to a shop on the corner. The sign above the door read *La Bonita*. *The pretty boutique*, she thought. This should be interesting.

The door buzzed as they entered to the heavy scent of flowery perfume. Within seconds, a stunning Mexican woman in a clingy magenta dress emerged from the back. Her hips gyrated softly from side to side as she walked toward them past rows of delicate silk shells and hand-woven scarves.

"Macaw, *mi amor*. How can I help you?" she purred, grasping his face between her red lacquered fingertips and planting kisses on each cheek. "I have a fabulous blue silk shirt that will look absolutely ravishing on you."

"Thanks, Ramona, maybe next time. Today, I need something for my friend here."

Ramona glanced at Alexa. "Oh, I see. I'm sure she wants something casual. Perhaps shorts and a blouse?"

"No, we need some edgy and hip threads."

Ramona raised her penciled-in eyebrows and clucked. "*Mi amor*, you do bring me challenges. But I guess you know I am a miracle worker. Give me a minute. I have some items her size in the back."

As Macaw watched Ramona's shapely figure wiggle toward the back of the store, Alexa felt irritated. Women with large busts and their come-hither way of walking always commandeered men's attention and shut off their minds. Minimally endowed like her mother, and tall and slender like her father, Alexa never competed with such sex appeal, and that always rankled her. Though men often found Alexa's long black hair and shapely legs appealing, she just couldn't show off her stuff like this woman.

Alexa felt Macaw's eyes on her, and she met them. His amused expression irked her even further. Then she admonished herself. She had no business worrying about his sex life. Like Macaw said, they had a job to do, and that's all she needed to concentrate on.

"What are you looking at?"

"Just watching you."

"Really?" she retorted. "I hadn't noticed."

Macaw opened his mouth to reply but stopped. She followed his gaze through the shop window to a black car parked next to the curb.

"Move behind that rack of clothes."

Alexa hesitated.

"Now," he ordered.

Macaw kept his eyes glued to the street while she stepped behind some jackets. He reached down and pulled up the leg of his jeans to extract a gun from an ankle holster.

Momentarily shocked, Alexa realized the probability he'd be armed, considering the life he led. The thought gave her an unexpected, yet welcome feeling of safety.

Macaw remained vigilant until the car finally pulled away from the curb and disappeared into traffic.

"Can I come out of hiding?" Alexa asked.

"Stay there. I'm not sure who our friends were, but they may be back."

"You didn't recognize the car?"

"No. But since every other car around here is hot, it's hard to know who was behind the wheel."

Ramona called for them.

"I'll go with you," Macaw said.

"What will Ramona think?"

"That I like to see my girl undress," he said, motioning for her to walk ahead of him.

About to protest at his caveman claim, Alexa instead smiled. It felt good hearing him say that, even if he was only joking. And what a luxury to have someone actually watching her back. Usually when she worked with a male partner—like Michael—she ended up saving his ass. The story in Tijuana awhile back was her last attempt at a partnership. Michael had whined like a baby about being harassed by the border patrol.

Ramona had several outfits waiting for Alexa. Despite the shop owner's obvious disapproval of Macaw's choice in companions, she had pulled out some cute clothing. Stepping inside the dressing room, Alexa whipped the curtain closed. No way would she expose her C-cup bra while Macaw and double-D Ramona watched.

Slipping into the first outfit—boot-cut jeans and a cream-colored shirt with multi-colored beading—Alexa smiled in approval at her reflection in the mirror. When she stepped out from behind the curtain, though, Ramona shook her head, her diamond pendant earrings swinging in protest.

"Very nice, yes, but I think I prefer you in another color."

About to object, Alexa decided to see what else Ramona had to offer. She pulled the curtain closed again and tried on another ensemble. Forty-five minutes later, Alexa's wardrobe now included two new outfits—hip-hugging, pencil-legged jeans, an emerald green, plunging V-neck top and black stilettos, and a tailored black skirt, paired with a burgundy blouse that exposed one shoulder. She chose a pair of soft, black suede boots to go with the skirt. The jeans, V-neck and stilettos were perfect for the Gomez visit, so she kept the outfit on.

When Macaw reached for his wallet, Alexa pulled out some cash and laid it on the counter. "No, Macaw, I'll get it." Unaware of his financial situation, she thought it best not to push things.

"It's no problem," he said, while Ramona waited.

"I'll just take it out of my travel allowance," Alexa insisted.

"Suit yourself."

"How nice it is to be a modern woman," Ramona said, picking the money up with her manicured thumb and forefinger and smiling at Macaw. "I'm an old-fashioned girl myself."

Macaw shook his head and chuckled.

As they turned to leave, Ramona reached out and put her hand on his bicep. "Come back and visit soon, *mi amor*. I have some fabulous shirts on order with your favorite jungle designs."

"Thanks," Macaw shot back. "I'll be in."

I'll just bet you'll be in, Alexa thought as the green-eyed monster clawed at her. When they got to the boutique's door, she jerked it open, nearly hitting Macaw in the face. As she stalked to his MG, he reached out and pulled her to his side. "Just cause you're pissed about Ramona doesn't mean you need to make yourself a target. Stay close," he murmured in her ear, his breath sending tingles along the side of her neck.

"I am not upset about Ramona," she said and smiled prettily. "You can be involved with whomever you want. Why would I care?"

Macaw's low laugh rumbled from his chest. "Believe it or not, Ramona's not my type."

"Yeah, right. She's everyone's type."

"Actually, she's Hector Hernandez's type. No one else touches her."

Alexa's eyes widened, and she whispered, "The Mexican Mafioso? She's his wife?"

Macaw laughed as he started up the car. "No, not his wife."

"His . . . his mistress?" she said.

"Lover. Something like that. So don't worry. Even if I wanted to, me and Ramona Valdez are definitely *not* an item."

Alexa mulled this over as he pulled the car into traffic. What on earth was wrong with her? Why so much relief at Macaw's unavailability to some woman? She absolutely had to get it together and concentrate on the most important assignment of her career.

They drove to an industrial part of town a few miles from where she and Rodolfo discovered the children the other night. Alexa's anxiety climbed the closer they got to their destination. So much depended on this meeting. One wrong move and they would never find the children. Or she might be added to the list of missing journalists. Sensing her anxiety, Macaw placed his hand on her shoulder.

"Let me do most of the talking, at first," he said. "Like we discussed, I'm going to say that your old man is loaded and wants some photos. To Imelda, there's only one reason to do anything, and that's cold cash. Once we start throwing money around and let her know how much your 'source' can benefit us all, she'll give us access to the kids."

Alexa patted the small purse stuffed with lollipops that she bought at a little shop near the hotel that morning. For now, the symbol of carefree childhood was the best she could do. Would she even get a chance to give them to the children, she wondered?

The MG bumped up and down as they pulled into an asphalt parking lot riddled with potholes. When he shut off the engine, Alexa climbed out of Macaw's side and allowed him to help her exit the car.

"You'd think I was on ice skates or something," she grumbled, bracing her legs to steady herself in the stilettos. "I'm used to my tennis shoes."

"You're not getting any complaints from me. Your gams are killer in those spikes," he said as they turned and headed toward the brick building. She was working on a good comeback, but stopped when her eyes fell on the shiny, gold sign hanging on the front door.

"*Pasteles Sabrosos*. Tasty Desserts," Alexa read. "What a front."

"From the looks of things, it's a new front. Imelda's jumpy. She thinks someone's onto her; she comes up with a new con quick to cover her tracks."

Inside they found a receptionist sitting at an empty wooden desk filing her fingernails. She looked up through a fringe of black bangs when they entered. "Can I help you?"

"Tell Fernando that Macaw is here to see him."

"I will ask if *Señor* Fernando is available," she said.

When she left the room, Alexa commented, "I don't smell any tasty desserts cooking."

"Damn, I was hoping for at least a chocolate chip cookie."

"Do you think he's here?"

"He's here," said Macaw. "So's Imelda. I checked with a source this morning."

The receptionist returned. "I'm sorry. *Señor* Gomez is unavailable."

"Okay, tell Imelda we'd like to see her."

"*Señora* Gomez is preparing to leave. Perhaps another day?"

Alexa tensed at the mention of waiting.

"We don't have another day," said Macaw. "Tell Imelda Macaw wants to see her immediately about a lucrative business matter. Tell her either you show us back, or I'll make myself at home and find my own way."

Eyes wide, the receptionist scurried out of the room, returning a few minutes later. "*Señora* Gomez says that I can bring you back for a brief meeting."

She led them down a dark passageway, past two empty storerooms and arrived at the end of the hall. Smiling self-consciously at Macaw, the receptionist pointed to an open door and then eased her way past them and back to the front office.

They entered the room to find a stocky woman roosting behind a large Steelcase desk. After her keen eyes scoured Alexa's face, Imelda turned to Macaw.

Qué pasa contigo, Macaw? *Vienes para más?*" Imelda asked him if he returned for more. What was she getting at? Alexa wondered. Another slashing to his face? The idea of this witch hurting him shot a hot bolt of anger through her.

"I couldn't stay away," Macaw said, halting in the center of the room and filling the space with his presence.

"Always too dramatic," said Imelda, waving them to sit down on a leather couch opposite her desk. "Who is this *puta* with you?"

"A friend who might be interested in a little action."

Imelda snickered as she leaned back in her chair. "Why come to me? You should be able to give her more action than she can take."

Alexa studied the woman's ugly face, with its heavy jowls and greasy, pockmarked skin. Deep lines—no doubt from cigarettes and alcohol—cut the flesh surrounding her eyes and mouth.

"I can't give her the kind of action she wants—or should I say, her old man wants," said Macaw.

"What kind of action are we talking about? Don't tell me you've stopped transporting. Are you going soft?"

"I'm still transporting, but she's not looking to get high like that," said Macaw.

"What is she looking for? I'm a busy woman, and I don't have time for games."

"I'll get to the point. I heard you're transporting a different type of merchandise nowadays. This one isn't inanimate."

Imelda's eyes narrowed.

"The word gets out. You know that."

"Since when have you been involved in *that* kind of merchandise?"

"Since never. That's why I'm here. She's willing to pay big for it, and I thought I'd pass on the business."

"You expect me to believe you're doing me a favor?" Imelda gestured to Macaw's scar.

"I got my own selfish motives. This means a huge cut for me, and I could really use a cash infusion right now."

"Can't we all," Imelda said, inspecting Alexa more closely. "She looks like a spoiled rich girl to me. And she's a half-breed."

"We come here to talk about our roots?" said Macaw. "You interested in providing my client with what she's looking for, or do we go elsewhere?"

"What, exactly, is she looking for? And for who?"

"Her old man is into stuff on the Internet. He wants her to take some photos."

"And why doesn't he come?"

"Too important. Never shows his face, but he doles out cash like candy." Macaw pulled out a huge wad of bills. Alexa could see greed warring with caution in Imelda's eyes.

"Most women are too soft for this. She looks like a cookie that will crumble," Imelda sneered.

"I'll crumble if I don't go home with pictures," Alexa tried to sound desperate.

"You poor rich girl," Imelda mocked. "Your man slaps you around? Try getting gang-raped by your uncles at a family reunion." She nearly spat at Alexa, who grew uneasy at the unsettling look in the older woman's eyes.

"Listen, Imelda, we didn't come here to hear your life story," Macaw intervened. "Are we in, or not?"

Imelda looked at the wad of cash again and licked her lips. "We can probably arrange something. But we're talking major cash. This is a rare commodity, involving a lot of risk for me. I've also got a couple high-profile government officials panting over this, and they're paying big. Maybe too big for you."

"Mexican government officials couldn't pay as much as my client is willing to pay," said Macaw. "They don't make that much in a year, even with bribes."

"I never said they were Mexican officials," Imelda said slyly.

"He just wants his lady to take a few pictures so he can get his rocks off and pass around the fun. He'll pay. You can count on it. Do we have a deal, or not?"

Alexa remained impassive as Imelda's eyes bored into her.

"I'll think about it."

"Don't think too long," said Macaw, rising to leave. "She's on business here for another week or so, and then she's headed back to the States."

Imelda gestured for them to leave. "I'll let you know within twenty-four hours."

A few minutes later as they drove away in Macaw's MG, Alexa asked, "So, what do you think she'll decide?"

"I don't know. Imelda's always been a wild card. Like I said, she likes the money, and you did a good job of convincing her that you're some dumb broad doing anything for her pervert old man. But she's no dummy. We'll just have to wait and see."

5

Macaw came to Alexa's door early the next morning. Still in her pajamas, she answered and ushered him in.

"Looks like I'm a morning regular around here," he said, and then added, "I like the threads."

"Thanks," Alexa said of her pink cotton shorts set. "In Mexico, I always make sure to sleep in something I can dash out the door in."

He raised his eyebrows. "Is this where I ask what happens when you're not in Mexico?"

Alexa flushed. "You're up early. It's only seven."

"I've never needed much sleep."

"What's the story? Did she call?" she asked.

"Yeah, it looks like she's going to pull the stuffing out of her mattress to make way for the dough."

Alexa's pulse quickened at the good news. "When do I go?"

Macaw corrected her. "You mean, when do *we* go? Today, if you want."

"Of course, I want."

"Imelda's licking her fangs over the funds."

"So much money," Alexa shook her head, thinking about how Peter, her editor, had intimated that the publisher expected a Pulitzer contender for the investment. Nothing less.

"Must be a lot of pressure for you," said Macaw.

"I'm used to pressure. Getting the little girls away from those vermin —that will make it all worth it."

"Little girls. That really bothers me. I never had any sisters. Good thing with my old man."

"Is your father still around?"

"No, he finally keeled from a heart attack. I almost danced on his grave. My mother wouldn't have survived much more of him. I cracked him hard after he beat her really bad one night, and he finally quit that shit, but the yelling never stopped."

"Sounds painful for all of you."

"You're talking like you know."

"Not quite the same, but yeah, I know."

"Your old man sounds like an okay guy."

"My papa is great. His brother, my Uncle Freddy, was a mean drunk."

"Live with you?"

"Yes, for a little while. My father could never say no to his only brother."

"The bastard finally kick the bucket?"

"Yes, lung cancer—he chain-smoked, too. His funeral was one of the best days of my life." Her words hung in the air, and she gasped. "I can't believe I just said that." Until now, she rarely thought about the day when she stood at her uncle's gravesite and secretly thanked God for removing him from the earth.

"Why can't you believe you said it? It's the truth, isn't it?"

"Yes, but—"

"But what? An asshole is an asshole, and his being dead doesn't change the fact. He made his own crummy decisions. Never apologize for how you felt about him."

"You're right. You know, you're easy to talk to."

"Shit, I usually don't talk," said Macaw. "I've found that it's better to keep my mouth shut."

Alexa looked at Macaw's mouth and strong jaw and remembered his kisses. She distracted herself by picking her hairbrush off the bureau and running it through her morning tangles.

"I'll wait downstairs while you get dressed. Want breakfast? Scrambled eggs and toast, right?"

"Not only are you easy to talk to—you're observant," said Alexa.

After Macaw left her room, she sank onto the bed and rested her head in her hands. This was by far the most pivotal assignment of her career. She absolutely had to keep it together! Getting involved with Macaw went against her career code—way too messy and distracting.

After donning her new black skirt and burgundy blouse from Ramona's boutique, Alexa locked her door and headed downstairs to the restaurant, determined to steer the day back to business. Her emotional moat crumbled the second she saw Macaw hunched over a newspaper wearing an earnest expression she'd come to recognize.

"You do read! And in Spanish."

"You caught me," he said, setting down the local rag. "Just boning up on some changes in Panama."

"Good changes?"

"Looks that way. I might be able to go back sooner than I thought."

Alexa slipped into the booth just as the waiter delivered their orders. The idea of Macaw leaving for Panama made her feel oddly anxious. She concentrated on her plate, shoveling in a mouthful of eggs and washing it down with orange juice.

"Imelda probably won't want me to go in with you to see the girls," he said.

"Why not?"

"Gives her more control that way."

"But I need you in there with me."

He grinned. "You finally said it."

"What?" She looked up.

"You need me."

"You're the Gomez expert, remember? You said she's, I quote, "an unpredictable wack job."

"That I did." His faced clouded over. "Don't worry. I'll make sure I go in with you."

"Thanks," said Alexa, surprised at the sense of relief she felt.

When they got to Imelda's office, the receptionist informed them that she was in a meeting and would get to them as soon as possible.

"She just wants to throw us off our game," Macaw whispered.

Alexa nodded and braced herself for what promised to be another unsavory meeting. Glancing around the sparsely furnished office, she tried to imagine living the kind of life that Imelda and Fernando did. What was the allure, she wondered? How did you get up every day and know that today might be the day you were found out and thrown in prison, or worse, killed? Better yet, how did you live with yourself doing the terrible things they did? Obviously, these were questions that Alexa would thankfully never be able to answer. But the queries did present her with a disturbing dilemma as a journalist. She'd been trained to see all sides of issues and then report them. This was one side she'd never fathom.

As he watched Alexa's wheels turning, Macaw thought how he'd never met any woman with so many sides. Nervous, sure, but she hid it well. Fiery, determined and unstoppable. She'd held her own with Imelda yesterday and would no doubt do the same today. And that was saying a lot. He'd seen grown men nearly crap their pants in her presence, and without even flinching, Alexa stared her down.

Nearly an hour later, Imelda came out of her office and motioned them inside.

"Somebody needs to work on some time management skills," complained Macaw as they all sat down.

Imelda ignored his comment and said, "*La Princesa* goes in with me. You wait outside."

"Bullshit. I go with her or the deal's off."

"As usual, Macaw, you think you are a big *hombre*." Imelda's leather chair groaned as she shifted her stocky frame.

"The way I see it, I am in control," he shot back. "I have the greenbacks from my client here, and you're lucky I brought her to you."

Imelda sniggered. "I have never felt lucky around you, *cholo*," she said, referring to the derogatory Mexican term for a low gang member.

"We can sit here and throw around nasty shit all day, or get to the business at hand. What will it be?" Alexa watched Macaw stiffen as he glared at Imelda.

"Why I even speak to you, I don't know," she said, rolling her eyes. "You can go in with the bitch, but I'm adding an extra $500 onto the $1,500 I quoted you, and I'm still going to be with you this first time."

"You okay with her being there?" Macaw asked Alexa.

She shrugged. "This first time it's okay, I guess."

"Next time we go in alone, if there is a next time," said Macaw. "Let's see if you've got something we actually want, or if you're just pissing our time away."

"Another one of your shortcoming's—impatience," Imelda retorted.

Alexa saw Macaw's jaw clench at that last comment, but he kept his cool as he pulled a wad of cash from his pocket. "Like I said, money is no object."

Imelda's sausage fingers reached out and grabbed the cash. "You finally got yourself a paying job. There's a hotel on La Jolla Avenue called *La Luna*. Go to room twenty-four. A guard is on duty. No weapons allowed. I don't want my merchandise marked up. I'll see you there." Imelda cast a scathing look at Alexa and added with a smirk, "This better be on the up and up. If you want to know how I treat traitors, just ask Macaw."

"As usual, Imelda, you're the hostess with the mostest," Macaw replied as they rose to leave.

Back in the car, Macaw glanced at Alexa as he turned on the ignition. "You ready for this?"

"As ready as I'm ever going to be. I mean, how do you get ready to act like a child pornographer?"

"Shit if I know."

When they approached *La Luna* hotel, Macaw said, "Be careful what you do and say in the room. There's a good chance that Imelda's taping. The blackmail opportunities are too irresistible."

They pulled up in front of an old motel, its exterior pitted from chipped paint. Weeds grew in the cracks of the erupting black asphalt surrounding the building and moss stained the walls. As they exited the car to the smell of trash burning in a nearby parking lot, Alexa thought about the English translation of *La Luna*—The moon. Coming here felt surreal enough to be a trip to the moon, she thought, angry at the sinister reason they were subjected to the stench and decay surrounding them. At room twenty-four, Alexa took a deep breath and let it out slowly as Macaw knocked on the door.

One of Imelda's guards opened it immediately and pointed a handgun at Macaw's face. Without skipping a beat, he said, "We're here to see Imelda."

"*Está bien*," cried Imelda from within the room.

The guard lowered the gun and searched them both carefully. When he opened Alexa's purse and eyed the lollipops, Macaw's eyebrows raised, but he said nothing. The guard motioned them to enter the room and went outside and shut the door.

Alexa hadn't known what to expect, but what she saw threatened her eyes with hot, panicked tears. Imelda stood next to a little girl, no older than nine or ten, sitting on the edge of the bed, her bare legs dangling. She wore a purple party dress, black patent leather shoes and a look of raw fear in her large, dark eyes.

Alexa approached the girl and knelt down in front of her. "It's okay," she spoke softly in Spanish, reminding herself to carefully weigh keeping the girl calm with not arousing Imelda's suspicion. "We just want to talk a little bit. That's all."

The little girl seemed to relax at the gentle words, but then flinched when Imelda told her in Spanish to obey or she'd be sorry.

"Hey, you have to intimidate the kid?" Macaw asked Imelda. "Her old man doesn't want pictures of kids looking like they're just about to shit their pants."

"No photos today," Imelda said, leaving the girl's side and walking over to Macaw, who had sat down in a chair next to a small table on the other side of the room.

"What the fuck are you talking about? We had a deal."

"Once again, *cholo*, you're confused about who is in charge," said Imelda, sitting in the chair across from Macaw.

"We get it, you're in charge," said Macaw loudly. "Always throwing your weight around—literally and figuratively."

Alexa realized that Macaw argued with Imelda to give her a chance to talk to the child without supervision.

"What's your name?" she asked the little girl, who looked at Imelda and Macaw, worry in her eyes.

"Don't listen to them," Alexa urged. "They are just being silly. I have a lollipop for you when we're done talking."

"I am Rosalita," the little girl said softly, looking down at her lap.

"What a pretty name. I bet you have a lot of friends with pretty names."

Rosalita hesitated, and then nodded.

"Tell me some pretty names," Alexa said, speaking as low as she dared, while quelling the overwhelming urge to grab Rosalita and run.

"There's Susana and Alexandra and Josephine," said Rosalita, getting more comfortable speaking to Alexa. "And there's Sofia and Maria and Silvina and Liana."

Alexa's ears perked up at the mention of the last name.

"It must be nice to live with all those girls with such pretty names."

"The little girl frowned and whispered, "Can I go home now?""

How Alexa wanted to cry out, you're going home right now. Instead, she jerked her mind out of her heart and pretended to ignore the comment.

"Okay, time's up," said Imelda, getting up from the chair.

"Already!" Alexa tried to sound irritated. "I was just getting her to relax!"

"This was a goodwill gesture. To see how serious you are. Next time you two can come in alone," Imelda said, opening the door and leaving, but not before instructing the guard to make sure they left immediately.

When she handed Rosalita a lollipop, Alexa felt heartened to see a huge grin creep across her face. Fighting another intense wish to run with the girl, Alexa wrenched herself away and grabbed Macaw's hand for support. Determined to walk away without a backward glance, she felt her knees grow weak at the realization that she wasn't any better than Imelda for leaving the poor little girl all alone with the guard. Where were the other children?

"You okay?" asked Macaw when they got in his car.

"Yeah, I'll be okay." She refused to reduce herself to tears. "Good work with Imelda."

He snorted in disgust as he pulled out of the hotel's parking lot. "That wacko is so predictable. I knew I could distract her with arguing —it's definitely her favorite sport—that and breaking every law possible."

When they parked in front of Alexa's hotel a few minutes later, Macaw shut off his car and got out. Usually after a difficult assignment she craved alone time. Not now.

"Shitty day, huh," he said as they walked into the cantina's late afternoon rush. The comforting smell of warm tortillas and pinto beans filled the air, and families talked and laughed noisily as they ate.

Once they sat down amid the cacophony, Alexa finally replied. "I keep seeing that little girl's face. So frightened. We left her all alone with that guard. Who knows what he'll do to her. And then we come here with all these happy families." Alexa tried to swallow the hot ball of anxiety in her throat, struggling to get out the question she most dreaded the answer to. "Do you think....?"

"It's hard to say what Imelda has been doing with them," Macaw said. "There's a good chance we're her only customers so far. She's careful like a cockroach, which is what makes her so dangerous. She lies in wait until she knows the coast is clear. She's still looking pretty antsy with this, which tells me this is her first time with girls this young. Most likely they're just living in some dump somewhere and that's the extent of it so far. And even though there's a huge market for child porn, the guard didn't seem like the type."

Alexa nodded, clinging to Macaw's words.

He covered her hands with his. "I know it's hard. Believe me, I wanted to choke the shit out of Imelda until she told us where the rest of them are stashed, but I know her. She has no heart. She'd never tell out of spite and hate, even if I threatened to kill her. Not to mention the army she had surrounding us. We gotta keep our eye on the prize—finding out where the rest of those little girls are, and who's backing her and Fernando. This isn't the US. Not a lot of people are paying attention, and hell, even in the States victims are lost in the woodwork every single minute of the day. You know that. You also know we're just scratching the surface here. There's a lot more kids in jeopardy out there. The cooler we keep our heads, the faster we find what we need and get those girls out of there, and hopefully stop this whole thing altogether."

"Thanks for the reminders," Alexa said. "One bit of good news. Rosalita confirmed that there's a Liana in the group."

"Fantastic," said Macaw.

"You hungry?" asked Alexa. "I don't think I could eat right now."

"Me neither. I'll walk you to your room."

On the way up the stairs, Alexa could feel Macaw's comforting presence behind her. What touched her so much about him? Why, in so many years of boring dates and occasional go-nowhere relationships, did she have to fall for *him* of all people? A relationship doomed from the start. When they got to her door, she turned to give him a quick peck.

"Want me to come in?" he asked as he moved closer, tilting her face up toward his.

"Yes," she said, her resolve turning to jelly.

Once inside, Alexa turned to Macaw and crawled into his arms even before turning on the light in the waning daylight.

"What the—" Macaw reached for the gun at his ankle.

Alexa saw it in the dim light. The meager contents of her room strewn throughout the small space.

"Looks like our friends in the car yesterday might have paid you a visit."

"Did you get an ID on the sketch we made?" asked Alexa, annoyed to find her laptop case empty.

"No—not yet. Still waiting for word from one of my sources. We'll find them, though. They got your laptop?"

"Yeah, but that's okay. It's clean. I kept decoy files on it of benign travel articles. Whenever I write a story, I put it directly on my flash drive and erase it from the computer." She pulled the small electronic device out of her purse and held it up. "Someone is translating my enthralling articles on the joys of snorkeling in *Cabo Pulmo* and sipping a margarita while watching a sunset at Land's End. Really good stories, I might add."

Macaw chuckled. "You are a kick in the pants."

Alexa felt touched by his statement, remembering a similar comment he made at dinner the other night about Randy, the high school friend he lost.

They cleaned up the mess, and Alexa was relieved to find all of her clothing still there. She'd call Peter tomorrow and have him order her a new laptop. All of a sudden, she felt overwhelmingly fatigued from the emotions of the day.

"You must be beat," said Macaw, picking up on her mood. "Especially with this break-in shit."

"I am." If only she could say the words, please stay.

Macaw said them for her. "You want me to stay? They're probably not coming back, but I'm not too hip on leaving you alone."

"All we've got is that sad excuse for a bed."

"We'll fit. Let's get some shut-eye. I'm beat, too."

They lay down on the narrow bed, Alexa facing away from Macaw, her back nestled against his torso. She smiled as she felt her eyelids grow heavy with exhaustion.

"I never thought I'd lie in a chick's bed and do nothing."

"Is it bothering you?"

"Nah, it's great. Get some sleep. Forget for a little while how fucked up the world is."

Soon Alexa slept. Nice dreams at first. Mama waving to her from the car and her father swinging her in the air. Then suddenly she stood at Uncle Freddy's gravesite next to a black hole. Relieved about his death, but afraid of falling into the hole with him, she stood at its edge, clinging to her father's arm. A crow flew at Alexa's face and she shrieked, turning to her father for assurance. But the face she met was not her papa's. Uncle Freddy held her arm in a vice grip and laughed a cavernous sound.

"You're dead!" Alexa tried to scream the words. "Dead! Don't you understand?" She awakened and bolted upright. "You're dead." The words filled the dark room.

"Shhh." Macaw massaged her shoulders. "I'm right here. It's just you and me." He pulled her back down and tight against him.

"Oh, Macaw," Alexa buried her face in the warm arms that encircled her. "I'm sorry to wake you. I don't know what's wrong with me lately. I've had so many bad dreams. You must think I'm a big baby."

"A babe, yeah." He stroked her hair. "It sounds like you have plenty of reasons for bad dreams. And after tonight, I wouldn't be surprised if I had a few myself."

"You? The tough guy? I can't picture a problem you can't take care of," said Alexa, wiggling around to face him.

Macaw laughed, his breath warm against her check. "Why not?"

"You seem so cool and collected. Always in command of situations."

"Not every situation. Believe me."

"I do believe you," said Alexa, her words drifting off as she fell asleep.

· · ·

The next morning, Alexa woke to find Macaw splayed out in the rickety chair sipping a cup of coffee.

"What time is it?" she asked, shielding her eyes from the bright sun ricocheting from under the thin curtains.

"Early. About seven."

"That's your hour, huh?"

"Guess so. Sleep okay?"

"If I hadn't been so emotionally worn out, I probably would have tossed and turned. I'm just glad it's morning so we can get back to the case."

"I got you some coffee to give you the energy for that. Not bad for Mexican brew."

"So after Panama, you lived in California for a while, right? You miss living there?" asked Alexa, raising herself up on an elbow and reaching for the coffee.

"Sometimes, but I visit."

"You do? I thought you were stuck here. Steering clear of Gonzales."

"A lot of people have forgotten about the Noriega fiasco stateside. Everybody there moves quickly to the next story, and it's easy to get lost in a crowd in a big city like LA or New York. Panama is different. It's a lot smaller country, but like I said, there's been an encouraging shift in power there recently."

"What's your favorite part about Panama?"

"The countryside and the beaches—they'll blow your socks off," he said and smiled. "Miles and miles of soft, white sand, ultra-blue ocean and peace. That's the best part—the peace. A spot in the interior of the country called *El Valle* is probably my favorite place on earth. It's a true valley that sits below sea level. Rolling green hills, spectacular ocean views, and the sweetest people you'll ever meet."

"It sounds blissful," said Alexa. "Does your mother live by the ocean?"

"Yeah. I got her a little place with a view on this military base in the Canal Zone when the GIs moved out after Carter signed the treaty. You'd like Mama." He gazed at Alexa for what seemed like an eternity. "She'd like you, too."

Alexa's heart quickened at his comment. "How do you know?"

"I just know."

"How can you just know? What has she liked about your other girl-friends?"

"I never brought anyone to meet her."

"No one? Not ever?"

"Never. Why? You surprised? You brought people to meet your papa?"

"Only in high school. But Papa's different. Always has his head and heart in the avocado groves. I don't think he ever noticed."

"He noticed," said Macaw. "He's just not a mama. They talk and talk and talk. But your father noticed. He just didn't say anything."

Silence ensued as they sipped their coffee until the phone rang, jarring them both.

Alexa put her cup on the floor and reached for it.

"Alexa Kent."

"Ms. Kent? This is Dr. Smythe, your father's physician."

"Oh, yes, Dr. Smythe, is everything okay?"

"Everything is fine. In fact, it's so fine that your father is ready to go home. I think he will heal more quickly if he gets back to familiar surroundings."

"How soon is soon?"

"Tomorrow. I was hoping you could come in the next couple of days and help him get situated. I understand that a neighbor, I believe her name is Violet Hanks, can watch over him temporarily."

"Violet, yes, she's a good friend. I will get a flight out tomorrow."

"Great. There will be a temporary nurse on duty when you get there. She can explain everything to you in terms of his requirements, so you can choose a good caretaker. He needs a firm hand to make sure he takes his medicine and rests to build strength."

"Thank you so much. I'll call if I have any questions."

Alexa put down the phone and sighed.

"Your old man needs you?"

"Yeah, I've got to fly out tomorrow morning. What terrible timing for the case. I'm so afraid of what could happen to those girls while I'm gone."

"Hey, don't worry. Imelda's not going anywhere now that we've thrown money her way. I'll use your absence to make her black heart grow fonder."

"You don't have to do this, you know."

"I don't do anything I don't want to," he said, moving toward the bed.

Alexa eyed his well-muscled frame with approval as he approached. Just as he leaned down to kiss her, a sharp tap on the door made them both jump.

"Aw, shit," said Macaw, quickly reaching for his gun, which he had stored beneath the bed.

"*Quién es?*" Alexa called out.

"It's Rodolfo, *Señorita* Alexa."

She opened the door and motioned for him to enter. Her informant showed no surprise at the presence of her visitor.

"*Señor* Macaw." Rodolfo nodded.

"Hey Rodolfo."

"I have some important information for you," Rodolfo said, as usual getting right to the point.

"Tell us," said Alexa.

"There is a *padre* at my church who might know something," Rodolfo said in a hushed voice.

"A priest? How could he know something?"

"I saw Fernando Gomez at the confessional this morning. When he left, I went in. The *padre* was in a bad way."

"How do you know?"

"He did not listen to my confession. I could have told him I killed the Pope. He would not have heard."

"So our boy Fernando has a conscience," said Macaw.

"Do you think Fernando told the father what's going on with the children?" asked Alexa.

"I don't know," said Rodolfo. "But whatever he told him, it was bad."

"Can we approach the father?"

Rodolfo shrugged his shoulders. "If you do, don't mention my name.

My family and I are well respected there, and I do not wish for anyone to know that I am involved."

"Of course, your name will never come up," said Alexa, who understood. Fernando's filth would rub off on anyone associated with him.

"Thank you," said Rodolfo. "The name of the church is *La Christiana* on Paloma Street downtown. And now, my wife and children are waiting for me. You will contact me if you need help?"

"Of course," said Alexa, pulling out a hundred-dollar bill and handing it to him.

After Rodolfo walked out, Alexa turned to Macaw.

"Are you Catholic?"

"Don't be thinking of me and church in the same sentence."

Alexa put her hands on her hips. "I asked you a question."

"Damn. Yeah, I'm Catholic. You?"

"My mama was Catholic, but I'm Protestant like my dad, so I'm not sure how the whole Catholicism thing works as far as confession."

Macaw took a step back and threw up his hands. "Hey, don't look at me. I haven't set foot in church for years."

"Well, it's time you went back."

"Oh, man, do I have to?"

Alexa pouted. "Please? Just go in with me when I come back from my trip."

"My mama would have a heart attack if she got wind of this. Okay, sure. I'll go."

"Thanks." Alexa smiled and then frowned when she realized that she didn't look forward to being away from Macaw. What on earth was she going to do when this case was over?

6

During the taxi ride from the San Diego airport to the farm, Alexa usually enjoyed the drive into the countryside, past avocado orchards and acres of espaliered grape vines. But this time Alexa barely saw the vegetation sweeping by. Instead, she brooded about Rosalita and the other little girls. By the time the taxi approached the turn-off to the ranch, she felt so anxious about having left the story that part of her wanted to ask the driver to point the car back to the airport. Then he turned down the tree-lined drive to the main house, and as they coasted past dense rows of her father's avocado trees, the air cooled perceptibly, and Alexa felt her blood pressure go down several notches. Staying here a day or two would be good, she reassured herself. Help her get perspective. And her father needed her.

When they pulled up in front of the modest California-style ranch house, she smiled as she paid the driver. Stepping out of the car and inhaling the rich scent of mulch, she heard the contented twitter of birds as they rummaged around in a fig tree loaded with purple, sugary fruit. Alexa let herself in with a key, and a no-nonsense woman in a nursing uniform immediately greeted her in the entryway.

"You must be Alexa. You've arrived at a good time," she said, her eyes peering through the tiny spectacles that sat toward the tip of her nose. "Your father is awake, and I've just finished taking his blood pressure."

"I hope the numbers were good," said Alexa, putting down her small travel bag.

"I'm happy to report they were very good."

"How is he otherwise?"

"He's holding his own, but don't expect him to talk much. He was lucky to survive the stroke—hopefully without any long-lasting damage. It will take him quite a while to regain his strength."

Alexa left the entryway and walked down a hallway, peering into the first room she came to.

"Papa?"

"Lexie? Is that you?" her father's voice quavered.

Alexa held back for a moment as her eyes focused on the pale figure engulfed in the double bed. What had happened to her once strong, vital father?

"It's me, Papa," she said, approaching his bed.

As Alexa took his cold hand in hers, Tom tried to smile, but it came out as a grimace.

"How are the trees?" he asked her.

Alexa smiled. He still breathed the one thing that really mattered to him.

"I haven't had a chance to look at them. I just got in and came straight to see you."

"Enrique was supposed to start harvesting today."

"I'm sure he did. He has worked for you, what, twenty-five years now? He always starts harvesting on time. Don't worry, Papa. I'll check on things and report it all to you."

"How is your work?"

"Good. I'm investigating a really big story right now. I think it will put me on the map."

"And I took you from it."

"Hush. I needed a break, and it's good to see you."

"Not so good to see me like this."

"You'll be back to your old self in no time, Papa. As long as you take your medicine!"

"I have no choice. That battle-ax of a nurse practically stuffs it down my throat, and Violet is no better."

"Where is Violet?"

"I'm right here child," said the older woman, who bustled into the room and held out her short, chubby arms for Alexa. She stepped into their neighbor's warm embrace and inhaled the familiar scent of lilac perfume.

Once they had finished hugging, Violet eyed Alexa critically. "You've lost weight again. Don't they let you eat?"

"I eat plenty. The Mexicans just don't have the money to cook fattening foods like we do. I have plenty of beans, eggs, homemade tortillas, and rice and fresh vegetables."

"Sounds dreadful," Violet clucked, her short, gray bob of hair swinging as she shook her head. "I'll fatten you up while you're here. There's left-over roast in the fridge, and first thing tomorrow I'll make that cheesy chicken dish you like so much."

"Yummy," said Alexa, glancing at her father, who had dozed off.

"I'm so glad you came," Violet whispered, steering her out of the room. "Your father wouldn't say it, but I know that he really wanted to see you. Can you stay for a while?"

Alexa felt a pang of guilt when she replied. "For a couple of days. I'm on a big story right now."

"That job of yours has taken you so far away." Violet shook her head as they headed toward the kitchen. "I've never understood it. You could have run the ranch. You're so good with the trees."

"I know, and I love it here, but it wasn't enough. I had to find my own way."

"You young people. What is enough, anyway?"

Alexa didn't answer, because she didn't know.

"Oh, well, it's nice to see you." Violet smiled and took Alexa's face in her hands. "Give me two days, and I guarantee you'll gain at least five pounds!"

Alexa laughed. "I'll give you two pounds, but that's all!"

As she watched Violet work in the kitchen, Alexa admired how she shuffled pans, chopped, sautéed, organized, cleaned and talked all at once. Ever since she could remember, Violet lived next door. Her husband, Phil, had died ten years earlier. Unable to have children of her own, Violet had always shown great interest in Alexa. She babysat for years, especially after Alexa's mother died. Since her husband's death, Alexa suspected that Violet had her eye on Tom and his on her, but neither one of them had appeared to make a move in that direction, which Alexa had always hoped for, because they'd be such a good fit.

Violet placed a roast and vegetables into a stainless steel pot and put it on a gas burner on the stove. "Make me a happy woman. Say there's a nice man in your life. And don't tell me again that the men you meet just aren't enough, because no man will ever be enough for us women."

Usually, Alexa would sigh and tell Violet she had no time for a man, but instead she thought of Macaw and her face flushed.

When Alexa stayed silent, Violet looked up from the stove and exclaimed, "My lands! Praise the Lord! Tell me all about him. Every juicy detail!"

"There's not all that much to tell."

"By the expression on your face, I can tell that's nonsense. Go on with you now. Spill."

"Well, he's very nice. And handsome. He's been helping me with the story I'm working on."

"Oh, another writer? Or a photographer?"

"Not exactly."

"What exactly?"

"Well, he's a businessman of sorts. He owns a bar."

"An entrepreneur, huh? Where's he from?"

"He's Panamanian and Italian. His father was Italian, and his mother is Panamanian. He grew up in Panama in the Canal Zone."

"Oh, so he's cross-cultural, like you."

"Exactly."

"Must have something to talk about in that department, then?"

"Yes."

"And what else do you talk about?" Violet's eyes dug into hers. "Or do you talk at all?"

Alexa laughed out loud. "Violet!"

"Drats! And I thought I was going to hear something really good. So, where's it all headed?"

"We're really from two different worlds. I'm not sure that we're headed anywhere."

"Except maybe to some good pillow talk?" she said, spooning a generous helping of roast and veggies onto an earthenware plate and pushing it toward Alexa. "That's something anyway. A girl's got to have some fun."

"Are we talking about me or you, Violet?"

"Me? It's too late. I'm just an old fart."

"Nonsense! As you would say, it's never too late."

"Your father...what I mean is…" She stopped. "Well, anyway, he's in no condition for anything more serious than a game of cards or rocking on the porch."

"My father." Alexa grinned. "I don't recall mentioning my father."

Now Violet's face colored up. "I was just talking in general terms," she sputtered.

"You and I know he's strong. He'll come out of this. When he does, I expect you to ask him out on a real date. He's too shy to ask you. And if you're worried that I'd find it disrespectful to my mother, don't. Nothing would thrill me more than seeing you and Papa together."

Violet's eyes twinkled as she replied, "Maybe I will, and maybe I won't. You'll just have to wait and see. Now back to fattening you up. After you're done with that, how about some homemade apple pie à la mode?"

"Sounds terrific. How are the avocado trees?"

"Pretty good, although the drought last year did some damage to a few of them."

"And what about Enrique? How's he holding up?"

"He's the Rock of Gibraltar. Your father is lucky to have him, but he knows that. It's because of that man that the farm is still running."

"Maybe we should give him a raise."

"I think he'd be happier with a new kitchen floor and bathroom," said Violet. "That old farmhouse he and his wife are living in is in bad shape. Why they don't complain is beyond me."

"Papa has never really noticed when things fall apart, has he? Maybe it all started when Mama left."

"Fact is, part of your father fell apart when your mother died," said Violet. "Augustina, what a beauty she was. And such a kind, gentle soul."

Alexa stopped eating, hungry for any tidbit about her mother. But she had never asked the burning question she was afraid to hear the answer to—why her mother left her and went on that fateful trip to Mexico? Why hadn't she taken Alexa with her?

Violet had a faraway look in her eyes. "I'll never forget the day she came home from the hospital with you all wrapped up in a big, pink blanket. Lordy, it was near ninety degrees out, but she had you all covered up. You looked like a big, pink cream puff. When she took off all those layers so that I could get a look at you, I thought she'd burst with pride. And the way she handled you, like a porcelain doll."

Alexa's heart ached at the thought of her mother gently swaddling her and holding her to her breast.

"Augustina was a truly fine woman, and so are you," Violet said, patting Alexa's hand. "Eat the rest of your dinner, child. I'll heat you up a piece of pie."

They talked awhile longer about Mexico and her current assignment. Alexa had to be vague, but Violet got the idea that lives were at stake.

"The world is a better place with people like you," she said as she finished up the dinner dishes and dried her hands. "I'm going home now. You look beat. Get some rest. The nurse is on duty for the night, and you've got a big day tomorrow looking for someone permanent to take care of your father. Didn't you say you'll be visiting your editor, too?"

"Yes, Peter's expecting a visit from me. You're right, I should turn in. I'll check on Papa before I go up."

After Violet bustled out, the house became so still that Alexa could hear the tick of the old grandfather clock in the living room. Although her gregarious neighbor talked nonstop and could sometimes be intrusive, Violet had always been fair, and had never felt sorry for Alexa. When she was a child, other women had talked about Alexa as if she couldn't hear. *"Poor thing,"* they'd whisper loudly. *"Her mother just ran off and left the country. Of course, she said she was coming back, but you know foreigners. They said it was a terrible accident. She was gorgeous before, but they had to do a closed casket. They say her body was nearly unrecognizable. Like I always say, here in the States we have a speed limit for a reason."*

Then, after talking about her mother in her presence, the women would turn to Alexa and tisk, or straighten the hair bow it took Papa ten minutes to put in.

Alexa sighed and eased herself down from her chair at the kitchen island. Walking lightly into her father's darkened room, she found the nurse sitting by the bed reading with a book light.

"How is he?"

"He's resting comfortably," the nurse replied. "Probably out for the night."

"You stay until morning, don't you?"

"Yes. Another nurse is coming at six-thirty."

"Goodnight then," said Alexa. "Please wake me if there is a problem."

"Of course. Good night."

As Alexa passed out of the room and into the hallway toward her old bedroom, she noticed how worn out and tired everything looked. The baseboards held a thick layer of dust, and the wallpaper showed loose seams and watermarks. It wasn't surprising, she supposed. Papa hadn't changed anything since Mama died nearly thirty years ago. Down the hall, Alexa pushed open her bedroom door, and it creaked like it always had. For some reason, the creak put her nerves on edge and made her glance around the room.

A while later as she lay on her back and listened to the faint echo of coyote howls in the distant hills, she glanced at the clock beside the bed—eleven. Though exhausted from traveling, she suddenly found it difficult to sleep. Eyeing the hulking dresser in the corner that always made her think of an oversized bear as a child, her mind traveled to the little girls in Mexico and their very real fears.

At some point, Alexa finally dozed off, but she woke with a start when the door creaked open. A scream lodged in her throat until her eyes adjusted, and she saw Felix, her father's old tabby cat.

"Oh, Felix, it's you," she breathed, getting out of bed and scooping the cat into her arms and lying down again. "You silly thing," she said, stroking his soft fur. "You scared me half to death. How have you been?" At the familiar sound of the cat's purring, she soon fell into a deep, dreamless sleep.

Alexa woke early the next morning. She slid out of bed and pulled on jeans and a sweater. Southern California mornings were often nippy. Downstairs she found the bleary-eyed night nurse sipping a cup of coffee in the kitchen.

"How did my father sleep?" she asked.

"Just fine. Not a sound from him. The relief nurse is in with him now. I suspect he'll be up soon."

"Thanks for the report," said Alexa, pouring herself a cup of steamy coffee.

"Violet told me that you'll be the one setting up permanent care for your father. I left the number of two services, including mine, next to the telephone. They should be opening in an hour or so. If you're only here for a couple of days, I'd suggest calling right away so the agencies have time to set up some interviews for you with available nurses."

"I will. Thanks," said Alexa. She took a sip of the coffee and waited for the brew to warm her insides. When the nurse said nothing more, Alexa slipped out of the kitchen door and into the crisp morning air. Mug in hand, she strolled to the avocado orchard. No way could she go in and see Papa without first inspecting the avocado trees. He'd know if she hadn't done a walk-through, and he wouldn't be pleased. As she entered the first stand of trees, Alexa immediately felt the soothing moisture given off by the trees' transpiration. Of every place in the world—and she'd traveled quite a bit in the last few years—this was her favorite place to be. Out here with these massive trees, their comforting canopy and emerald-green fruit, Alexa felt safe and at peace.

She walked the spongy, well-tended earth, making her way to her favorite spot—a giant old tree standing at the edge of a small meadow filled with daisies. Her father could have planted trees in the meadow, but it had been her mother's favorite spot to picnic, so he'd left strict orders to leave it alone. Alexa found the spot on the trunk that always brought tears to her eyes and traced the heart and initials with her forefinger. *TK con AGV* it still said. Tom Kent plus Augustina Guzman Vasquez. This is where it all began. Where her mother and father met and fell in love.

Augustina had come to the ranch when Tom's father ran it. The daughter of a Mexican migrant fruit picker, she was only seventeen when she arrived with her family to harvest avocados. She was shy and beautiful, and Tom Kent fell in love with her immediately. Unfortunately, Tom's father strictly forbid his two sons from running around with the help. He wanted his only offspring to set their sights on local farm owners' daughters. But Tom Kent couldn't keep away from Augustina. They started to talk, and then met secretly in the groves. By the time Tom's father found out, they were madly in love. When Tom said that he intended to marry Augustina, his father raged. He called her trash and fired her father, sending them back on the road to fend for themselves. The next week, however, Tom's father became ill with pneumonia. Unable to get out of bed to continue the annual harvest, he'd been forced to rehire Marcos Vasquez, Augustina's father, because he had been his best and most responsible worker.

It was Tom who searched for and found Marcos, his daughters and wife, living in an abandoned field a few miles away. Aunt Lupe said he rode in on a horse, like a knight in shining armor. He requested that Marcos and his family return, and then swept Augustina, who had just turned eighteen, onto his horse and asked her father for her hand. When the stunned Marcos agreed, Tom galloped away with Augustina clinging to him, her long black hair whipping in the wind. A week later, Tom returned with his new bride. At first, Grandpa Kent blustered and yelled, but he'd been weakened by the pneumonia and eventually gave in and began teaching the young couple about the farm.

The wind kicked up, sending avocado flowers into Alexa's hair. She shook her head in vain against the shower of tiny, lime green buds. They always clung that way, only to be pulled out by persistent fingers. As a child, she imagined that the flowers had magical powers if she let them remain in her hair. That if she had enough, all of the bad things would go away, and the good things would return, like her mother. Were the little girls in Mexico grasping a similar hope, Alexa wondered?

"*Señorita Alexa.*"

Alexa turned around. It was Enrique Medina, Papa's right-hand man. "Enrique! How are you?"

"I am well," said the older man, his back humped from cultivating the earth under the trees for so many years. "But your Papa is not well, no?"

"No, Papa's not doing very well, but I think he's going to get better soon."

"Of course, because you are here."

Alexa felt that all too familiar pang of guilt at Enrique's comment. "He has wonderful medical professionals taking care of him, too. How is the harvest going? He wants a report."

"Well enough; a little drought last winter. The trees are strong like your father."

"Will there be enough avocados for our main markets?"

"Yes, and there will be some for the specialty buyers. Now that we're certified organic, all of the health restaurants in Northern California want our avocados. At a good price, too."

"Sounds like we'll do okay then, but I suspected nothing less with you in charge."

Enrique gave Alexa a pleased smile. "You are staying for a while *Señorita?*"

"Just a couple of days, but I'll come back as soon as I can."

"Good. Please excuse me. I have much to do."

"Of course. Tell Maria I will visit her before I leave."

"She will like that." Enrique crouched under the canopy of a nearby avocado tree and stooped down to examine the soil.

Alexa turned back for the house. Time to call nursing agencies, check in with Papa, and head into San Diego for the day. Once inside the house, she ran into the new nurse, a deliriously chipper early bird who offered Alexa coffee.

"I already had my morning cup, thanks," she said. "How's my father?"

"Much better. You can go in and wish him good morning, if you like."

"I'll do that as soon as I make calls to the nursing agencies."

"Yes, of course!"

Alexa quickly called the agencies, explaining the situation and giving them insurance information. By the time she hung up ten minutes later, she had set up appointments with four nurses the next morning. Hopefully she'd like one of them and feel secure leaving her father in his or her hands.

Time to visit Papa. "You're up," Alexa greeted him. "You look rested."

"I feel better, little one," he said, reaching out to take her hand. "How did you sleep?"

"Great. It's nice to be back in the States. In Mexico, I sleep with one eye and ear open. And before you ask, I just checked on the trees. Everything's fine. The harvest will be good, despite the drought. Enrique has the crews working double-time."

"That man is a lifesaver."

"I'd have to agree."

"Where are you off to?"

"To San Diego to see Peter, and then I'm hoping to surprise Esperanza for lunch."

"Tell Esperanza hello for me."

"I will. Can I borrow the truck?"

"That old thing. Of course."

"Will it get me there and back?"

"It may be old and battered, but Enrique keeps it up."

. . .

A few minutes later, Alexa dressed in tailored brown slacks and a white blouse. Slipping the band out of her hair, she let it hang free, and then grabbed the truck keys out of the kitchen.

She actually liked the old Ford Ranger, even though the back bed had a mess of stray avocado leaves and the brown leather seats cracked with age years ago. Sure enough, the engine reliably fired up, and the truck puttered down the driveway and out onto the paved road. After the dusty roads of Mexico and the continual stench of burning trash, the fresh breeze of Fallbrook was nirvana. She cranked open the old truck window and let the wind course through her hair.

Driving along the road and passing orchards and the occasional farmhouse, Alexa thought of the happy times she and her father spent carrying avocados to market. They would rise in the wee hours of the morning, having loaded the truck the night before, and travel to a farmer's market in the city. There they'd set up their table and wait for local restaurant chefs to swoop in and pick up and admire the deep-green, oval fruit. Though many of the avocado ranches had started switching over to the Haas because of its better shipping durability, Papa had insisted on sticking with the Fuerte avocado because of its creamier texture and bigger fruit. His insight proved successful. It was his avocados that the chefs always swarmed to first.

As she cruised along, Alexa thought about Macaw. They came from such different backgrounds, and yet she felt so close to him—closer than she had ever felt to any other man. Did he feel the same way about her, she wondered? Or was she just a passing flirtation for him? Alexa would love to know, but it wasn't something she could easily ask him. And that brought up the next question. Why him? Why not one of her co-workers, or better yet a nice stable accountant or someone in the publishing world? Someone from her world. Who are you kidding, Alexa, she laughed and asked herself aloud. What is your world, anyway? Isn't this your world? Working undercover in other countries and writing stories about the seedier side of life? When she thought of it that way, Macaw fit nicely into her life. Amazing what a little rationalizing could do for one's psyche.

The briny scent of the sea hit Alexa's nose seconds before the ocean unfolded to her right—its deep blue water flashed with sparks of morning sun. Temperatures hovered around eighty. Splayed on shore were dozens of sunbathers, their colorful umbrellas and bright beach towels scattered across the caramel-tinted sand.

Forty minutes later, she approached downtown San Diego. The newspaper offices were located in one of the few skyscrapers in the city. The joke among the newsroom staff was that they wouldn't be able to cover an earthquake, because they'd be a pile of rubble. Alexa parked in the underground parking garage. As the elevator swept her up to the tenth floor, she mused about the journey journalism had taken her on so far. She had arrived from a mid-sized daily in Fresno where she started working right out of college. Alexa made a reputation for herself by exposing a garment factory scandal, profiling the life of a seamstress with five children, who worked her fingers raw sewing for ten to twelve hours a day for very little pay. When Alexa interviewed for her current position at the *San Diego Union Tribune*, her reputation came with her—mostly because her former boss was friends with Peter and put in a good word for her. At first, Peter was skeptical about giving her a chance with the Latin America beat that had been vacated. He had asked her point blank, since she came from a mid-sized daily in a medium-sized town, what did she know about foreign affairs?

Alexa stood her ground during the interview with Peter, emphasizing that she hoped Peter would give her a try for a month, and then if he thought she couldn't cut it, she'd leave quietly.

Peter hesitantly agreed to Alexa's deal. Her first assignment involved a drug smuggling case at the Port of San Diego. Reporters from other papers also covered the case, but Alexa claimed a coup when she discovered a connection to a local, well-respected shipping magnate. By the time she finished, Alexa had also pinpointed a high-powered judge. After that and a few more successful stories, Peter said that Alexa had a knack for sniffing out slime and handed her free rein. Was the ability to pinpoint corruption innate, she sometimes speculated? Or had years fending for herself emotionally without a mother's input honed her detection skills?

The editorial department hummed when she arrived. Several reporters greeted her as she cruised to Peter's office. He sat at his desk with a big red marker reviewing that morning's paper.

"Peter?"

"Alexa. Welcome home. How's your father?"

"He looked better this morning than he did last night. But I have to admit, I've never seen him so weak and defenseless."

"It's hard, I know," said Peter, his eyes softening.

Alexa remembered that he had lost his mother to Alzheimer's a couple of years before.

"I guess you would know," she said quietly.

Peter nodded. "So, bring me up to speed with the story."

Alexa shut his door and began unraveling the sordid events of the last few weeks.

"How do people get so sick?" Peter said when she finished.

"I don't know, but I do know that I have to blow this wide open and get those poor little girls out as soon as possible."

"I won't argue with you there. Do you still have enough money to back you up?"

Alexa thought about how Macaw still held most of the cash and hoped that Peter wasn't going to engage her in a conversation about how much was left. Though she had felt safe leaving the money with Macaw back in Mexico, now that she was so far away, anxiety crept its way into her thoughts. "I have enough for now," she replied. "I'll let you know, though, and I'll get you a detailed accounting in the next few days."

"Thanks, I've got a meeting with the higher-ups next week, so I'll need it."

They sat in silence for a moment.

"So, this source you've been using. He's a big help?"

"Tremendous. I wouldn't have gotten as far as I have without him."

"That's good to hear. With his connections, he should be able to keep you safe. And you trust him?"

Alexa nodded and changed the subject, picking Peter's brain on how to access certain Mexican government files.

As she prepared to leave a few minutes later, Peter asked, "So you think you'll be ready to go back tomorrow?"

"Yes, please get me a flight out tomorrow late afternoon."

"You sure you don't need more time with your father?"

"It would be nice, but I don't have the luxury. I'm afraid to let this trail get too cold. I don't want them to get spooked and move the little girls."

"I'll feel better when you're done with this one," said Peter. "I know it's been a nail-biter for you. I have to admit, it's keeping me on edge, too. Call or email me every day. No exceptions. Find an internet café, if you have to. Oh, and stop in administration on your way out. Your new laptop is waiting."

"Thanks. I'll try to keep this one safe."

"You just take care of yourself, okay?" said Peter.

"I promise."

Back in her father's pickup a few minutes later, Alexa jockeyed in traffic as she made her way toward the eastern part of downtown. She hadn't had a chance to call her childhood friend, Esperanza, earlier, so she hoped that lunch would be possible.

When she parked in front of the glass building of Korman Law Offices, Alexa checked her reflection in the rearview mirror and grimaced. Digging around in her purse, she pulled out her beat-up tube of burgundy-colored lipstick. Sliding it over her lips, she wished that she had some eye shadow or blush. Esperanza was the queen of fashion—always had been. When they met in junior high, she tried with no success to get Alexa excited about flipping through teen magazines and salivating over the latest designer clothing. Now a high-powered criminal attorney, she could afford all of the latest trends, and even in her more conservative lawyer clothes, she always came off incredibly stylish.

At the reception desk, Alexa asked, "Esperanza Perez, please."

"Do you have an appointment?"

Alexa was about to reply when Esperanza breezed out of her office dressed in a pale gray, silk suit.

"Sonia, where are those notes from yesterday's meeting? I need them by—" She stopped short when she saw Alexa.

"Alexa! Where in the world did you come from?"

"I'm in town for a couple of days and thought I'd stop in to see if you can do lunch."

"This is such a great surprise. Luckily, there's no court for me today. Come on in. Thanks, Sonia, I'll get those notes later," she said to her secretary, gesturing Alexa into her spacious, elegantly appointed office with floor to ceiling windows overlooking the bay. Esperanza walked to a plush red couch that sat in the corner of the room and plopped down, kicking off her dark gray stilettos. "Have a seat."

Alexa sat down and sighed.

"What's the matter, Lexie?" she asked.

"Who says anything's the matter?"

"You're talking to me, remember? What's up?"

"Papa had a stroke."

"Oh, no!" Esperanza gasped. "Is he okay?"

"I think he's going to be alright. But you can never tell for sure. And he's so weak."

"I'm so sorry. I had no idea. When did it happen?"

"Last week. I just got in last night."

"Alexa! Your dad had a stroke last week, and you're just now making it here?"

"There wasn't anything I could do at first. He was in the hospital for several days, and they didn't even tell me about it until a couple of days after it happened."

"But Lexie—"

"Essie, I feel bad enough already, believe me."

"Okay, okay. I won't say anything more. Dare I ask how long you're here?"

"I have to go back tomorrow afternoon."

"Back where? Mexico again?"

Alexa nodded. "And before you ask if I can make my stay a little longer, I can't. I'm in the middle of a really big story, and—"

"I know you have to get back to it. That part I understand. I'm a working girl, too. What I can't for the life of me understand is your fascination with that country. I know I was born there, and my mama still loves going back whenever she can, but I just don't get it. It's so backward, and they have absolutely no fashion sense!"

Alexa laughed. "Fortunately, I don't report on the latest and greatest in attire."

"What are you reporting on?"

"A sordid mess in Mexico."

"Need any legal advice? I have plenty of pals in our Mexico office."

"I might." Alexa spilled a few vague details.

"Those poor baby girls! You have to get them out of there."

"I will. But I'm just wondering about the laws in Mexico. Are they as severe as here for child pornography? I'd hate for them to wriggle out of this whole thing."

"As far as I understand, the laws in that area are as strict as they are here."

"Good."

"Do you want to go to that Italian place on the corner?" asked Esperanza.

"Yes, the food is scrumptious."

"Anything would be scrumptious after the slop they feed you in Mexico."

"It's not all slop!"

"Okay, I've had some good food there, I'll admit. And the margaritas are fabulous."

A couple of doors down, they walked into Antonio's. The host greeted them with a big smile and directed them to a prime table in front of the window overlooking the street.

"So what's up besides work?" asked Esperanza. "Anyone new in your life?"

"You and Violet!" Alexa shifted uncomfortably in her chair.

"Me and Violet, what? It sounds more like you and someone. Tell me. Now!"

Alexa told Esperanza about Macaw.

"A bad boy, huh? So how is he in the sack? Did fireworks go off?"

"We haven't gotten that far. Yet."

"At least there's a yet. You lead such a boring love life. Take the plunge —or should I say, jump, and get to bed with him as soon as you get back."

Alexa laughed. "You never mince words. Speaking of love, how's Mike?"

"Great. I can't believe we've been dating for more than two years now. We're thinking about getting married."

"You are! That's great."

Esperanza frowned.

"What's wrong? Don't you want to get married?"

"Yeah, I think so," she said, nibbling on bread sticks from the basket on the table. "I don't know. I hate to give up my freedom, but then again, I don't really do much of anything but spend time with him anyway."

"It's just cold feet," assured Alexa.

"Probably."

They finished their lunch chatting about old friends they hadn't seen in a while and Esperanza's mother, who couldn't stop meddling in her life. "She has already picked out my wedding cake!" she exclaimed. "I don't know what I'm going to do with that woman." Her friend stopped. "I'm sorry Lexie. I don't always think. Here I am complaining about my mother. It sounds really juvenile."

"It's okay," said Alexa. "You don't have to apologize because of my mother, but I appreciate your sensitivity."

When they finished eating, Esperanza checked her watch. "It's getting late, and I have a deposition in a half hour."

They both headed back to the law offices and hugged out front of Esperanza's building. Alexa took the parking garage stairs down to her truck. When she pulled out onto the street, she noticed a gray sedan behind her. Not a big deal, she assured herself, but she soon became apprehensive when she saw that the sedan made sure no cars got between them. Unease pricked the hairs along the back of her neck. She turned right quickly. The sedan followed. Up ahead at the next stoplight, she stayed in her lane, but took a hard right at the last moment. The sedan slid by, but not before she got a quick look at the driver's stony profile. It must have been a tail, she thought, concerned. But who? Who else knew about the story? It didn't make sense.

Alexa cruised slowly for a couple of minutes, checking around to make sure that she'd lost the tail. When she felt confident she'd ditched him, she headed for Pacific Coast Highway and kicked the speed up to sixty on the open road. She'd feel better when she got back to the safety of the ranch. Hell, she'd feel better when she got back to Mexico and Macaw. There, she admitted missing the guy to herself. Not so bad. After a while, the ocean unfolded to her left and she began to breathe easier.

A half hour later as she neared Fallbrook, she hummed a song from her high school days and thought about Papa. He loved chess. Maybe he'd feel up to playing after dinner. Trying to remember where she put the game the last time they used it, Alexa didn't notice the gray sedan until it tailgated her. Spotting it in the rearview mirror, she nearly drove off the side of the road. Who was he? What did he want? Could it be about a previous story? Or was it this one? She pushed the speedometer higher and racked her brain for the best approach. She would soon reach the ranch driveway. But what if he followed her up? She couldn't put her father in that kind of danger. Should she call 911? Was she really certain the sedan followed her?

Just a half mile from the ranch, she had an idea. Putting on her emergency flashers, she began to swerve wildly. Glancing back, she noted the driver had been taken off guard by her behavior. Good—it was just what she wanted. She quickly stopped the swerving and sped up, turning off her hazards. After passing the ranch driveway and a bend in the road, she swerved off on a side road she knew. Her assailant's car raced on ahead and down a hill. She brought the truck to a halt, then slammed it into reverse, did a quick U-turn, and floored it to return to the ranch. Speeding down the drive, she pulled off into the orchards, praying that Enrique was nowhere about. Hopping out, she looked cautiously from her vantage point and saw the sedan speed past, heading back in the direction they had come from. There was a good chance that he hadn't even seen the driveway opening.

Ironically, for years Alexa had bugged her father to make the entrance more prominent, because visitors were always passing it by and getting lost. He had refused, saying that the ranch was his own private oasis, and the fewer people who knew about it the better. Right about now Alexa would have to agree. After waiting a good fifteen minutes, she pulled the truck out of the trees and headed back to the house. For now, she decided to put the incident out of her mind. She'd go inside and enjoy her father's company.

7

When Alexa returned to *La Cantina Cantata* the following evening, she found a note from Macaw on her threshold. It said, "Call me," and underneath he'd drawn a macaw. Smiling, she marveled at the contradictions of the man. Was that why he fascinated her? She never knew what new side of him she'd see?

She punched in his number on her cell phone.

"Hey. Get back okay?"

"Yeah, I'm standing in my room looking at your note. Nice drawing."

"Thanks. I'm no Picasso, but I try."

"So, anything exciting happen while I was gone?"

"I worked on Imelda and defrosted her frozen heart. She's going to let us see three of the girls tomorrow."

"Great! Hopefully Liana will be one of them."

"Just promise me you won't try to do anything heroic."

"It'll be hard, but I know it would jeopardize getting all of the girls out of there. Imelda could disappear with them forever," said Alexa as she lay down on her bed and gazed up at the ceiling.

"So, how's your dad?"

"He improved some while I was there."

"That's good. Sounds like it was a worthwhile trip. I got some info on the creeps that stopped in front of Ramona's the other day. Want me to come over and share it?"

"That'd be great. I had a visit from another unwanted friend when I was driving back to the ranch from San Diego."

"You shitting me? Sounds like you're getting more and more popular by the minute. I'll bring some of my *empanadas*. I made a batch this morning."

"And you cook," she said, smiling into the phone. "My hero."

While Alexa waited for her *empanadas*, Macaw snapped his cell phone shut and slipped it into his jeans as he walked through the crowded bar. Things were humming for a Thursday night. That was good. He needed the cash, because he had just about stopped distributing pot. Since Alexa came along, he didn't have the time, and he had to admit, he didn't have the heart for it anymore. Helping her made him reach inside and pull out the good stuff he had hidden away. He realized he was only fooling himself, though. Sure, she liked him, and even seemed attracted. But their two worlds were so far apart he might as well live on the moon. In a way, he felt irritated with himself—rushing over to see her the minute she got back. He couldn't help himself, though, and he needed to tell her about the two goons that had turned up at Ramona's the other day. The news wasn't good. For now, he'd do what he'd always done. Live in the moment and take what seemed like the next logical step. He didn't know any other way.

Alexa's mouth watered for the *empanadas* even before she pulled open the door. As Macaw entered her room, she held out her hand for the bag he held.

"So now I find out the truth," he said, raising the bag of savory pastries above his head. "You only like me for my cooking."

Alexa laughed and attempted to reach the *empanadas* by standing on tiptoe. "There are a few other reasons I like you, but for now, I have to admit the *empanadas* are on the top of my list. C'mon, they smell fantastic. Give them to me."

"Not before. . . ." Macaw trailed off.

"Before what?"

"Nothing."

"No, go ahead. Before what?" Alexa's eyes twinkled.

"Here," he said, handing over the *empanadas*. "I feel so used."

"That's terrible you feel that way. I don't have any cash on hand," she stopped and moved in close, giving him a quick kiss on the mouth, "but hopefully that can serve as payment."

Macaw grinned. "Partial payment. Maybe."

Sitting down on the edge of her bed, Alexa ripped open the bag and inhaled the scent of ground beef and onion. She bit into an *empanada* and moaned in pleasure. With her mouth full, she asked, "Aren't you going to eat?"

"I scarfed a bunch right after I finished making them a couple of hours ago. I'm still full."

Macaw liked watching her devour the *empanadas*. Unlike most chicks, constantly worrying about their weight and agonizing over every bite, Alexa dug in and savored her food. When she finished every last morsel, she sucked the golden juices from several fingers and then sighed contentedly. "I lied to Violet."

"The neighbor with the hots for your old man?"

"Yeah, I told her that the food in Mexico was edible, just bland. I forgot about how luscious your *empanadas* are."

"I'll cook for you anytime, babe."

Alexa's eyes caught his, and she gave him a slow smile.

"You're fed, so it's back to work," said Macaw. "Those guys that stopped at Ramona's the other day work for someone high up in immigration."

"Immigration? "

"US Naturalization and Immigration."

"Who is it?"

"I'm not sure yet. My sources are still digging."

"I guess that explains how they're getting girls across the border without incident or anyone noticing."

He nodded. "I've got a source inside who's supposed to get in touch with me soon. Now tell me more about the guy in Fallbrook."

Alexa explained how she'd been followed in the city but thought she'd lost him.

"Damn, he sounds bold. You sure you've never seen the guy? Could it have been one of our pals from Immigration?"

Alexa shook her head. "I only saw his profile as he drove past, but it was definitely someone else." A tingle of anxiety slid down her spine. "How worried should I be?"

"I'm not gonna lie to you. We've got a lot of players here—the guys at Ramona's—the ones who almost nabbed you after the bank—now Fallbrook, and we have no idea who ransacked your room. We're obviously pissing off a lot of people, but that's okay. It means we're getting close."

Alexa nodded. "That's what usually happens."

"Yeah, I'm sure you know," agreed Macaw. "You've done some heavy stories. Covering that drug bust on the San Diego border must have gotten really rough. I seriously can't believe you did that one on your own."

"I look back, and I can't believe it either," said Alexa, thankful that this time she wasn't alone.

As if Macaw read her mind, he replied, "I'm here for you on this one. You're covered. So tell me about your visit to your dad's. What'd you do?"

"Talked mostly. About the ranch. My job."

"Not about him and Violet?" Macaw grinned.

Alexa laughed. "I tried to steer the conversation to her, but he either didn't understand what I was up to, or he was avoiding the topic."

"I vote for the latter."

Alexa liked the easy banter. She considered asking him to get a beer in the cantina when his cell phone rang.

He listened to a torrent of Spanish on the other end with a furrowed brow and then answered, "Who? Did you break it up? How bad's he hurt? How much damage?"

Macaw snapped his cell phone shut and frowned. "I gotta get back to the bar. Some dumb asses got into a fight."

"Of course," Alexa said, following him to the door.

"I'll pick you up tomorrow to see the girls."

"Let's pray Liana will be there. I'd love to give her parents some hopeful news. And if we have time tomorrow, we need to go to the church Rodolfo told us about."

"I was hoping you forgot about that."

"You can hope all you want, but we're going." She watched him make his way down the stairs, marveling again at how nimble he was for such a large, muscular guy.

The next morning, they headed out, camera in tow. As Macaw predicted, now that money flowed Imelda's way, she set caution aside and eagerly awaited their arrival. On the ride over to Imelda's, Alexa thought about people who actually enjoyed this kind of thing, and she inwardly cringed. With other stories she'd been able to imagine, even though she thought it wrong, what it might be like to use drugs, for example, until you were so high you couldn't remember your name, or the thrill of smuggling guns and getting away with it. But kidnapping and selling children? Not in any universe could she imagine understanding that.

Macaw ran inside to pay Imelda before they headed to the hotel, and Alexa was glad for that. The less she saw of that toxic woman, the better.

When he hopped back in the MG beside her, he snorted in disgust. "That wacko told me not to hurt her babies."

A few minutes later, they walked into the hotel room at *La Luna,* and Alexa's heart cried out. On the bed sat three forlorn little girls. One girl, no more than eight or nine, sucked on the hem of her skirt. Another clung to Rosalita, who looked up, relief crossing her face when she saw Alexa.

Oh, how Alexa wished she and Macaw could swoop Rosalita and the other two up and give them a real reason to be relieved!

"Hi Rosalita," Alexa said. "Who are your friends?"

"This is Liana," she said of the little girl clinging to her. "And that is Lily."

"We're just going to take your pictures, and then I have lollipops for you all."

Rosalita didn't reply as Alexa, hands shaking, struggled to pull the camera from its case. Macaw took the camera from her. "I'll take the shots. You pose them like your old man wants," he said. Alexa watched him scan the room—most likely searching for a hidden camera.

"You're right," she said, kneeling on the floor next to the girls. "He definitely likes things a certain way."

Macaw proceeded to take photos and talk loudly about how good they were turning out, while she made a show of arranging their hair and clothing. As she did this, she asked them questions in a low voice.

"How long did it take you to get here?"

"Not a long time," replied Rosalita. "I'm hungry."

"Do they feed you?"

"Yes, but it doesn't taste good. It makes my stomach hurt."

"Do you remember anything about where you're staying?"

"It's in a basement," said Liana.

Now they were getting somewhere! "Describe the basement," she said.

"It's dark and scary," said Liana. "I want to go home."

"Anything else you can remember about the basement? Can you see outside?"

Liana shook her head, but Lily piped up. "There is one window. I can see—"

The guard rapped on the door at that moment, announcing their time had ended, which caused the girls to shut down. Alexa willed away the tears threatening to erupt as she gave each of them two lollipops.

Macaw watched Alexa give the girls the candy and turn to leave. As they headed for the door, he thought, now comes the hard part—throwing them back to the wolves. He pictured Imelda's greedy face and wondered about the identity of the head honcho, and rage boiled in his veins. If he found the guy right then and there, he'd easily rip his arms and legs off.

Outside, the guard stood with his chest puffed, blocking their path.

"What's your problem?" asked Macaw. "We paid Imelda."

"She wants to see the film," said the guard.

"No way. We had a deal. She can go to hell."

"She wants to see the film," the guard repeated, waving a gun in their faces.

"Look, brain surgeon, there is no film. This is digital—it's in the camera."

"We'll go back and show her the photos, okay?" said Alexa, working to avoid gunfire.

The guard hesitated.

"You need the camera to show the film," she explained. "We have both. Let us go back and talk to her."

"You don't want to piss Imelda off, *hombre*," said Macaw. "Trust me. I've seen her cut off balls. Let us take care of this."

The guard clearly had no idea what to do, so he pulled out a cell phone. When he started to speak, Macaw grabbed the phone from him. "Look, you crazy bitch. We didn't pay you two grand to have your goon fuck with us. You want any more business, you tell him to let us be on our way."

Imelda spewed out a string of vile Spanish cuss words and then Macaw handed the phone back to the guard. He listened to Imelda's order and stepped aside to let them pass.

Back in the car, Alexa tried to calm down, but couldn't get the image of the gun out of her head. What a weakling she was. That minor altercation couldn't begin to compare with the nightmare the young girls were enduring. She laid her head back against the car's seat and closed her eyes.

"After she finished bitching me out about the photos, she asked if we'd be back tomorrow," said Macaw. "She must have one of Fernando's loan sharks breathing down her fat neck."

"What'd you tell her?"

"That we'll be in touch. She threatened and said that she's moving them soon."

Alexa grabbed Macaw's arm. "We have to get them out—now. Just pull your gun!"

"We can't, not yet," he said, looking down to where her fingernails dug into the skin on his arm, bringing blood to the surface.

Alexa removed her hand and threw her head back against the car seat. "I'm sorry. I don't even know what I'm doing. I feel like screaming, crying, yelling, punching down a brick wall. The thought of losing them—I seriously don't think I could live with myself."

"Listen, I know this sucks major, but don't worry about Imelda moving them. It's just a scare tactic. She's not going to do that until she feels like we're tapped out. You did a really good job in there. I'm sure she won't suspect a thing, even if she watches the tape. As you and I both know, we've got to hold out for the big name behind this. And that was only three of the girls. You saw a lot more in the warehouse—like twelve or thirteen, right? And that was just a recent shipment."

As they headed back to the cantina, Alexa felt trapped inside of the MG. "It's so hot and muggy in this blasted country," she said, a volcano of emotion in her chest. Watching the sights of downtown La Paz pass steadied her. Art galleries, restaurants, vegetable vendors, people walking the streets. By the time they pulled up in front of the cantina, she said,

"You're right. We do need to get to the top dog. Those little girls will have to hold on a while longer."

She hoped that her proclamation would make Macaw relax, but it didn't appear to. He scrutinized her. "I've got an important meeting in a half an hour in the bar, otherwise I'd come up. You going to be okay? I'll come back in a while and we can go to the church, if there's still time."

"Yeah, I'm good," Alexa assured him. "Go do what you have to do."

He waited until she entered the cantina and then drove away.

Alexa plodded upstairs to her room and lay down on the bed, remembering another time she felt this helpless.

She had been given the privilege of assisting Enrique in the avocado orchard. A storm had ripped through the night before and avocados littered the ground. Hoping to salvage as many as possible, Enrique had the whole crew—including six-year-old Alexa—gather them.

When she had returned that afternoon with a bucket of avocados, the house creaked with stillness. Papa sat at the kitchen table with his head in his hands.

"What's the matter, Papa?" Alexa had asked, an uneasy feeling gripping her.

Her father turned to her, his face masked with pain.

"Your mama had an accident, Lexie."

"What do you mean?"

"She died in a car accident this morning."

"Mama's in Mexico. She said she's coming home soon."

"I'm sorry, little one. Your mama isn't ever coming home."

"No!" Alexa screamed. "No! I want my mama. Give me my mama!"

Her father tried to calm her, but Alexa continued to yell and kick as if possessed by something unseen. Not until Violet took her in her arms and spoke to her in low, soothing tones did Alexa finally stop screaming. And even then, she whimpered all night. Violet stayed next to Alexa's bed rocking her back and forth in her arms, and later coaxing her to eat and drink.

At one point, they thought she slept, but Alexa heard them.

"I'm worried about her Tom. She's so torn up."

"We're all torn up."

"That no good brother of yours doesn't look too upset. Went off to the bar like nothing ever happened, and he was the reason Augustina left in the first place."

"Freddy had nothing to do with it. Augustina left to see her family in Mexico."

"Excuse my French, but that's a bunch of crap, and you know it, Tom Kent."

"He lost his job, Violet, give him a break. Being part of the Secret Service meant everything to him."

"Your brother had a bright future, I'll give him that, but he lost his job because of his drinking. That was his own choice, and the sooner you see he has a problem, the better. Where's he getting all of that money, anyway? Not on a government pension, I'll tell you."

"Freddy brought Alexa back from Mexico, didn't he? Thank God, too. If Alexa had been in that car with Augustina, I don't know what I would have done."

"Haven't you asked yourself why, Tom? Why didn't Augustina bring Alexa back? Why did your wife stay, and why did Freddy return?"

"I don't have the energy to talk about this now Violet."

"Well, you better get the energy. You've got a very sad little girl in there, and this is one hurt you can't fix with a cookie or a pat on the back."

Pulling her thoughts back to the present, Alexa distracted herself by listening to the clatter of pots and pans below as the kitchen crew prepared the midday meal. Eventually, her eyelids grew heavy, and she drifted off, waking a few minutes later to the sound of a trash truck in the street. Her eyes focused on the camera. She wanted to visit Liana's parents and get a positive ID; then ensure them their daughter was still alive.

Alexa picked up the camera and turned it on to inspect the photos. She could kiss Macaw. In the headshots he'd taken of each girl, somehow, they didn't look terrified. They could show Liana's parents their daughter without alarming them any further.

Shaking the sleep out of her head, she sat down at her new computer and began to write. Sometimes it was best this way—letting the words tumble out and just typing them as they came. She wrote about the little girls in the hotel room—their sad eyes and rumpled clothing. She likened them to rag dolls separated from their owners, lost and alone. As Alexa wrote the words, her own despair filled the computer screen. Not until a knock on the door did she notice the tears on her cheeks.

"Who is it?" she called out.

"It's me," said Macaw.

Alexa wiped tears from her face with the back of her hand and opened the door.

"What's the matter? Your old man okay?"

"I was writing about the girls in the hotel room."

"Heavy duty, huh?"

She nodded.

"Macaw sat down on Alexa's bed and studied her. "Anything else up? You sure you're okay?"

"Yeah. It's just those children. It's killing me to leave them there."

"I hear you. I want to move on this thing, too, and get them out of there. What's the latest?" He saw the camera on the table. "Photos okay?"

"They're great. We need to go and have Liana's parents ID her and then assure them she's okay. After that we'll go to Rodolfo's church."

"Visiting the parents sounds okay, but church?"

"We need to move on that lead Rodolfo gave us about Fernando Gomez talking to a priest."

"I know. The trouble is when the *padre* hears how long it's been since I've been in church, he might kick me out."

"So, don't tell him."

"I can tell you're not Catholic. They ask you the last time you confessed."

"Shouldn't they be happy you're confessing and not worry about the technicalities?"

"The Catholics are big on technicalities, but I'll live through it. I lived through Catholic elementary school."

"That I'm trying to picture," said Alexa, giving him an amused smile. "There's a lot about you I don't know."

"I'll have to fill you in one of these days. But for now, you ready to go? We've got a mother to make happy and a priest to drive crazy."

Liana's brothers and sisters saw Alexa and Macaw coming from a distance. By the time they arrived in the dusty courtyard, Elvita and Juan waited. Alexa's heart fell to her feet when she saw their hopeful expressions.

"You don't have our Liana?" Elivita's eyes reflected worry.

"I think we found her. She is doing okay," said Alexa.

"You saw our little girl?" asked Juan.

Alexa pulled out the camera and pressed buttons until the little girl's face popped up.

"Liana!" cried the woman, caressing the camera's screen as tears rolled down her cheeks. "Where is she? You did not bring her home to us?"

"We're working around the clock to get her home."

"Tell me where she is. I will go get her myself," declared Juan.

"Sorry *Señor*, we can't do that," Macaw spoke up. "But you've got my word that we'll get her home soon."

"*Gracias, Señor*," said Elvita, nodding at Macaw. "Forgive my husband. His heart is heavy since Liana left."

"We understand," said Alexa. "We will work as quickly as we can to bring Liana home to you. We won't rest until we do."

"I know you will bring her home. Juan and I will continue to pray for God to assist you both."

As Alexa and Macaw walked away, he grasped her hand and said, "Elvita is right. We'll get them out of that hell-hole soon."

Twenty minutes later when they arrived at *La Christiana* Cathedral, Alexa looked up at the massive, ancient building.

"What a beautiful old church," she marveled and then turned to Macaw, "Ready to confess your deepest, darkest secrets?"

A shadow fell over Macaw's face. "The father doesn't have enough time to hear about all of my sins."

"Just tell him about your most recent ones."

"That could take days. Plus, I'm a steak lover, even on Fridays."

Alexa smiled. "I don't know if that's such a big sin."

"Like I said, you're definitely not Catholic. What's the priest's name again?"

"Father Pedro."

Inside the church, the hushed, cool air embraced them. It took Alexa's eyes several seconds to adjust to the dim light. Once they did, the first thing she noticed were the mass of creamy white candles flickering in front of the pulpit and lining long tables on each side. Though the streets of La Paz and many other Mexican cities were often littered with trash, the inside of the church was pristine. Where the candlelight hit the rows of wooden pews, the wood gleamed. And the silence. So deep and serene. The only sound was a slight murmur coming from one of the confessionals.

As Macaw waited to confess, Alexa slid into a pew and sat down to watch visitors reverently cross the polished concrete floor to light candles. Within a couple of minutes, she heard the muffled rumble of Macaw's deep voice. Running her hand along the worn wooden seatback in front of her, Alexa thought about her mother. She felt so close to her here—as if she might even be sitting next to her.

"Something weighs heavily on your heart, *Señorita?*"

Alexa looked up to see a balding priest with kind eyes.

She hesitated, but then replied. "Yes."

"A loss perhaps?"

Alexa felt a calm wash over her as the father sat down.

"My mama," she said, surprising herself. "She died tragically when I was only six years old."

"Ah, a loss that runs deep," he said. "That one is not so easily mended."

"No," said Alexa, who felt an unwelcome knot of emotion form in her throat. "I'm usually okay, but sometimes—"

"Sometimes you feel utterly alone."

"Yes."

"But I think you know, *Señorita*, that God is always with you, and so is your mother through him?"

"I would like to believe that."

"You can rely on it," he said, patting her hand.

She smiled at the priest. "Thank you, *padre*. You are very kind."

"God is the most kind of all. He wants to lift your heart in hope, child. Return whenever you feel alone or sorrowful. Now I have an appointment and must go," he apologized, getting up to leave. "But please, come back."

"I will," promised Alexa. "Who should I ask for?"

"*Padre* Pedro," he answered and glided from the pew down the center aisle, his robes rustling as he walked.

Momentarily stunned, Alexa followed after him, stopping when a parishioner took his arm in deep conversation. The two walked toward the front of the church and disappeared.

Pursuing the priest and asking him about Fernando when he was otherwise occupied didn't seem like the prudent thing to do. Alexa would have to wait awhile to see if she could catch him alone again. In the meantime, her mother on her mind, Alexa felt compelled to do something in her honor.

Macaw stepped out of the confessional, surprised. Getting some of that crap off his chest actually felt good. Scanning the sanctuary for Alexa, he spotted her in front of a table of candles, their fluttering light illuminating her face. She lit one and stood for a moment with her head bowed, praying for her mother, he wondered, or the little girls? When she turned to leave the table, their eyes met across the room, and he felt an unfamiliar strumming sensation in his chest. Shit, was that his heart? He didn't move as she smiled and walked toward him.

"Hi," she whispered. "How'd things go?"

"Good, but I don't think he's the priest we're looking for."

"He wasn't. I actually talked to him but didn't find out his name until he was walking away and someone else approached him," she said as she glanced around the church. A woman sitting in the front row gave them an annoyed look, and Alexa pointed to the door.

Exiting into a small courtyard, they shielded their eyes against the glare of late afternoon sun. When another priest approached, Alexa asked him where she could find *Padre* Pedro and was told that he had left.

"He told me to come back whenever I want," shrugged Alexa. "I'll try again tomorrow."

Macaw nodded.

"So how was your confession?"

"I never thought I'd say this, but it felt good to come clean. I did some praying to myself for the girls, too."

Alexa looked at him, eyes wide, surprised at his words. She took both his hands and imagined her mother watching over them.

8

It would rain soon, Macaw could tell. The thickening air hung around him like heavy mist from a waterfall. He undid the top couple buttons of his jungle print shirt and turned on the little fan at his office desk. As its motor whirred, he stared at the latest numbers from the bar without seeing them, and then threw the accounting book back down again. Closing his eyes, he leaned back in his chair and conjured up an image of his old home in Panama. Every rainy season, the backyard would flood, sending rivulets of water every which way. As a kid, he used to love playing outside during the rainstorms—especially when his old man was yelling at his mama. He'd take the fallen leaves from the mango tree and pretend they were big ships carrying him downstream.

Thinking about his childhood home always did this—gave him a gnawing feeling of emptiness that only a stiff drink could fill. He opened his eyes and pulled out a small bottle of Jack Daniel's from his desk drawer, uncapped it, tipped it towards his lips and then stopped. Shit, who the hell was he fooling? This wasn't all about Panama—it was about Alexa, too. He couldn't stop thinking about yesterday. Hell, he'd gone to a church with her, and it had meant something to him. She was getting under his skin, major. He hadn't felt this way about anyone—in the sense of feeling really close to someone—since Randy. When he lost his best buddy, Macaw shut down emotionally and started going through the motions of life. Until now. What was it about Alexa that got him thinking that maybe feeling was possible? Sure, she was sexy, but it wasn't just that.

Snorting in irritation, he tightened the cap, threw the whiskey back in his desk drawer and left his office.

"I'm going out for a while," he announced. "Call me if the shipment comes in. I want to do a close check on the vodka bottles. I think we got shorted last month."

His head bartender nodded in acknowledgement.

Macaw told himself that he'd just go visit one of his showgirl friends, Angela or Gabriella, get his rocks off and then go back to the bar, but before he knew it, he found himself in front of *La Cantina Cantata*. What the hell did he think he was doing, anyway? He had street-smarts, sure, but she was a brainy, successful chick. Way too smart for him. The only reason she was involved with him in the first place was the story—she needed his help. Just thinking about her got him hard, and he cursed himself, got out of his car and headed upstairs.

Taking the stairs three at a time, he stopped in front of her door and rapped hard. "Alexa, you there? It's me."

He heard her walk across the floor, and then she pulled the door open. Dressed in white shorts and a red tank top, she had her long hair wrapped in a bun on her head and held it with a pencil.

"Hi." She smiled. "Any word on anything?" Then she frowned at the look in his eyes. "Is something wrong?"

"Yeah, something's wrong," Macaw said, closing the door behind him and grabbing the pencil out of her hair. He sucked in his breath as her black, shiny mane fell onto her shoulders and over her breasts.

"You are so damned beautiful. That's what's wrong."

Alexa's eyes widened, and she blushed. "I guess this is where I say thanks."

He reached for her, pulling her close and covering her mouth with his. She responded, and as she melted into his chest, he felt her nipples harden through the thin tank top. Taking a hand full of her silky hair in one fist, he pulled her head back and ran his tongue down her sweet-tasting neck, stopping at the tender hollow.

Rain began pelting the cantina's roof, and Alexa jumped at the sound and pulled back.

"No," Macaw groaned. "Don't push me away again."

"I'm not." She gave a nervous laugh. "I have to close the window. The rain."

He sat on the edge of the bed and watched her pull the window shut and draw the curtains. Turning around, in one fluid movement, she peeled off her tank top, exposing her breasts. And then she unzipped her shorts and stood there backlit by the wind-whipped, gray afternoon light peeking through a part in the curtain.

C 'mere," he urged.

A faint smile on her lips, Alexa stepped out of her shorts and panties and came closer, each step causing his heart to flip-flop. Stopping in front of him, she kneeled on the floor, unbuttoning his shirt and planting a kiss on his chest with each button she released. His hot skin welcomed her cool, smooth hands as she pushed the shirt off his shoulders and smiled at the chest and pecs he had worked so hard to chisel. When she ran her tongue down his belly to just above the top button of his jeans, he felt a grenade go off in his head. As if waiting for the explosion to stop, for a suspended moment Alexa hesitated, and his heart fell. Was she changing her mind? Realizing who she was with? He let out a breath he didn't know he'd been holding when with quick fingers, she unbuttoned his jeans, releasing him. Moaning and nearly coming right then and there, he reached into his back pocket for a condom and then kicked off his pants. As she unfurled the rubber onto him, Alexa's sweet, gentle movements pushed him so far past excitement that when she finished, he lay back on the bed and pulled her on top of him.

When Macaw picked her up, as if on cue, thunder rumbled outside, and the rain thrummed even harder on the roof. Breathless with desire, she had difficulty distinguishing between the storm and her own heart. She looked down at Macaw—powerful and good-looking enough to get any girl he wanted. Something had stopped her the first time they had gotten this far, but this time, though she still felt a tinge of the odd anxiety, she let herself fall into the sweet abyss of pleasure, need, desire that filled her like nothing else could. He took one of her breasts into his mouth and she cried out, thankful for the storm's masking roar. Never had she felt so alive or exposed, and for once in her life, she didn't care. She just knew as she lowered herself onto him and he filled her that she wanted this moment of time suspended in eternity.

Smiling down at him, she ran her hands over the mound of his biceps and slowly started to rock her hips, flirting with his desire to hurry. When he wrapped his strong hands around her bottom and began to lift her in an effort to quicken things up, she laughed and pulled his arms away.

"You think I'm made of steel or something?" he said. Reaching up, he cupped her breasts and rubbed the nipples with his thumbs, then encircled her waist and pulled her hard against him.

"Go slow," she breathed in Macaw's ear, running her tongue down his throat all the way to his taut, salty nipples—licking one and then the other. He started to speak again, and she shut him up by covering his mouth with kisses, probing his tongue with hers. When she came up for air, Macaw grabbed her behind again, this time in a vice grip. His unexpected move took her by surprise, catapulting her to the top of the pleasure wave. Arching her back, she took him fully, crying out as the orgasm slammed her body.

When Macaw, who had pulled out restraint he never knew he had, felt Alexa let loose, he cried out her name and came hard and fast. After, as her breasts pressed warm on his chest, he felt her heart beating against his and thought how right it felt. For the first time ever with a woman, he didn't want her to hurry up and disentangle so he could make a quick exit.

Minutes passed, and then Alexa sighed in his ear. "I guess I should move."

"Suit yourself," he replied. "You're alright where you are."

She slid off Macaw onto her side, so she faced him.

"That was wild," he said.

Alexa grinned. "I would have to agree."

"You okay with it? I mean, I probably took you off guard."

"I thought I took you off guard," said Alexa, easing her head onto his chest and breathing in his musky scent. That was the best sex she'd ever experienced, and she felt so peaceful and protected. From her vantage point, she had a clear view of the macaw tattoo on his arm. Obviously drawn by a gifted hand, the bird appeared life-like. The vivid green head and orange chest represented strength and vitality. In black letters underneath it read Panama.

She kissed the tattoo and asked, "Do you miss Panama?"

"Every single day."

"Do you ever go back to visit?"

"Haven't been able to until recently, because of Gonzales. Things have calmed down enough finally that I think I can get in under the radar if I need to."

"Jesse McMillan told me they would never have stopped Gonzales's drug operation if it weren't for you," said Alexa. "He said you were amazing."

Macaw shrugged. "To tell you the truth, I don't remember all that much about that time. I was still so consumed by Randy's death. I wasn't going to stop until Gonzales paid for...." he trailed off.

"For the death of Randy?"

"Yeah, he was the reason my buddy died."

"What do you miss the most about Panama?"

"You mean, besides my mama?"

Alexa laughed. "Yeah, besides your mama."

"Hard to say. There are so many cool things about Panama. The beaches, the mango trees, the jungles, the macaws, the *empanadas*."

"Are you kidding me? Your *empanadas* are fabulous!"

"They're better in Panama. Everything's better in Panama. Except you, of course." Macaw rubbed Alexa's back, sending a rush of contentment into her belly.

"Mexico doesn't measure up, huh?"

"Nah—it tries and even gets close sometimes, but there's no place like home."

"I could take offense to that since I'm half-Mexican, but I understand what you mean. Fallbrook's home to me."

"You miss it, too?"

"All the time, but I like Mexico. I feel closer to my mother here. Almost like I'm rediscovering her roots, which is why I chose to be a Latin correspondent."

"I can understand that. What do you miss about California?"

"Like you, everything. But if I had to point out a few things I'd say the first would be the avocado groves on the ranch. Ever since I was a kid, they were my favorite place to be. So cool and tranquil, especially on a really hot day. I like being there even when the avocado flowers fall and get tangled in my hair. Everyone else I knew whose parents owned an avocado ranch would whine about the flowers getting stuck in their hair and on their clothes, but I loved it. I'd be sitting in class and find an avocado flower on my sleeve, and it would make me feel like I'd taken a little bit of home with me."

"That's nice," said Macaw, kissing the top of her head.

"You're nice," she said, kissing his chest.

"There you go again calling me nice. I told you I'm not even close to nice. How do I prove it to you?"

"You can do bad things to me."

"That sounds promising. What kind of bad things?"

"This requires some demonstration. Let me show you."

A couple of hours later when the rain had stopped, they decided to dress and slip downstairs to eat. As they arrived in the now quiet cantina, the last stragglers filed out into the humid night. Miguel Aguilar, the manager and chief cook, appeared to be the only one around.

"*Señorita* Alexa," he said, smiling at her, and then giving a slight nod of the head to Macaw.

"Miguel, I know you're closed, but is there a chance you still have some food left? Anything will do. Everything you cook is fabulous."

"There are some *taquitos* left—that is all."

"Can we have them?"

"Of course, *Señorita* Alexa, they are all yours."

"Thank you! Do you know Macaw, Miguel?"

The head cook hesitated and then replied, "Like everyone here in La Paz, I know of him, of course." He bowed his head again at Macaw and glanced at the floor.

Suddenly, Alexa realized how isolated Macaw must feel. Certainly, he had everyone's respect and fear, but their friendship? It didn't look that way.

"He won't bite," Alexa said.

"Only her," Macaw replied, holding out his hand to Miguel, who smiled shyly and shook it. "Let's taste your *taquitos*. See if they're better than my *empanadas*."

"I will get them for you." Miguel left the deserted dining room and ducked into the kitchen as Alexa and Macaw pulled up two chairs and sat down. Moments later, he came bursting through the kitchen's swinging door wielding a platter of *taquitos*, plates, cups and two Tecate beers. Setting it all down on the table in one quick movement, he pulled napkins out of his back pocket and waited for them to take a taste.

Alexa bit into her *taquito* and said, "Delicious as usual, Miguel."

Slower and more methodical, Macaw chomped two bites, chewed and swallowed, before he shared his opinion. "Excellent. Just enough *jalapeño*, and I like that the beef isn't too stringy."

Miguel beamed at the review and then turned to leave the dining room, but walked back to the table with a question in his eyes.

"Do you need us to pay tonight, Miguel? Or can you just put it on my tab?" Alexa asked.

"It is on the house, *Señorita*. There is something else."

"What?"

"I should have told you this sooner."

"Told me what?" Alexa thought of her father and alarm bells sounded.

"There were visitors to your room a couple of days ago."

"Visitors? Was I here?"

"The boy on duty thought you were, so he sent them up, but you weren't. *Gracias a Dios*."

"That must have been the day of my break-in," she said. "Did you get a good look at them?"

He nodded. "I believe I know their names."

"Who were they?"

"Javier Torres and Alejandro Soto."

Alexa asked Miguel, "Can you wait a minute while I go up to my room for a couple of drawings?" He nodded, and she ran upstairs and removed two pieces of paper from behind a loose section of wallpaper in her room that she held flush to the wall with tape. Back downstairs, she handed him the drawings of the two men on the sidewalk that Macaw had done.

He nodded. "That is them."

"Thank you for telling me, Miguel," said Alexa.

Macaw pulled out his cell phone and dialed, holding up a finger to quiet Alexa when she started to speak.

"Hey, what's up? Listen, I got a couple of names for you to run for me."

Macaw listened to the male voice on the other end.

"Sorry to bust up the party, but this is important. The names are Javier Torres and Alejandro Soto."

Alexa stared at Macaw's determined face as he waited. The voice finally came back on the line, and Macaw let out a low whistle, thanked his source and flipped his phone shut.

"We're pissing off the wrong people."

Alexa's breath hitched. "Who are they?"

"Better question, what are they? Answer—assassins."

"I am sorry that I did not tell you before, but you were away," Miguel apologized as he collected their dishes.

"It's okay," Alexa assured him. "And I understand that you have to protect your employees and your family. If you want me to leave, I will."

"That is not necessary, *Señorita*. With *Señor* Macaw by your side, we will all be safe."

Instead of finding offense at obviously needing help in the protection department, Alexa sighed in relief. But she couldn't help thinking about her father. It would crush him to lose her, too. The other day she'd truly thought the men were just after the cash she carried from the bank. It never crossed her mind that they would want to kill her.

Macaw broke the silence after Miguel returned to the kitchen. "Well, shit, nothing like a little pressure."

Alexa's eyes flew to his.

"I'm no friggin' superman."

Somehow, despite the seriousness of the news, Macaw's words lightened Alexa's heart, and she replied, "I beg to differ after your performance upstairs."

"Yeah. Ready for an encore?"

"Yes," she said and laughed, thinking that if her days were numbered, then she wanted to lay with this beautiful animal of a man one more time.

9

The next morning, Alexa woke up alone in bed, surprised that she hadn't stirred when Macaw left. After enjoying each other again following their nighttime snack, she slept soundly in his arms. Figuring he had work to do and would call later, she got up and took a sponge bath, dressed and headed downstairs for breakfast.

Miguel flashed Alexa a knowing grin when he put scrambled eggs, toast, coffee and juice in front of her. He didn't ask if Macaw would be joining her, which made Alexa think that he must have seen him leave.

After eating, she tried Macaw's cell again. It went straight to voicemail. He obviously wouldn't be going to the church with her to see *Padre* Pedro, but that was okay, because she felt comfortable enough going solo. The hired guns they'd learned about last night hovered at the back of her mind, but she'd be heading out in broad daylight. And she actually looked forward to visiting the huge, peaceful cathedral.

The air hung heavy with the scent of burning wax when Alexa arrived at the church. Several worshippers stood lighting candles and murmurs floated from the confessionals. She slipped into a back pew and sat down, gazing forward to the altar and its floor-to-ceiling stained glass windows that glowed from the morning sun. Intricately pieced together, the glass highlighted vignettes of Christ's short life. The baby Jesus cradled in the Virgin Mary's arms, the adolescent Jesus working as a carpenter, the grown Jesus advising his disciples over his last meal. That last scene always struck Alexa. How could Judas sit there and break bread with Jesus, knowing what he would do? How did betrayal work so easily for some people?

Alexa's heart skipped a beat when someone sat down next to her.

"*Padre* Pedro!"

"Forgive me for alarming you. Maybe you don't wish to be disturbed?"

"No, please stay," said Alexa, half of her wanting to pump him for information, the other to question him about faith and the human condition.

"Something still troubles you?"

"Is it bad to hate the dead and buried?" she blurted out.

"Hate is always a strong emotion and often leads to self-destruction. It is not an emotion that God encourages, but it is one of our most basic and sometimes understandable. Did the dead do something that consumes you?"

Alexa swallowed. "I'm not sure," she whispered. "I just know that when this person came to live with us, things were never the same, and then I lost my mother. She died, and he didn't care."

"That is a terrible tragedy," said *Padre* Pedro. He enveloped her clenched fist with his thin hand. "Not easily overcome."

Alexa nodded and fought back tears. She rarely let these emotions surface—and certainly not in front of others.

"You were six when your mother entered heaven, no?"

"Yes, padre."

"Old enough to remember, but young enough to forget," he said.

"That's exactly the trouble. Sometimes it's hard to remember what she looked like. I have to pull out her picture to remind myself. I can still hear her voice, though, and her beautiful songs, but I can't remember the words—only the melody of one of them. My father doesn't remember any of the words. He's an American."

"You remember the melody. Hum it for me."

Alexa closed her eyes and drifted back in time. Long ago echoes of her mother's voice filled her head, and she began to hum.

"Ah, yes. That is *"Tú Eres Mi Cielo."* "You Are My Heaven." A well-known lullaby that mothers sing to their beloved children. Your mother loved you very much."

"I miss her so," said Alexa, struggling to stop the tears that threatened to spill onto her cheeks.

"But you also know that she is always with you? As is God?"

"I try to remember that."

"Remember that when your heart is heavy."

They sat in silence for a time, *Padre* Pedro seeming to fall into a sort of meditation. Finally, he interrupted their silence. "Forgive me, I would rather not leave you now in your distress, but I must prepare for afternoon Mass." He rose to leave.

"Please, *Padre*, there is something more," Alexa said, putting her hand on the arm of his linen robe.

"*Si?*"

Honesty seemed the best policy at this point.

"I have appreciated our talks. They have helped me very much. But they are not the reason I originally came here."

Padre Pedro waited.

"I am an investigative reporter for the *San Diego Union Tribune,* and I am investigating a ring of evil individuals exploiting children."

The priest's smile fell from his face. He looked around and leaned closer to Alexa.

"And you believe I have information about this ring?"

"I think you might. At least I know you heard the confession of one of the ring leaders. I'm not sure what he told you, and I know that you're not at liberty to share that, but the trouble is, children's lives are at stake."

The priest sighed deeply. A good time passed before he spoke, and when he did, he bowed his head as if in prayer, and whispered, "As you have said, the confessional is sacred. But considering that we speak of

God's most innocent lambs, I believe that he would think badly of my silence. Is it Fernando Gomez?"

Alexa nodded.

"He told me that he experienced fanciful notions. That he did not actually do those terrible things, but had thought about them. I wondered. I have prayed about this for some time. For God to give me a message. It seems you are that message."

"I hate to be the bearer of bad news, *Padre*, but I have seen it with my own eyes. They are holding innocent children captive, and I must help them."

"*Ay, Dios mío*," *Padre* Pedro said, crossing himself. "You are a brave *señorita*. How can I help?"

"At this point, I honestly don't know, but I'd like us to put our heads together—see what we can come up with. I'm working with someone named Macaw, and he may know what to do next. Our real goal is to remove all of the children as soon as possible and get to the chief of the operation. Someone is financing the Gomezes. That's who we really want."

"If I see Fernando again, I will try to get some information from him," said the *padre*.

"Please be careful," said Alexa. "These are dangerous people."

"*Gracias, Señorita*, I will be careful, but I always remember that God is with me. He will guide me. You must remember that he is there for you as well."

"I will," said Alexa, getting up to leave. "In the future, it is best if we communicate by messenger, and in private."

"There is an old church in the east end of town. *St. Caterina's*. Few people visit. A good friend of mine is the *padre* there. We can meet there if we must. Where are you staying?"

"*La Cantina Cantata*."

"God go with you," said *Padre* Pedro. "Your mother would be proud, *Señorita*. You remember that."

"*Gracias*," said Alexa as she turned to leave the church.

. . .

When she returned to her room, Alexa tried calling Macaw again to tell him about the meeting with the priest, but still no answer. A vague feeling of unease started to creep into her belly, but she pushed it aside and turned on her laptop to work on the story. He would call soon—probably just stuck in meetings this morning.

When Alexa's cell phone rang later that afternoon, she jumped up and grabbed it. "Hi!"

"Wow, what a greeting," said Peter. "Expecting someone else?"

"Uh, no, well, yes. I thought you were my source. Sorry I haven't checked in since yesterday."

"Actually, you haven't checked in since the day before yesterday. I was getting worried," said Peter. "Everything okay there? You sound kind of strange."

Alexa had been so wrapped up in going to bed with Macaw yesterday that she missed an entire day. And now she hadn't heard from him in hours. Although they'd only known each other for a couple of weeks, until now, he'd checked in a few times a day. As a matter of fact, she was getting so used to his checking in that she hadn't really noticed how regularly he'd done so. Until now. All afternoon, every time she heard a noise in the hall, she stopped writing and waited for his familiar rap on her door.

"It's a strange case," said Alexa.

"That's an understatement. So how are you and your source getting along?"

"Fine. I was just expecting some news from him."

"Are you sure everything is okay? He's not causing you any trouble?"

Alexa pictured Macaw naked in her bed and almost laughed. "Trouble? Not at all."

"Okay, because I'd be really worried right now if I thought there was a chance he was a plant or something."

"He's not a plant!" Alexa exclaimed.

"Whoa. Listen, I have a right to be a little worried, don't I? You said that he's living on the dark side, and he has worked with your sources in the past."

Alexa paused. Peter had a good point. A glimmer of doubt raised itself in her mind, and she felt her stomach clinch.

"Look, I know he's not a plant. Call it woman's intuition or something. I'm certain he has plenty of other things to do. He does have a life, and he's been spending a lot of time helping me."

"Okay, you've always had a good sense of people, so I believe you. Tell me what's up with the story."

"I may have a hot lead really soon." In a low voice she told him about *Padre* Pedro and the information she waited on.

When they hung up a few minutes later, Peter sounded convinced that things were okay, but she wasn't feeling the same. She'd given Macaw almost all of the money, not to mention opening up to him emotionally and physically. Was he the upstanding guy she believed him to be?

A couple of hours later, Alexa began to nod off at her laptop, so she lay back on the bed and began to dream. She stood alone on the edge of the jungle, afraid to enter the thick tapestry of greenery where the boa constrictors slithered through the padded earth. Then she was a little girl again, walking down the hallway at the ranch. She heard a muffled cry and her mother plead, "Please! No!"

When she peered into her parent's room, she saw Uncle Freddy on top of Mama.

"What are you looking at, you worthless half-breed?" her uncle sneered.

"Leave Mama alone!" Alexa screamed, running into the room with her fists raised. "I'll tell Papa."

"Your papa ain't here, and he won't believe you anyway, you little liar."

"Papa will believe me, and I'm going to tell him."

Uncle Freddy rose from the bed and knocked her to the floor with the back of his hand. Then he turned back to Augustina. "You tell your brat to keep her mouth shut, or I'll kill you both. I got friends in high places, and you know it." He buckled his belt and then stalked out of the room and stormed down the hall, leaving the stench of alcohol and sweat.

Alexa ran to her mother, who lay on the bed pulling her clothing around her.

"Did he hurt you, Mama?"

"No. Thanks to you. You're the angel God sent to save me."

"Papa should make Uncle Freddy leave."

"I will talk to your father. *Te quiero mucho, mi amor.*"

"I love you, too, Mama," Alexa said as her mother locked the bedroom door and invited her to curl up in the nook of her arm.

Alexa woke with a start, the weight of the memory long since buried pinning her chest to the bed and sucking the air out of her lungs.

After all of these years, she finally remembered why she hated Uncle Freddy so much! He attacked her mother. Was that why Mama had left? To get away from him? But why didn't she take Alexa with her? A timid knock on the door interrupted Alexa's memories. "Who is it?" she called out.

"It is Arturo, *Señorita* Alexa."

She pulled the door open and smiled down at Miguel's child as he handed her a small piece of paper.

"*Gracias,*" she said, giving him the five *pesos* in change she had crammed in the front pocket of her jeans after breakfast.

"*Qué bueno!*" Arturo smiled, and then ran back downstairs.

Alexa closed the door and sat on her bed, opening the small piece of paper that simply said—*St. Caterina's* seven o'clock.

She glanced at the time. Almost six o'clock. She needed at least forty-five minutes to make her way to the old church, which sat on the outskirts of town. Macaw wasn't answering, and Rodolfo didn't want his church to know he was involved, so she'd have to go alone. This lead could be the big break that she needed, and who knew if *Padre* Pedro would risk another meeting.

She dressed in what she had come to call her "undercover" clothing—black jeans and a T-shirt, with her room key, passport, cell phone and flash drive stuffed into her pocket. Out in front of the cantina, she caught a taxi and told the driver to drop her off at the east end of the city in front of some shops about a half mile from the church. She decided it would raise less attention to appear to be shopping, as opposed to going to an out-of-the-way church.

Just to make it look good, Alexa wandered into a leather shop.

"*Hola, señorita,* you like?" said an eager Mexican woman, who held up a bright yellow, fringed purse.

"*No, gracias,*" she said, shaking her head. Then, so as not to disappoint the poor woman, who may not have had a sale all day, she bought a small leather change purse.

Outside again, she decided to make her way to the church. Walking west and leaving the shops behind, she headed into the burnt orange sunset down a dirt road that eventually ended at the old church. As she arrived in front of the cathedral, which lay no more than a quarter of a mile from the ocean, she admired the majestic building's steeple in the fading light. In the States, they would have made the building a historic attraction where you could have a fairytale wedding or bulldozed it down and put in luxury hotels. Mexicans, people with history, preserved it without questioning geographic riches.

Alexa pressed her lips together to steady her nerves and stepped into the dimly lit sanctuary, waiting a moment for her eyes to adjust. The sight of a long table glimmering with candles comforted her. She approached and gazed down at the flickering lights, wondering how many prayers had been uttered right here. Glancing at her cell phone, she noted the time at nearly seven o'clock. Perhaps the *padre* hadn't made it here yet. In the last row of pews, she sat and waited, remembering what the father had said about the power of prayer. Then she recalled her uncle and the deeply held memory that had come loose that afternoon. Suddenly, she felt an intense anger at her father. How could he not have noticed that Uncle Freddy was bothering her mother? Why didn't he kick him out? Papa was always defending Uncle Freddy and saying that he was just having a bad time.

Apprehension snaked its way into her stomach, and she checked the time again.

The priest was late now. How much longer should she wait, Alexa wondered? Thinking that the whole thing could very well be a set-up, she jumped when the *padre* slid in next to her.

"You received my message, I see."

Alexa nodded.

He spoke quietly. "There is an American woman, who lives right now in a hotel in La Paz. I don't know her real name, but they call her *La Rubia.*"

"What does she have to do with things?" asked Alexa.

"I am told that she may lead you to the head of the organization. She lives in *Los Hermanos* hotel on *Diablo* Street.

"A very bad part of town," said Alexa.

The father nodded. "No doubt she is also doing bad things. I'm sorry, but that is all I have for you."

"That's more than enough, *Padre*. Thank you so much for your help. I hope you haven't put yourself in danger."

"I am in far less danger than those poor little girls. God help you bring them home. And a safe passage to you on your dangerous journey."

"God bless you," said Alexa, who hugged him and walked out the doors into the balmy evening air. As she made her way back to town humming the nursery rhyme her mother sang to her, Alexa pictured the *padre's* concerned face and words of encouragement. He relied on her to do what he couldn't—to intervene for those young girls. Not with God, but with a part of life that was evil. Those little souls were her Mexican sisters, in a way. If they slipped through her fingers, she would not only be letting *Padre* Pedro and the parents down, she would be failing herself.

A few minutes, later when she passed the shop where she bought the coin purse, she sensed someone behind her. Making a quick escape down a narrow street, she glanced back quickly and saw a tall man with a baseball cap pulled low over his eyes gaining on her. Up ahead sat a bakery she had often visited. She suspected the owner, a man named Manuel, would still be there counting his *pesos* and preparing to lock up for the night. She prayed the door would still be unlocked. A throng of raucous American tourists heading Alexa's way gave her the perfect opportunity. She slipped through the crowd and out the other side, dashing into Manuel's shop. Once the door clicked shut, she locked it, flipped off the lights and turned the open sign to closed. As she flattened herself against the wall out of sight of passersby, Manuel stepped out of the kitchen and stared at her, opening his mouth to speak. She put a forefinger to her lips, and he went back inside the kitchen.

Heart pumping in her ears, Alexa stood in the dark with the kitchen's light seeping out from under the door. Once she sensed that the stranger had walked past, she slipped into the kitchen. She and Manuel exchanged knowing glances, and he offered her a tray of pastries.

"*Sopaipillas!* Just what I needed, Manuel."

She chose the largest one and bit into the honey-butter-filled fried pastry. The air inside puffed in her face and the filling melted in her mouth. As she licked powdered sugar from her lips and savored the pastry, she forgot for a few minutes about the plight of the little girls and Macaw's disappearance.

10

"Let me get this straight. You went all the way out to that abandoned church last night on your own without backup?" Peter sounded pained, as if someone plucked hairs from his head one at a time.

"It's not an abandoned church. It's still fully functional, just not all that popular. And I met a priest, chief, not some Mafioso."

"When you call me chief, I know you're hiding something. What happened to your great source and protector? What's his name? Parrot?"

"Macaw. He wasn't available."

"Define not available. Stuck at work? In the hospital? Working for the other side? Dead?"

Alexa hesitated.

"Lex? What aren't you telling me?" Peter started to whine. Not a good sign.

"I'm not exactly sure where Macaw is, but trust me, he'll resurface."

"And you're so sure why? Women's intuition?"

"Something like that." Alexa's mind burned at the memory of Macaw's fiery kisses. How could *that* have been an act?

"Look, Lex. I'm really worried. If you don't hear from Macaw by tomorrow, I'm sending Michael down. No negotiations on this one."

Alexa knew from Peter's final tone that he meant it, and there was no use in disagreeing. After promising to call in the morning, she hung up the phone and breathed a sigh of relief that she hadn't revealed where *Padre* Pedro's potential source, Shannon, lived. He would send in the National Guard. At breakfast, her discussion with Miguel about *Diablo* Street had been unsettling at best.

"That is a very bad street, *Señorita* Alexa," Miguel told her. "Why do you ask?" He stood balancing a platter of steaming egg burritos.

"I was just wondering. Have you ever been there?"

The cantina manager's eyes widened, and he shook his head.

"But you've heard of it?"

"Of course, everyone has."

"What have you heard? Besides that it's a bad street."

"There are drugs and stabbings there all of the time. You aren't going there, are you *Señorita* Alexa?"

"You're busy, Miguel, thanks for the information." She waved him on.

He stayed glued to the spot, despite calls from customers for the food he held. "Maybe *Señor* Macaw can go instead?" he suggested.

Alexa shrugged. "Anyone in the cantina ever been there?"

"Rodrigo in the kitchen."

"Thanks, I'll talk to him and see if I can get the background information I need."

Relief filled Miguel's eyes. "That is a much better idea, *Señorita*. He can tell you everything you need to know. *Ya, voy!*" he yelled as he made his way to the tables of hungry customers.

Alexa pushed speed dial for the millionth time. Macaw's message came on immediately. Throwing the phone on her bed, she thought, Macaw would be the best person to accompany her to find Shannon, but he was nowhere to be found. Besides the fact that she really needed him on this latest venture, he had just about all of the money. And he was her contact person with Imelda. The little girls' time bomb ticked louder with every minute that he stayed away. Okay, so she didn't have control over Macaw and really had no business expecting him to be available whenever she wanted. He had a life. But a frigging phone call would be nice. Was he like all of the other guys? Full of promises and talk and then fizzling out and fading away as soon as he got laid?

There was no use thinking about it now. She needed to move forward and get to *Diablo* Street and Shannon before the girl overdosed or got killed and couldn't tell her anything. Rodolfo would probably go with her if she asked, but she didn't want to. She'd feel horrible if something happened to him. Best to handle it alone. She consulted with Rodrigo in the kitchen about *Diablo* Street and what to take with her. If the fact that she planned on traveling to the street surprised him, he didn't show it. Instead, he gladly gave her a rundown—no cell phone or passport—just cash. The lunacy of going without any ties to the outside world gripped her with fear, but she knew he was right. All the wrong person had to do was open her passport, and she could disappear. A camera would obviously make her a target, so that was out, too. Time to use her journalistic eye and store all of the details so that she could write about the experience later.

After some thought, which involved her conscience disguised as Peter standing on one shoulder wagging his finger in disapproval, Alexa decided to make her expedition that evening. Traveling at dusk meant an even more dangerous mission, but she figured Shannon would probably be sleeping in the day and more likely to be up partying at night. Alexa lived with Uncle Freddy long enough to know that you don't disturb drunks or drug addicts when they're sleeping it off. Best to nab them just as the first excited buzz set in for the night, before they progressed to mean or disjointed.

That evening she put on jeans and a black T-shirt, pulled her hair into a ponytail, stuffed cash into her pocket and left the cantina. When she hailed a cab and told the driver she wanted to be dropped off at the corner of *Cortez* and *Diablo*, he shook his head and muttered something about crazy Americans. That irked Alexa, who felt like announcing her Mexican status, but decided that would make her seem even crazier. Stopping at the dreaded intersection, the taxi driver snapped his fingers for the fare, snatched the money from her hand and raced away as soon as she got out. Alexa peered down the narrow street teetering with rickety buildings and whiffed the unmistakable odor of raw sewage. A neglected quiet hung suspended in the air.

As she stood there unsure of where to start, a man shuffled towards her with an extended hand. Feigning ignorance, Alexa asked for *La Rubia*, and the man turned and walked away. Several more people tried begging, until Alexa spotted what looked like an American. He had stringy blond hair that passed needing a cut months before and wore a pair of blue board shorts pocked with cigarette burns.

"I heard you saying that you're looking for Shannon?" he said. "What for?"

"We have a mutual friend who wants me to check in with her."

"What's Shannon get for it?"

"I've got something for her, but I need to see her first."

"I'll go see if she wants a visitor," he said, disappearing into a building with a charred exterior and sagging roof.

Alexa eyed the structure and hoped there wasn't an earthquake—even a minor tremor—or she'd end up under a pile of rubble. Running on adrenaline now, she shoved aside feelings of panic that threatened to trip her up. She could freak out later over the fact that she stood on one of the meanest streets in La Paz. Now, she had to stay focused, get what she came for, and get out as fast as possible.

Minutes passed and the scruffy blond finally emerged, gesturing for her to follow him. She ducked through the doorway as she entered a dark corridor that stank of a noxious cocktail of vermin and vomit.

"She's in that room back there," he said, pointing to a door yawning open at the end of the hallway. "I got something to do." He went through an open side door and stepped back onto the street, and Alexa turned toward the milky yellow light leaking from Shannon's room. Stepping forward, she strained to listen for any sound that would indicate what lay ahead, hearing nothing but her own breath.

When she got to the room's threshold, Alexa peered inside. Her eyes fell on a girl with dull brown hair enthroned on a cot.

"Shannon?"

"Yeah, that's me," the girl said, pushing herself up on bony elbows. "Who we both know?"

Alexa entered the room and threw out the first name that came to mind. "Maria."

"Maria Hernandez! Shit! That bitch still alive? I thought her *cholo* boyfriend would have killed her by now. He was always beating the crap out of her."

"Maria's tough," said Alexa. "She's still around, just like you."

"I don't get out much these days," said Shannon, plopping back down and exposing track-stained arms. "Jack says you got something for me. Any goodies?"

"No goodies, but some cash."

"That'll do. Fork it over," she said, licking her lips. "I haven't had a fix since yesterday."

"First, I want to talk," said Alexa.

Shannon's watery blue eyes narrowed. "Talk about what?"

"About a missing girl."

"What girl? What's this all about?"

"I've been told that you may have information on some disappearances."

"I don't know what the hell you're talking about. What did Maria say? She's a lying bitch."

Alexa scrutinized Shannon, sensing cracks beneath her veneer. "I don't want to cause you any trouble, really," she said, moving closer to the bed. "I'm just trying to find out whatever I can about the little girls who turned up missing a couple of weeks ago."

Shannon struggled to sit up. "Did my father send you? If he did, tell him I'm never coming home. Ever. He hurt me for the last time."

"I don't know your father. I'm interested in the little Mexican girls who were abducted."

"Talk to my father if you want to find out about missing girls," Shannon spat. "He has made an empire off of them."

Alexa's pulse quickened. "Are you saying that your father runs a human sex trafficking ring?"

"If that's the fancy term for selling girls for prostitution and pornography, then yes, he runs a human sex trafficking ring. When I found out what he was up to a few years ago and tried to turn him in, he made everyone think I was drugged up and crazy, so I ran."

"No one believed you?"

"Are you kidding me? You think anyone wanted to believe that the squeaky-clean senator could do something that horrible?"

"A US senator?"

Shannon gave Alexa a sidelong look. "My old man must not have sent you. You're totally out of the loop. US Senator Frank Roth of California. Ever heard of him?"

Alexa nodded, stunned at this revelation.

"What are you going to do with the information?"

"If what you're telling me is true, I'll stop him," promised Alexa.

"Good," said Shannon, who appeared spent from her outbursts. "Now where's the money you promised me? I need my medicine."

Alexa handed over a roll of cash. "Here's two-hundred."

Shannon took the money and smiled for the first time. "Thanks. This will last me two weeks here."

A rush of sadness at the waste of a life washed through Alexa, who reached out to touch the girl's shoulder, her fingers hitting bone. "You take care of yourself," she said. Lame, Alexa thought, but really, what else could she say?

"Me and Jack are going to get out of here soon," said Shannon. "Find a sweet little place along the coast and swing in hammocks all day."

"That sounds nice." Alexa started to turn and leave, but then stopped and asked, "Where's your mother?"

"She died of cancer when I was fifteen. Left me with my freak of a father," Shannon trailed off. She didn't appear to notice when Alexa left the room.

Emerging from Shannon's building to find that darkness had swallowed up the street, Alexa's exhilaration at the scoop immediately dampened at the realization that she hadn't planned her exit as well as her entrance. Crossing her fingers, she scurried toward Cortez, but soon cried out when a hand clenched her arm and snapped her sideways.

"Hold it, *chica*," growled her captor, a Mexican man whose breath reeked of garlic and beer. "We want to have a talk with you." He flung her forward through the doorway of a building. As she scrambled to regain her footing inside, her back went ramrod straight when she came face-to-face with a muscular bald man.

"Nice of you to visit. Have a seat," he said.

"I can stand," Alexa replied.

He gestured to the man helping him. "Gerardo, show our guest to her seat."

The assistant grasped her shoulders and threw her on to a worn couch.

"What do you want? Money?" asked Alexa. "I've got plenty of cash. Just let me go."

"We don't want your money, yet," said the bald man. He leaned over and put his face in Alexa's. "We want to know who you work for."

"Shannon and I have a girlfriend in common, that's all. The friend was worried about her."

The bald man stepped back and laughed. "You come all this way just to say *hola*? I don't believe it."

"That's all there is to it," said Alexa, gasping when he put his foot on the bottom of the sofa between her legs, and with one great thrust propelled the couch across the floor. As it slammed against the wall, she bit her lip, sending the sharp taste of blood into her mouth.

"Your mama never taught you that it's bad manners to lie?"

"I told you. I was just visiting Shannon for a friend. The friend paid me big bucks to come, okay."

"Check her," he ordered his companion, who yanked her to her feet and pulled the wad of cash from her pocket.

"I told you that they paid me to find her," said Alexa. "You can have it. Just let me go."

"You're a narc, aren't you?"

"No narc is stupid enough to walk in here and visit someone without backup," Alexa tried not to plead. "I'm just doing someone a favor."

The leader pulled a knife from his pocket and waved it at Alexa.

"I wouldn't do that if I were you, Pepe," said a familiar voice from the doorway. "She's a wack job, but she ain't no narc."

The bald Mexican swung around and cried, "Macaw!"

"That's my girl you got there." Macaw motioned to Alexa, who thought she'd never been so happy to see anyone before.

"Your girl?" Pepe's face fell. "I didn't know, Macaw. She comes asking a lot of questions and waving money around."

"She gets bored when I'm out of town and likes to pretend she's on one of those cop shows," Macaw said as he approached Alexa and grabbed her by the wrist. "I leave you for a couple of days, and you're in trouble again! You lose all the money I gave you?"

Pepe dutifully handed over the bundle of cash, and Macaw peeled off a fifty and gave it to the stunned Mexican.

Outside in the muggy night air, Macaw had a car waiting. They slid in and the driver quickly pulled away.

"You are one crazy broad. I hope you got what you were looking for."

"I got it. I know who's behind the ring. It's a US Senator."

As the car made its way back to the cantina, Alexa's adrenaline ebbed. She vacillated between fury at Macaw for acting like he picked her up from preschool, to sheer relief. Eyeing his solid shoulder, she longed to rest her head on it, but stopped herself. Where the hell had he been this whole time?

11

"So, how'd you find me?" Alexa asked when she slid the key into her hotel room door and pushed it open.

"I had a guy follow you while I was gone. Good thing, too."

He stood in the doorway and watched Alexa stomp to the window and throw it open, sending a wave of cool night air into the stuffy room.

"Hey, what gives?" he asked.

She spun around. "Don't get me wrong. I was thrilled to see you, but I didn't give you permission to have me followed!"

"Chill. If I'd asked for permission, you would have shot me down. Look at you now!"

Alexa crossed her arms over her chest. "That was your guy following me last night? I should have figured. I nearly gave myself a heart attack giving him the slip."

"Last night? You shitting me? I didn't get any reports about last night."

"Don't act all innocent. You know I was followed last night."

He came in and closed the door. "My boys assured me things were quiet. What happened?"

He watched Alexa scan his face, and then she sat down on the bed and told him what transpired on her return trip from *St. Caterina's*.

"Good thing you ducked into that bakery. But this sucks. Our boys are getting too close for my comfort. Now I definitely can't let you out of my sight."

"I know it's none of my business, but where were you?" she asked.

"You're right, it isn't your business, but I'll tell you anyway. My mama needed me."

"Your mama?" Alexa leaned forward. "You went back to Panama to see her? Is she okay?"

"Not really, but I did what I could. Her sister, my Aunt Francesca, died."

"How sad. I thought business pulled you away."

"That would have been much easier. Sorry I didn't call. No time to set up my cell service there, and I couldn't get away from the family to rent one."

He eyed Alexa. "Looks like I got back just in time. You having doubts about me?"

Alexa got up and peered into the refrigerator. "Are you hungry? I've got some of Miguel's *chiles rellanos.*"

"I already ate. You were, weren't you?"

Alexa opened the cardboard container, picked up a fork and shoveled in a mouthful as she stood.

"I was what?" she asked, her words muffled by the food.

"You were doubting me. I can tell."

He watched Alexa set the fork down on top of the refrigerator and waited. Had she decided to call it quits while he was away? Damn, he knew he should have found some way to contact her.

"Okay, so I was a little uncertain. The truth is—" she trailed off.

"Yeah?" He waited, afraid to take a breath and not hear what she was about to say. "Mostly, I think I just missed you," Alexa blurted.

"You think?"

"Okay, I know."

Glad relief pushed him toward her. "Funny thing happened to me, too." He moved even closer and stroked her silky hair. "I kept thinking about this crazy, beautiful chick who might get herself killed if I didn't hurry up and get back."

"I like the beautiful part."

"Sorry again for not calling you. That was shitty."

She smiled. "How are you going to make it up to me?"

"Let me show you," he murmured, taking Alexa's face in his hands and pressing his mouth to hers. Smooth and slow, the kiss lingered between them, until his core caught on fire, and he picked her up and lowered her onto the bed. Reaching with one hand to whip off his T-shirt and throw it to the floor, he stopped at the look on her face.

"What?"

"Nothing. You're just so beautiful."

"That's the first time a babe has called me beautiful. You're the one who's beautiful."

"No, I'm not. I'm average, but..."

Macaw laughed and kissed her again. When he finished, he unbuttoned her blouse, then unclasped her bra and nodded in approval at her hard nipples.

"Now I know you missed me," he said, leaning down and languidly drawing his tongue around the outside of one breast, then the other—lapping up the sweet taste of her honey skin. When he finished his trail and took one breast in his mouth, tickling her eager nipple with his tongue, she moaned and reached down to unzip her jeans. Grabbing her hands and pulling her arms to her sides, he smiled and said, "Let me."

The zoom of metal teeth releasing punctuated the quiet room as he slid her zipper down. She lifted her hips and he tugged her pants off, dropping them to the floor. Drawing a finger along the top of her pink, lace panties, he marveled at how firm yet supple her skin was.

When Alexa met his eyes and guided his fingers beneath her underwear to an even softer, sweeter spot, he felt himself strain against his jeans.

"Take off your pants," she urged, as if reading his mind. "Please."

"You definitely missed me. You're even saying please." As his fingers explored her silky insides, she closed her eyes and moaned. When he felt her quiver, he stopped, and she opened her eyes.

"No point in rushing things. We're in no hurry."

Alexa arched her back, grabbed his hand and guided his fingers back between her legs. He let her desire and excitement build, slowly at first, until she cried out. "Take off your pants now," she groaned, lifting her hips and sliding out of her panties.

"Bossy," Macaw grinned, "I like that." Standing, he unzipped his jeans and slid out of them and his underwear. He had hoped to stay this way, teasing her into begging even more, but all of his self-control jumped out the window when she sat up and embraced his erection, urging, "C'mon, let me be your home."

He lowered himself onto her and entered, straining to keep things slow and steady, but the dam broke and he found himself hammering her —all the while at the back of his mind her words repeating—let me be your home. This felt like home, he thought, like nothing ever had before. Alexa buried her fingers in his hair when she came, calling out his name, and in seconds he followed.

Afterwards, as they lay sandwiched together, he kissed her on the neck and murmured, "We need a bigger bed. You'll have to come to my place next time."

"Next time," Alexa said, planting a kiss in the middle of his chest. "Sounds like you're already missing me."

They lay in silence for a time, each aware of the other's heartbeat. The old building creaked as they dozed.

When Alexa's cell phone rang some time later, it jerked her awake and had her reaching over the edge of the bed and fumbling around until she found it. She squinted at the caller ID—*Peter*. Placing a forefinger to her lips, she flipped the phone open with her other hand and answered, "Hi, Peter. I was just thinking about calling you."

Macaw started to laugh, and she kicked his shin.

Her boss jumped right in. "Hopefully you were going to call because you've made some significant progress on the story. Bifford is checking in with me five times a day, and you know that one of my main goals in life is to not hear from him."

"As a matter of fact, I've got fantastic news. I found out who's heading up the organization. It turns out he's a bigwig in US politics."

"Sounds potentially juicy. What's the name?"

"California Senator Frank Roth."

There was silence on the other end of the phone. Peter cleared his throat. "That is a serious accusation. You have a solid source?"

"Yes, his daughter." She explained her visit to Shannon Roth, leaving out the part about going alone.

"This is big. Let me check with Bifford, and I'll get back to you tomorrow morning. Everything else okay? You found Macaw?"

"Yes."

"Why do I feel like you're not telling me everything?"

Alexa felt her face coloring up in the dark room. "Nothing else to tell. Like I said, he had some business to take care of, and now we're back on track."

"Lex, we've worked together what—five years now? I know when you're holding out on me. What is it? We can't afford any surprises right now."

Alexa sat up in bed, her bare back sticking to the wall. "No surprises, Peter. Honest. Everything's moving along just as it should. What aren't *you* telling me?"

Peter was quiet. "Like I've been saying since you took this assignment, Bifford is just about out of patience. To be perfectly honest, he's considering pulling back on the investigative budget. He's thinking he might get his money's worth in another department—like real estate or sports."

"Since when can you get headlines like this with sports or real estate?" exclaimed Alexa.

"You just said the operative word—headlines. We need some, pronto. Look, I know you're busting your butt there. I get it. I've been in the trenches, too. But you've got to understand Bifford's side of things. He put a lot of extra cash into this—not to mention your salary. He wants results."

"The legwork's been done. All he has to do is give me the go ahead, and I'll give him results," vowed Alexa.

"I know you will. I'll call you first thing in the morning."

Alexa flipped her phone shut and threw it on the floor.

"That didn't sound good."

"It's worse than it sounded. I haven't got much time left to produce that Pulitzer. The publisher is getting antsy—talking about redirecting resources to other departments, which means I may be writing about rising home prices really soon."

"Damn, if the pressure isn't enough," said Macaw, rubbing her shoulder. "So what did he say about Roth?"

"He's going to get back to me tomorrow after he talks to the publisher. Hopefully with a go-ahead to bring in Roth and Imelda."

In her room early the next morning, Alexa opened her eyes to gray light filled with suspended dust. It'd been an interminable night of tense semi-sleep—her only comfort nestling up to Macaw's solid chest. She smiled at his peaceful face. Thank goodness he slept. Her squirming probably kept him up most of the night. With sparse movement, she reached to the floor and picked up her cell phone, checking the alerts—no call yet. Hopefully Peter called soon. Her knotted stomach couldn't take much more.

When her phone rang moments later, Macaw stirred. She flipped it open without checking the caller ID.

"Alexa speaking."

"Hi, it's Peter. I talked to Bifford."

"And?"

"Go ahead and turn in the Gomezes and get those girls out of there."

"What about Roth?"

"For now, there is no Roth. Bifford wants to steer clear of him until things are checked out. Make Imelda and Fernando out to be the villains they are, and really play up the girls' return. Write a tear-jerker—you've definitely got the material."

Alexa noticed a small catch in Peter's voice she hadn't heard before.

"But Roth's probably behind it all. This will give him time to cover his tracks."

"Probably is the operative word here, Alexa. We can't mar the guy's reputation without some confirmation."

"What about his daughter?"

"Her story checks out. Roth had a wife who died of cancer awhile back, and he has two kids—a son and a daughter. The daughter hasn't lived at home for several years. That's not enough, though. Plenty of kids get upset with their parents and leave."

"But there's probably a lot more little girls involved that we don't even know about. The only way to save them is to expose Roth."

"Didn't you tell me the little girls we do know about don't have much time left?"

"Yes, that's true. They are top priority. I'll go to the police station today."

"Great. I'll tell Bifford. Keep me posted. And be careful!"

"I'm always careful," she said, giving Macaw a warning look when he rolled his eyes.

Alexa hung up the phone and sighed. "I guess you heard that the publisher wants me to keep Roth out of things for now."

Macaw nodded. "And that's not making you happy."

"Of course not. This is so frustrating. We both know he's the ring leader. I'm not waiting for them and their corroboration on Roth. I'm going to email Esperanza and see what she can dig up on the senator."

"Your friend, the lawyer, in San Diego?" said Macaw, who put his arms behind his head, displaying his ample biceps. "That's an excellent idea. Then we'll go down to the station and ask them to do a raid on Imelda. Now *that* will be satisfying."

After Macaw made a call to Imelda pretending to set up another visit later that afternoon to see all of the girls, they dressed and headed downstairs for a quick breakfast. On the way to the police station, Alexa kept checking the time. Now that she had gotten the green light, every single second seemed to matter.

When they arrived at headquarters, they asked to see Alexa's source, Captain Hidalgo, who directed them to Police Chief Jose Cordova. A compact, brisk man, Cordova ushered them into his office and gestured for them to sit.

"Captain Hidalgo says that you have the location where Imelda and

Fernando Gomez are holding *inocentes?*" said Cordova as he sat down at his desk, which was adorned with family photos.

"Yes, sir, we just verified the address on *Agua* Street."

"How many children are being held?"

"We believe there are between ten and thirteen," said Alexa, pulling out the photos of the three girls that Macaw had taken and handing them to Cordova.

When the captain flipped through the three pictures, the veins in his neck bulged. *"Ay, las pobrecitas,"* he said and shook his head. "We have suspected the Gomezes were up to no good for a long time, but not until now do we have concrete proof. Do you wish to go when we arrest them and regain the children?"

Alexa pictured Imelda's sneering face and hesitated. "Yes, I'd like to go."

"I'm going, too," said Macaw.

"We will make arrangements. Give us a few minutes. Please wait here." He reached for the door handle, when Alexa stopped him.

"One more thing. Once we retrieve the children, I would like to personally bring one of the little girls home. Information from her parents helped us locate the children in the first place."

"Her name?"

"Liana Garcia."

"We will make sure that happens," said the officer, smiling warmly at Alexa. "It is the least we can do for all of your brave work."

Once the door clicked behind the chief, Alexa asked Macaw, "How do you think Imelda is going to react?"

"Like a cornered panther. She'll try to scratch and snarl her way out and will tear up anyone who gets in the way."

Alexa flinched at the thought.

"I'm not looking forward to seeing the psycho either, believe me. But it'll be worth it to see them throw her in a cage where she belongs."

Alexa nodded and checked the time on her cell phone again.

After a while another officer burst into the room. He wore what appeared to be a bullet-proof vest and had a machine gun slung around his shoulder.

"Looks like they know Imelda as well as we do," Macaw commented as they followed the officer out of the room and into the back of a squad car.

When they pulled away from the curb, Alexa slid her cold hand into Macaw's warm one. How many officers had they employed for this job? she wondered, noting at least two cars behind and ahead of them.

At the intersection of *Agua* and *Puente*, the officer slammed on the brakes and instructed them to stay in the car. As she watched him and other policemen sprint toward the hotel and take stations outside with guns drawn, Alexa prayed out loud, "God, please get those little girls out unharmed."

Using a megaphone, the captain called for the Gomezes to come out with their hands up. Moments passed. "Nothing," Alexa breathed, "I hope they didn't get tipped off."

"Wouldn't be the first time with the Mexican police," Macaw commented.

"I can't stand this," cried Alexa. "I have to do something." She reached for the car door handle.

Macaw grabbed her arm. "Hold on. What the hell are you going to do?"

"I don't know, but it's better than just sitting here."

"What? Getting shot's better?"

"I just feel so helpless!" Alexa pounded the seat in front of her. "No one's coming. They're probably slipping out the back."

"The police have the whole place covered. I know this is tough, but there's not a lot we can do. Let them do their job—we've done ours."

Finally, a hotel room door opened slowly, and Fernando stood there cowering with his hands in the air. When he stopped advancing several feet from the building, an officer seized him and clipped on cuffs.

"There's the big, stupid papa bear. Now we need the mama panther," murmured Macaw.

Alexa watched Fernando talk to the cops and wondered what he was saying. Then the rest of the officers swarmed the hotel room. When the men began running out of the building with children, Alexa loosened her grip on the car seat. "They've got them! Did you see? How many girls was that?"

"Looks like at least eleven," said Macaw.

The door to the room remained open, and several minutes passed as the officers pushed Fernando into a squad car and led the children into a waiting van.

"Son-of-a-bitch," said Macaw.

"She's gone, isn't she?"

"Looks that way."

Chief Cordova approached the car, and Alexa rolled down the window.

"We have the children and Fernando Gomez, as you can see, but we aren't sure where Imelda is. It seems she was tipped off right before we got here."

"But she's the mastermind of this whole thing."

"We know," said Cordova. "We're searching for her. She is considered armed and dangerous. Do you want a police guard?"

"Yes," said Alexa.

"Can you give us a minute?" asked Macaw.

The chief nodded and stepped over to talk to another officer.

"We don't want a police guard."

"Why not?" asked Alexa.

"Bringing in the police will only make you more of a target. Imelda obviously has at least one cop on her payroll. Besides, you've got me. The Terminator. Remember?"

"Chief Cordova," she called out the window. "Thanks, but Macaw and I will be okay."

"As you wish. We are holding the children in the station tonight for debriefing with a psychologist. You are welcome to come in the morning and help with their return."

· · ·

When they got back to Alexa's room at the cantina awhile later, Macaw said, "Saving lives takes time."

"I know. I can't believe how late it is," she said as she put her room key down. "I'm not that hungry, but did you want to get an early dinner?"

"Nah, I lost my appetite when we found out Imelda escaped. I'm beat, though. I didn't get that many Zzz's last night. I wouldn't mind crashing for a few hours."

"Me neither," said Alexa. She slipped off her jeans and shoes and hopped into bed, scooting up against the wall to give Macaw room.

He undressed and lay down facing her.

Alexa smiled, then frowned. "Do you think Imelda knows we turned her in?"

"Probably, but right now she's got bigger issues to deal with, like saving her own ass."

Alexa touched the scar on Macaw's face with her fingertip.

"Don't worry about that wack job," he assured her. "I'll be ready for her this time. I would have been ready for her last time, but that's another story."

"Tell me."

She felt Macaw's jaw tighten. "Forget it. Sorry. I shouldn't have asked." Alexa closed her eyes and inhaled the odor of fried tortillas rising from the restaurant below.

Moments passed, and then Macaw broke the silence. "I told you about my little buddy, Randy. Maybe you also heard something from Jesse McMillan."

"Only that Randy died tragically."

"When I first came to Mexico, I was pretty broken up. Imelda took me off guard and got to my face."

"You mean you were broken up about what happened with Randy?"

"Yeah. We were friends since we could both walk. I never had any siblings, so he was the closest thing to a brother that I knew. In our sophomore year of high school, Randy started getting heavy into partying. I partied right along with him, but he really took to it. I've always been able to switch it off. Have a couple of drinks or a joint and then stop.

Randy had no switch, and I really began worrying, because it was hard to tell what he was taking. That's when I started dealing. I needed the money, because my old man kept losing jobs to fighting. And I thought it would give me a way to make sure Randy stayed safe." Macaw stopped. "You don't want to hear this shit."

Alexa put her hand on his chest, absorbing the steady thump of his heart. "Yes, I do. Go on," she urged.

"I did really well with dealing. Watching Randy party so much, I rarely touched the stuff, so I had a clear head most of the time. By our senior year, he was a mess. Couldn't think of anything but partying. I tried to talk to him. So did his girlfriend and Jesse, but he wouldn't listen to anyone. At first he just drank and smoked pot and did mushrooms. But then Randy met the new kid on the block—coke. It was expensive, and I wasn't comfortable dealing it. Randy begged me to try selling it so he'd have access to a continuous supply, but I didn't want to." Macaw stopped talking again.

Alexa brushed his face with her hands, wishing she could rub out the pain she saw there. "It's okay, I'm here."

He took a deep breath and continued, "A couple months before our high school graduation, some new coke players backed by Gonzales came into town and muscled in on the established cartel. They approached me about carrying their stuff, and I refused. As it turns out, not such a good move. Gonzales set me up, and I was busted by the Panamanian narcs and thrown in jail. That was hell, but not the worst part. Randy took over the business when I went in. Only trouble was, his judgment was clouded by a white haze. It took Gonzales about five minutes to approach Randy with a real sweet deal. If he took them on as the new distributor, he could have all of the coke he could handle. Of course, he jumped on the opportunity and ran with it. At first, he just distributed to local high school kids and upwardly mobile Panamanians. By the time I got out seven weeks later—thanks to paying my way out with all the cash I'd saved—they had him running massive amounts of the stuff into Panama City. I freaked and told him to get out of the mess, and he promised he would. He was committed to one last run, and there was no way out of it." Macaw's breathing had become shallow and uneven.

Alexa waited.

"I'll never forget that night. It was the last night that the Canal Zone was officially the Canal Zone. The Panamanians were set to take over at midnight. I'd planned on going with Randy for that last run, but somehow lost track of him. I never saw him alive again."

"What happened?" asked Alexa.

"Turns out someone must have tipped off the Panamanian narcs, because they were waiting for Randy at the drop-off point. When he saw them, he swallowed the load of coke he was carrying."

Alexa gasped.

"The cops didn't know what the hell was going on when he collapsed in the station. They rushed him to the hospital in the Canal Zone, but he died of a massive heart attack soon after he arrived there."

She slipped her hand into Macaw's as his last words hung in the small room. They stayed that way for a time, silent, as if each waited for the other to speak, and then as if no words needed to be said.

Finally, Macaw punctuated the silence. "That's what I like about you. You don't blab on and on about looking at the bright side."

"There's a time for the bright side," said Alexa. "And then there's a time for the dark side. And I'm not sure that the two are mutually exclusive."

Eventually, they both fell asleep.

Alexa woke several hours later to find Macaw sitting in the chair next to the bed.

"Is everything okay?" she asked, her voice fuzzy from slumber.

"You were talking in your sleep."

"Great," said Alexa sitting up and running her hands through her hair. "I hope I didn't say anything I'm going to need to deny."

"Looks like I'm not the only one with buried memories. Who's Aunt Lupe?"

Alexa stopped trying to tame her hair at his question. "My mother's sister, why?"

"She still alive?"

"Very much so. She lives in Todos Santos."

"I think you should go see her."

"Don't get me wrong, I'd love to see her. But why?"

"I don't know, but I think it's important you talk to her. You want me to come?"

This was getting weirder by the minute, she thought. "You want to go see my aunt?"

Macaw shrugged. "Why not? I'd like to visit that area of Mexico."

"I don't know, Macaw. I've got a lot going on here."

"You trust me, don't you?" he asked.

"Of course."

"It's a gut feeling, and my instincts are rarely wrong."

"Okay, fine, we'll go once the story is done. You getting back in bed?"

"In a minute. I want to listen for a while and make sure I don't hear anything suspicious."

Alexa yawned and said, "My bodyguard." And then, for the first time in years, she fell into a sound sleep.

12

The next day delivered an unrelenting heat that could melt an iceberg before noon. Alexa sifted through the chest of drawers in her room, searching for the perfect outfit. She wanted to stay cool and comfortable while returning Liana to her parents, but she also wished to look nice. Finally, she stood in her underwear debating between a shorts set and a simple cotton dress.

"The fashion show's great, but don't we need to get going?" asked Macaw, who had run over to his place earlier and changed into khaki shorts and a blue, button-down shirt.

"I don't know what to wear."

"I can guarantee that Liana's parents wouldn't care if you delivered her in your birthday suit."

Alexa sighed. "I don't know what's wrong with me. I slept great last night, but my head feels like a muddled mess this morning."

Macaw put a palm at the small of her back and rubbed.

"You're burned out, that's what's wrong. You need some downtime."

"You're not burned out. You never are. How do you do it? You're here every day helping me, and you manage to run your business. I wish I had that kind of stamina."

Macaw let out a throaty laugh and kissed the back of her neck. "You got stamina, baby, believe me. You forgot the other night that quickly? Maybe I should refresh your memory."

"I'm not talking about *that* kind of stamina," Alexa said.

"Why not? That's the best kind of stamina."

"Oh, you're terrible," she said, wrapping her arms around his neck and tilting her face up to his. He cupped her behind in his hands and nibbled on her bottom lip, sending a rush of desire straight to her heart. All she wanted was to fall onto the rumpled sheets with him—damn the heat. From the way he held her, she could tell he wanted that, too.

"We have to get going," she said, reluctantly extracting herself from his embrace.

"I know. It'll have to wait. I like the shorts and top."

Alexa took his suggestion and they headed to the police station. When they arrived a few minutes later, all was quiet.

"No one would ever guess that there's a bunch of little girls in here," Alexa whispered.

"All too scared to talk, I'm sure," said Macaw, steering her toward Chief Cordova, who stood near a conference room at the back of the building.

While it usually irked Alexa to be lead around by men, somehow she didn't mind it so much when the directions came from Macaw. Maybe because she trusted and respected him? At the thought, she removed her arm from his. No time for distractions. She needed a clear head for this. After all the abuse the little girls had endured, she wanted to help transition them back as safely and easily as possible.

"You'll do fine," Macaw whispered in her ear right before they shook hands with Chief Cordova. How did he read her mind?

"*Señorita* Alexa, *Señor* Macaw. We are honored to have you with us again," said the Mexican police chief, directing them to his office. As Alexa and Macaw sat down in chairs facing his desk, she asked, "Do you think you got all of the girls?"

"We talked to all of them, and yes, it seems we have everyone. Of course, this has been difficult since we didn't know many of these children were missing in the first place, and we wouldn't have known, if not for you and *Señor* Macaw. We are deeply grateful."

"How are the girls doing?"

"Most are in good health, but one little girl has pneumonia."

Alexa's heart sank. "Oh, no, not Liana Garcia?"

"I am happy to say that she is doing very well. Fernando Gomez did not resist arrest. It was almost as if he expected us. He went peaceably and is now in prison in the next town."

"What were the conditions like where you found the girls?" asked Alexa.

"I am ashamed to say worse than some of our barrios. The girls were living like animals, sleeping on filthy towels in a room with no air conditioning and not even a toilet or running water. *Señor* Gomez will be in prison for a very long time." The chief glanced at a photo on his desk of himself and his family. "In my line of work, I see terrible things, but this is one of the worst I have ever encountered."

"May we see the children now?" asked Alexa.

"Of course." Cordova rose to lead the way into an adjoining room.

Alexa's heart did a somersault at the sight of the girls. Although there were chairs, they had chosen to sit wedged together on the floor against the wall. When the children lifted their eyes to Alexa and Macaw, she sensed a ripple of unease run through the group. She thought she heard one little girl talk about candy—probably remembering the lollipops. Then Alexa saw Liana huddled at the end of the line. The little girl recognized them, uncertainty covering her pretty face.

Would she and the other girls live their lives fearful? Or finally forget? Alexa wondered, hoping that the ugly memories would fade in time.

"I know they did a little counseling last night, but I wish Liana's parents would take her in for more," said Alexa to Macaw.

"Compliance in that area may not be too good, but I'll talk to her old man. If I pay for a few sessions, he might actually agree. Bottom line, though, is that being part of a tight-knit family is going to be the best therapy for all of them."

Macaw's comment about family made her think of her father. When she had called Fallbrook that morning, Violet said he was doing much better. At least that was something she didn't have to worry about.

"You would cover the cost of professional therapy for Liana?" Alexa gazed at Macaw with a mixture of surprise and admiration.

"There's a good chance her old man won't accept the charity. He's probably embarrassed he let his wife talk him into letting Liana go in the first place. You know, the Latino macho thing. Glad I'm not like that." Macaw grinned.

Alexa laughed. "You're delusional. But seriously, that's a really nice gesture."

She watched Macaw's eyes soften as he replied, "I know what happened to those girls really tore you up, and I wish I could pay for all of them. Liana's therapy—I can swing that. And the truth is, I want to."

Alexa approached Liana, crouching down to her level and smiling. "We're taking you home to your mama and papa," she said in Spanish.

The child visibly brightened at the mention of home, but then frowned. "Will I be able to stay?"

"Yes," Alexa quickly replied.

Expecting another smile, Alexa's heart strings stretched when huge teardrops started crawling down the little girl's dirt-streaked face. "What's the matter, honey?"

Liana spoke softly. "I hope my parents are not angry with me."

The child's words sent a strong maternal surge through Alexa. How she wanted to cradle Liana and somehow magically wipe away what had happened with Imelda. "Your parents aren't angry, Liana. They miss you and want you home," Alexa assured her. "You're a good girl. You didn't do anything wrong. Those were bad people."

Her words didn't seem to comfort the girl. Liana's shoulders shook harder as the tears flowed.

To Alexa's surprise, Macaw kneeled down next to her.

"Be careful," he said to Liana, who looked at him quizzically through watery eyes.

"You cry too much, and you'll run out of tears."

Liana wiped her face with her palms.

"I'm serious. I had a good friend when I was your age. She ran out of tears. Cried too much one day, and all of the sudden she was completely dry."

An inkling of a smile appeared on Liana's face.

"You know how hard it is to be a kid without any tears left?" Macaw asked.

Liana shook her head.

"Really hard. My friend couldn't cry anymore when her little brother broke her toys or when her big brother stepped on her foot."

Now Liana had a big grin on her face. "My brother, Julio, steps on my foot all of the time!"

"See," said Macaw. "And you probably cry to your mama, right? And then she gives you a hug?"

Liana nodded vigorously.

"So, you better save your tears for when you get home. We're going there really soon."

"Are you taking me home?" Liana asked Macaw.

"Do you want me to?"

Liana nodded again.

"Okay, I'll take you home. Can she go?" He pointed to Alexa. "She steps on my feet sometimes, but I'll make sure she's good."

The little girl giggled.

Alexa smiled, relieved and amazed at how easily Macaw had dealt with the situation.

After they finished paperwork to sign out Liana, Alexa took the little girl's hand and led her out to Macaw's MG. She climbed in the car and accepted Liana when Macaw lifted her in. Hugging the little girl's birdlike frame as they pulled away from the police station, she told Liana, "Your brothers and sisters are going to be so excited to see you."

When they parked in Liana's *pueblo's* town square, the weariness Alexa had seen in the little girl's brown velvet eyes gave way to joy.

"Let's go see your family," said Alexa as they all climbed out of the car and headed down the path leading off the square that lead to Liana's home.

Elvita saw Liana first. Leaving her tortillas on the open fire, she grabbed her long skirt in both hands and ran toward them, screaming her daughter's name.

As her mother approached, Liana's thin face filled with delight, and she broke into a run. Arms outstretched, Elvita scooped her daughter up and thanked God, crying, "*Gracias a Dios! Gracias a Dios!*"

Alexa watched as mother and daughter held each other tight. Moments passed before Elvita stopped embracing her daughter and looked into Liana's face. "They hurt you little one, I can see. They will never, ever hurt you again." Liana smiled and buried her face against her mother's breast.

Juan appeared then, his weathered face glowing with relief and joy.

Liana looked at her father from her vantage point in Elvita's arms. "Papa?" she said cautiously.

Without hesitation, he joined the hug with his wife and daughter, praising God as well.

Feeling like an intruder, Alexa started to back away and give them space, but Elvita noticed and stopped her.

"You are an angel from heaven," she said to Alexa. "We can never repay you for bringing Liana back to us."

"There's no need to try. I was honored to be able to return your daughter."

"Our family will have a *fiesta*," announced Juan. "You and your friend will stay, no? We will invite our neighbors and tell them that Liana was sick, but now she is healed."

"We would like to stay for the *fiesta*," said Alexa, looking at Macaw, who shrugged and nodded his approval.

Though they had very little, Alexa watched amazed at what they pulled together on such short notice. Elvita flitted around her one-room, adobe home, measuring out corn *masa* to make stacks of tortillas. Giddy with gratitude, Juan pulled a change purse out of the recesses of his worn pants and extracted several *pesos*, calling to Liana's older brother.

Placing the coins in the boy's small hand, he instructed, "Julio, you will go to the market and ask *Señor* Lopez to wrap up a nice chicken for you."

"A great fat one, Julio, you make certain," ordered Elvita, busy patting out the *masa*. "Don't drop it. Bring it right back here for the feast tonight. Our Liana is home."

"But where has she been, Papa?" asked Julio, his chest puffed with pride at his important errand.

"No place important, *mijo*," said Juan. "No place important at all." He hugged both children to him.

Alexa glanced at Macaw and once again admired his ability to read any situation. To have offered to pay for the chicken—or ten chickens because Macaw could afford it—would wound Juan's pride. With this party, the Garcias wanted to thank Alexa and Macaw. To honor that wish, she and Macaw were simply required to sit back and gratefully accept their humble hospitality.

They were given the best seats in the house—two worn lawn chairs. Before long, Julio returned with the chicken, and Elvita had it cut up and sizzling on her outdoor stove. Then she simmered rice and tomatoes in a small pot, formed a giant mound of tortillas and expertly flipped them over the flames, all the while roasting freshly harvested chili peppers. Juan handed Macaw and Alexa worn plastic cups filled with an amber liquid. Taking a sip, Alexa tasted a thick, homemade beer that made her tongue tingle.

"I gotta sell this one," Macaw remarked after he took a long swig. She started to ask if he meant it, but Juan and two other men appeared with their *guitarrónes*. They tuned them and began strumming in unison, belting out a salsa tune of gratitude.

Alexa smiled at the boisterous music, clapping her hands to the quick beat and shouting her approval.

Macaw surprised her and asked, "Wanna dance?"

"That beer must really be getting to you. I thought you hate to dance?"

"Not with you. Besides, it'll make them happy."

Alexa let him pull her up and swing her around in a funky salsa routine that made everyone laugh. The *mariachis* responded by playing even louder, which drew more neighbors to the Garcia's house. When Alexa noticed Liana and her brothers and sisters standing on the sidelines watching her and Macaw dance, she reached out and grabbed Liana and Julio, and motioned for the rest of her siblings to join them. To see Liana dance and laugh with such abandon made Alexa's heart swell with thanksgiving. Surrounded by such love, surely her wounds would heal and the horrors of the last few weeks would fade in time. They danced for a couple of songs more, and then Elvita motioned for the men to stop playing so they could eat.

Liana had the honor of doling out the open-flame chicken to fill the warm tortillas, and Alexa marveled at how there seemed to be enough for everyone. When the plates were cleared, Juan poured more beer, and the men resumed their playing for another couple of hours as the sun fell behind the trees, and Elvita's fire became the only thing that lit up the dark night around them. Sitting and watching the Garcias and their neighbors, Alexa reveled in their obvious joy. She knew that Juan and Elvita danced for the return of their daughter, but there also existed an obvious contentment in their faces. They seemed overjoyed with their gift of celebration. It need not be bigger, better or grander. It was their hearts in their hands offered first to God, then Alexa and Macaw.

At one point during the night, when the men took a break from the guitars, Alexa saw Macaw pull Juan aside. As the two men talked, she felt relieved to see that Liana's father never appeared outraged.

Once the fire had nearly gone out and conversation lulled, Alexa and Macaw made their exit, promising to return for a visit.

On the way back to her hotel, Macaw said, "I talked to Juan, and he agreed to get Liana counseling, if I pay for it."

"That's great. I'm so glad she'll be getting some help."

"You're quiet. You okay?"

"I'm fine. That was a great party."

"They know how to party, that's for sure. What else is on your mind?"

"I can't help thinking about Roth and how his name has been dropped from this whole thing. And Imelda is running loose. It doesn't seem fair.

Don't get me wrong. I'm really grateful to get the kids back to their parents, but Imelda and Roth are just going to do it again."

"I was thinking the same thing. We gotta at least find that crazy bitch and turn her in."

"And what about Roth?"

"Didn't your boss tell you to write the story and leave his name out of it?"

"Yes, he said something about not opening that can of worms and how we only have the word of a druggy. Never mind that the druggy is Roth's own daughter. Like I said, I'm thrilled to get Liana home, but I hate to think of how many more Lianas there will be if Roth is allowed to go free."

"I hear ya," said Macaw. He was silent for the rest of the ride back to the cantina.

13

After the party at the Garcia's, Macaw pulled up in front of the cantina and told her, "I gotta check on the bar, but I can come back if you want."

Alexa shook her head. "I'll be okay. You've spent the last two days here. I'm sure you've got stuff to catch up on. I need to work on the story, anyway."

Macaw made her promise to call if she changed her mind and waited until she entered the cantina before pulling away.

Once in her room, she dialed Peter's number. It was late, but her editor had been adamant about her calling him regarding the sting. Otherwise, he'd most likely be on the next plane to La Paz.

"Lex, that you?" Peter's voice came across the line thick with sleep.

"Hi, sorry to wake you, but I know you wanted me to check in."

"Definitely, how'd the return of the girls go?"

"Great. Macaw and I delivered Liana home personally, and her over-joyed parents threw a party in our honor."

"You should be proud of your work, Alexa. I'm glad you got those little girls home safely. So, once you file the story tomorrow, you're ready to come home. I've got another front-pager in Peru for you. There's a ring of heroin manufacturers in the jungles there destroying natural resources and lives. Do you want me to book you a flight for the day after tomorrow?"

Alexa was silent.

"Lex? You there? Do we have a bad connection?"

"No, I just. . . . Never mind."

"What? I want to make my star reporter happy. What is it? Do you need a few extra days?"

"I can't stop thinking about Roth," she blurted out. "How that evil bastard is getting away with this, and I'm just supposed to move on to the next thing."

"The next thing is important, too, Lex. And you saved a lot of lives. You should be happy about that. As for Roth, we aren't even sure that he's involved. You just have the word of his doped-up daughter. She could have an axe to grind. We don't know anything for sure."

"I just know he's involved—up to his armpits. And with a little more time I can prove it."

"Listen, Lex, like I told you. The powers that be forbid you to spend any more time or money on this story. They made it very clear that they want you to write the article without Roth and move on. Why? I don't know. Is someone trying to cover someone else's ass? Maybe. I do know that my conversation with Bifford got a little hostile, and you know I don't like hostile. That's why I'm an editor and not out in the field."

"Doesn't that make you wonder? Why is everyone so jumpy when the name Roth comes up? What is everyone trying to hide?"

Peter sighed. "I like my job. I know you like your job. I want to keep mine. Just put this bone down, get on a plane and come home so I can brief you on Peru."

"What's Michael doing?"

"Why?"

"I was just curious what he's working on. I get out of touch when I'm on location."

"He's working on an inner-city story about slumlords. What's with the change of subject? Something you're not telling me?"

"No, everything's fine. I'm going to finish writing the story now so you can read it first thing in the morning."

"Okay. Happy writing."

"Goodnight."

Pushing her conversation with Peter to the back of her mind—including the fact that he wanted her on location in Peru within the next few days, which meant leaving Macaw—she opened her laptop, powered it up and stuck in her flash drive. Worrying and wondering about what to do next only led to writer's block, and she wanted to write about Liana's return while it was fresh in her mind.

Before starting, she removed water from the refrigerator and rubbed the cool bottle against her forehead. Unscrewing the cap, she took a sip and then skimmed the words on the computer screen. Emotion burned in her chest as she read the passages about the girls in the hotel room. Swallowing hard, she held back the tears. What was wrong with her? She couldn't remember ever having been so emotional over an article. Sure, it was the first story where little girls were being bought and sold like inanimate objects, but still. Maybe that was the point, after all. Maybe it was a sign that she should harness the anxiety she felt and channel it into the story.

Taking a deep breath, she focused on the computer screen and entered her favorite altered universe where only words mattered. On this plane of consciousness as a wordsmith, time stood still while she crafted the story of the little girls' harrowing experiences, quoting heavily from a child psychologist, who commented on the trauma they experienced and would continue to struggle with for many years to come. Then she chronicled the rescue, relating Cordova's description of the filthy, airless room where they were held captive. At points, the words rushed out from her mind so fast that her typing fingers could scarcely catch up with her thoughts. When she finished, she felt emotionally and physically spent. Hooking the computer up to her landline, she modemed the story to Peter, saved it on a flash drive, which she shoved deep in her pocket, and erased the file from her computer.

Lying down on the bed, she closed her eyes and almost immediately fell into an exhausted sleep.

In the early morning hours, an insistent scraping sound—metal on metal —nipped at the edges of her awareness. Was it part of her dream? The sound seemed so real, wire jimmying a door, breaking into her consciousness. Too late. While she was still surrounded by semi-darkness, a large, decidedly male hand clamped on her mouth and a knee buried itself in her stomach. She scrabbled to remove the hand from her mouth but stopped when the knee dug in deeper.

"Listen closely, bitch. You're done playing junior detective. You hear? You shut your mouth and keep all of this out of the newspaper, or you'll be sorry," he hissed, filling her nostrils with the acrid scent of mentholated cigarettes. "And don't think lover boy Macaw will stop us. We'll teach him a lesson, too. While you watch. Get the hell out of Mexico, before we cut you up in little pieces and feed you to the tourists."

The darkly clad figure slipped out the door, and Alexa sat up coughing and gulping air, the pain in her stomach worse than anything she could have imagined. When she could breathe evenly again, a sudden revelation struck her. Even though her intruder spoke excellent Spanish, he wasn't Mexican. Definitely American. And he wanted information. She didn't have to check the room to know what he'd taken. Her computer. Again.

She rolled out of bed and struggled to the door. The lock had been forced and was broken. She'd call Miguel to come fix it pronto, although she didn't think the intruder would be back. At least not right away.

When she finished dressing and brushed her hair, she felt a little more in control and ready when Peter called.

"Lex, the article is fantastic! It's a page-turner. Can't wait to run it. And the photos are perfect. They protect the little girls' identities, but really show their plight."

"I'm glad you like it."

"How about coming home tomorrow?"

"I want to talk to you about that."

"What about it? I'm not liking the tone of your voice."

"I need some personal time."

"Personal time?"

"I've got an aunt in Todos Santos. My mother's sister. I haven't seen her in forever. She's getting on in years, and I thought this would be a good time to visit."

"It's not the best time, Lex. Remember Peru? That story may not wait. What is this really about?"

"Just some personal time."

"I know you're not telling me something. Are you planning on going after—? Look, Lex, I know things seem unfair, but you're a big girl. Life is unfair. Someone always profits. We all do our best."

She cut him off. "Like you said yesterday, boss. You like your job. I like that you like your job, so all I'm going to say is that I really need this personal time."

"And like I also said, this is a terrible time to slow down. Bifford is happy with the latest article, but he's carrying around a short fuse when it comes to canceling overseas investigations. I hate to sound harsh, but this personal time might cost you your job as you know it."

Anxiety clutched at Alexa's throat at his last comment, but there was really no alternative. If Roth was running a human sex trafficking ring, then Alexa wanted to try one more time to nail him.

"This is something I really need to do, Peter," she finally replied.

"Okay, so personal time to see your aunt. That's your official story?"

"Yes, that's my official story."

Alexa could hear Peter breathing on the other end of the line, no doubt weighing his words carefully. "Tell your aunt I wish her all the best and to not keep you away from us too long. Tell her that we really need you here and that we've come to rely on you. Tell your aunt to send you home safely to us."

"I'll give her the message. I'm sure she'll promise to make sure I'm safe and sound and back home as soon as possible."

"Promises can't always be kept. What is it they say in Mexico? *Vaya con Dios?*"

"That's what they say," replied Alexa. "Go with God."

"I won't stop worrying about you," said Peter. "You know that." And then he hung up.

It wasn't as if it was all a lie, Alexa thought as she flipped her cell phone shut. She did plan on visiting Aunt Lupe. She just also planned on hunting Roth down and stopping his operation. The next step was figuring out who could help her do that.

She opened a notebook and began jotting down possible leads. Visit Roth's daughter, of course, but what if she couldn't find her now? Druggies tended to move around, or worse overdose. Who else could shed some light on this case? And then a random thought entered her head that even surprised Alexa. Why hadn't she thought of it before? Fernando. They had him in custody, and he was, after all, the weak link. If he could confess everything to a priest, maybe with a bit of persuasion from her and Macaw he could at least give them some crumbs of information about how to find Imelda and Roth.

She called Macaw, who answered on the first ring.

"Hey," his deep voice calmed her nerves. "What's up?"

"A lot. Can you come over?"

"I'm on my way."

When Macaw arrived and listened to the details of her break-in, his eyes hardened. "I shouldn't have left you alone. I had someone watching the place, but the idiot obviously screwed up."

"I'm okay," she said. "It was actually a good thing."

He let out an exasperated puff of air. "Only you would think that having your life threatened was a good thing. Enlighten me on how good it was."

"I was waffling—thinking about giving up on exposing Roth and moving on to the next story, but I can't. This break-in shows me we're getting close to busting that slimeball, and now more than ever I want us to stop him."

"I noticed you said us."

"Only if you want it to be an us. If not, I understand. You can't stop your life to accommodate my problems. And you haven't been able to live your normal every day since you met me. I can go it alone."

He studied her for a second before replying. "I don't doubt that you would take this on alone, and there's a good chance you might even be successful. But it'd be way too dangerous for one person. I want Roth and Imelda as much as you do, so I'm in."

"You sure?"

"When have I ever said anything I didn't mean?"

"In that case, I've got a few ideas."

"Tell me."

Alexa laid out her plan to visit Shannon and Fernando at the penitentiary.

"A visit to old Fernando is a killer idea." Macaw nodded in approval. "I'll make a few calls and get us in. Meanwhile, we can go look for Shannon."

When they headed to *Diablo* Street a while later, Alexa thought about her last trip there all alone and how much safer she felt this time with Macaw at her side. Before they left her hotel room, she watched him load his gun, and a surge of excitement raced through her when she thought of the uncertainty that lay ahead for them. Until now, she avoided thinking about her own vulnerability. If she'd thought about it too much in the past, she would have talked herself out of the crazy things she'd walked into over the last few years. Without those experiences—even if they were dangerous—she wouldn't be here with Macaw at her side, ready to do almost anything to stop a human sex trafficking ring.

One of his guys had driven them, and as they exited the car, Macaw warned him to be ready to move.

"Classy address," Macaw commented as he followed Alexa to the building where she'd last seen Shannon. When they entered the dank entryway, he warned her, "Whatever you do. Don't sneeze."

Alexa giggled under her breath and then ventured, "Hello? Anyone here? Shannon?"

She led Macaw to the back of the building and into Shannon's makeshift room. The cot was empty.

"Crap," said Alexa.

"You looking for Shannon?" said a voice from behind that put Alexa's nerves on edge and had Macaw reaching for his gun. Alexa swung around to see the blond guy who led her to Shannon the previous time.

"Hi. Remember me?" she asked. "Shannon's friend? Any idea where she is?"

The blond guy's hair looked even dirtier than before—if that was possible—and his glassy eyes took a good minute to register Alexa. "Oh, yeah. You're that rich friend who gave her a ton of money. Cool."

"Where is she?" asked Alexa again.

"She's gone."

"I see that. Any idea where she went?"

"I don't know where they took her."

"Who took her?"

"A couple of guys. Something about her old man wanting to see her. She didn't want to go, but two guys with guns come in, I listen. You know what I mean?"

Alexa nodded. "No idea at all where they took her?"

He shook his head and frowned. "It sucks. She's my girl. Now I'm all alone."

Alexa felt grateful for the information and pulled out a fifty-dollar bill, even though she knew he'd probably spend it on drugs.

As they headed out of the building, Alexa said, "Obviously Roth's associates came in and removed her. Who knows where she's at now."

Macaw signaled his driver to pick them up.

When they were settled back in the car, Alexa complained, "Well, that was a totally useless trip."

"No, it wasn't."

"What do you mean? We have no idea where Roth is."

"Yeah, but we know that Roth is running scared and that he's definitely our man."

"True. I guess it's good to look on the bright side."

"Want to go to my bar for lunch? I need to check on a few things."

"Sounds great. What's on the menu? The usual?"

"I've been a little busy, so no *empanadas*. But Pablo makes a killer fish taco."

"Sorry."

"For what?"

"For keeping you so busy. You have a life, too."

"What could be better than fighting crime with a hot babe?" He squeezed her hand.

Alexa laughed. "Nothing."

"No, seriously. Life hasn't been this interesting since I don't know when. I was sick of staring at the four walls in my office and breaking up bar fights."

They pulled into Macaw's parking space at the back of the bar and headed inside to a hopping lunch crowd.

"Hey, Pablo," Macaw addressed his cook, who lowered a heaping plate of tacos onto a table. "Bring a plate of those and some iced tea into my office."

Pablo nodded and continued to another group, handing them a plate stacked with steaming tortillas.

Once inside Macaw's office, Alexa felt his pure maleness take over the small space. Without thinking, she slid into his arms and planted a hungry kiss on his mouth. He reciprocated, sitting back on his desk and pulling her close. As they lost themselves in one another, she felt him harden. Remembering Pablo and the tacos, she pulled back.

"Hey, I thought I taught you not to play tease," he breathed deeply.

"Well, if you're complaining, I guess I can busy myself dusting the bookshelves. Besides, Pablo could come in at any minute."

"I trained my employees to knock. So, don't sweat that. We got plenty of privacy. What gives?"

Alexa searched Macaw's eyes. What was it she wanted? An assurance that he felt the same deep connection that she had obviously come to feel? That he couldn't live without her? That he could see them having a future?

"What's bothering you?" Macaw pulled Alexa closer and rubbed her behind, making everything in her ignite.

"It's just, do you think...?"

Pablo rapped on the door. "Got your tacos and tea, boss. Okay to come in?"

"I see what you mean about privacy," said Alexa, slowly extricating herself from his grasp.

"Hold on!" he yelled to Pablo and redirected his gaze at her. "Tell me. What were you going to say?"

"It can wait. Get the door. He's busy."

"Okay, but you're going to spill."

What could she say to him, she wondered as he took the plate of tacos and teas and placed them on the desk. That she had fallen hard for him? That she had no idea how this would play out, but she didn't want it to end? Saying those things went against all of her beliefs about staying professional, keeping a clear head and not ever getting involved. Those rules had led to her success. They kept her moving forward.

Macaw handed her a taco and bit into his. She watched his jaw work as he chewed and swallowed. "Tell me. You freaked about going to see Fernando? I can go myself, if you want."

"I'm a little scared. I haven't heard the best things about Mexican prisons. But I definitely want to go."

"They're a trip, that's for sure. Ironically, in some ways they're a lot better than American ones."

"Surprising. How so?"

"Well, for one, the inmates have a lot more freedom than American prisoners do. Family and conjugal visits are the norm, and if you have the dough, you can have whatever you want—like a big screen TV in your cell."

"You're not talking from experience?"

"No. But some of my men have been inside. Like I told you, I did spend some time in a Panamanian jail, and that was far from a country club existence." His cell phone rang. "*Si?*" He listened for a few minutes and then thanked the caller. "I owe you, *hombre.*"

Clapping his phone shut, he grinned. "We're in. Fernando's expecting visitors."

"Does he know who's visiting?"

"Hell no, I thought it'd be better to surprise him. Give him something to worry about."

Alexa nodded and scarfed down her taco.

An hour later, they approached the maximum-security prison. When the facility loomed in the distance with its mammoth metal fences topped by giant spools of barbed wire, Alexa's heart sped up. Convincing Fernando to talk was key. Without Shannon, he was their only hope.

"We'll get our boy to talk," said Macaw as they got out of his car. "No problem."

"Tell me where you get your confidence."

"Fernando likes to eat—a lot. Mexican prisons aren't known for their cuisine. There's very little of it, and what there is sucks. You got money inside, though, you can eat like a king."

"I hope you're right," said Alexa.

At the guard shack, Alexa let Macaw do the talking. "Hector Hernandez sent us. Said we can visit a new inmate—Fernando Gomez."

Alexa thought of Hector's mistress, Ramona, the boutique owner, and wondered if she'd approve of the jeans and T-shirt she wore. What *do* you wear to visit a prisoner? She wondered.

The guard checked a list and then activated the large metal gate to slide open. When Macaw took Alexa's arm and pulled her in close to him, she gratefully let him shield her with his body. As soon as the gate clanged shut, trapping them in the testosterone-charged space, the catcalls and whistles started. When they walked past the prison yard, one muscular inmate leered at them and called out, "Hey, *hombre*, you bring us a present?"

The atmosphere was different in the visiting room. Children ran around as their mothers talked to prisoners. After a few minutes, Fernando walked into the room, his eyes taking on a veiled look of relief when they fell on Macaw and Alexa.

They had handcuffed him and chained his legs together. As he shuffled toward them, Alexa wondered how he'd gotten himself into the life he led. She felt nothing but disgust for the man.

"Fernando, my man," Macaw boomed, motioning to the prisoner to sit across from them. "I would ask how they're treating you, but I'd say from your thin, yellow face, not too good. The food suck? You poor bastard. Before we came, I pigged out on a plate piled this high with tacos." He raised his hand a foot above the table in front of them.

Fernando's eyes turned needy and desperate. "Yeah, Macaw. You come here to tell me about your dinner plans?"

"No, but we can talk about how yours might get a whole lot better if you tell us what we wanna hear."

"And what's that?"

"Where's your old lady? And where's her backer? We're planning to shut them both down."

"Good luck." Fernando shrugged, his left eye twitching.

"From where I'm sitting, you're not too lucky, *amigo*. Imelda left you to take the fall. Let me know where she is, and she can pay her dues, too."

"I told that woman the kids were a bad idea." Fernando shook his head. "She wouldn't listen." Then he stopped and eyed Alexa. "Since when you work with someone, Macaw?"

"Since now. She and I have our different reasons for talking to your wacko wife. Whatever you say to me, you say to her, too. Think real hard, and you might just get a cheese pizza tonight. We got the cash—just need the info."

"She has a lot of safe houses. Hard to keep track of all of them. You can bet she's holed up in one, though, and not poking even her fat little pinky out."

"Tell me about them," ordered Macaw.

"Screw you. I give Imelda up, I'm a dead man."

Macaw laughed. "You and I both know she has never taken you seriously. I know that pissed you off. How about paying her back for her disrespect?"

Fernando crossed his arms over his chest. "I'm not telling you shit."

"Fine," said Macaw, leaning back in his chair and smiling. "You like *empanadas*? I make mine with fresh ground beef—you know the brand you used to order? Then I mix in plenty of onions and garlic. I love garlic, don't you? A little tomato, but not too much. Of course, currants, and then—"

"Okay, okay. Stop talking about food," Fernando sniveled. "I'll tell you about the safe houses, but I want a lot of cash."

"Go on," commanded Macaw.

Fernando leaned in close. "There's the place in Veracruz, but I doubt she went that far. Another one here in La Paz, but that's too close. I like the one outside of Mexico City, but she said it was too far away from the night life." He paused. "I'm sure she's in Cabo, near the action. We have a piece of property near Land's End."

"That sounds like our Imelda. Tell me about security."

As Fernando filled Macaw in on the intricate details of disarming the alarm system, and how many guards he thought she'd have on hand, Alexa studied Fernando closely. He appeared to be telling the truth.

"And what about her backer? We know he's big time. Where can we find him?"

Fernando ran his thick fingers through thinning hair. "She always met him in private. Afraid I might say something stupid."

"There has got to be something you can pass our way," said Alexa. "Any little detail."

Fernando concentrated for a moment and then his eyes lit up. "He liked a really expensive cigar. She always made sure to take him a box when they met."

"What cigar?" asked Macaw.

"Hold on. Let me think. I'm not a cigar smoker. I remember! Montecristo A. One of those stupid things was like seventy bucks."

"Sounds like a big spender. No surprise. That all, *amigo*?"

"That's all, Macaw. Now where's my money?"

"One more question. What the hell did you ever see in Imelda?"

Fernando got a faraway look in his eyes. "My mama always liked her," he mused. "*Qué bueno* she died before she could see this."

"Imelda must have put on quite a show for your mama," said Macaw.

"My wife is always putting on a show."

Macaw extracted a wad of cash and quickly passed it to Fernando. "Have a nice dinner."

Fernando gripped the money in his hand and glanced grimly about him.

Alexa thought she felt Fernando's eyes follow them as they walked away.

Once in Macaw's MG, she asked, "You think we've got the location?"

"Yeah, I think that's the most likely place that she'd be headed. I know my Mexico geography pretty well. Isn't that on the way to your aunt's in Todos Santos?"

Alexa nodded. "I won't be lying to Peter after all. I will be visiting Aunt Lupe."

Macaw began to chuckle.

"Cheer me up. What's so funny?"

"I'm guessing Fernando won't be asking for conjugal visits from his wife."

Alexa threw back her head and laughed until she cried. "Thanks, I needed that," she said, wiping tears from her eyes.

When they got to *La Cantina Cantata*, Macaw and Alexa ordered some tacos from Miguel and carried them up to her room. They ate in silence, both contemplating their next move. After she had swallowed her last bite, Alexa spoke, "I think we should head out as soon as possible. Can you go tomorrow?"

Macaw yawned. "Yeah, I think I can clear my schedule for a few days. We want to get to Imelda before she really goes underground. I'm beat."

"Me too," said Alexa, who pulled off her clothes and climbed into bed in her underwear.

Macaw put his gun under the bed, stripped and crawled in next to her. "I'm not complaining, but what happened to the threads you always wear to bed in Mexico in case of an emergency exit?" he asked.

"I'm too tired to put them on."

They drifted off; both sleeping so soundly they didn't hear Miguel's muffled cries in the middle of the night.

14

Later, Alexa would marvel at the irony of her final words before they both fell asleep that night. Though she slept soundly in Macaw's strong arms, there was one enemy neither had considered. They both woke in the middle of the night coughing in the haze of smoke that filled her room. Macaw jumped up immediately, pulled his jeans on and grabbed his gun from under the bed. She slid on the blouse from the night before, slipped into her pants and pushed on tennis shoes.

"Get valuables!" cried Macaw, shielding his mouth and nose with his T-shirt.

Alexa patted her pocket. Flash drive, passport and cell phone accounted for. Computer gone. Her mother's rosary! She ran to the wall and ripped back the wallpaper, extracting the beads and slipping them around her neck.

Macaw pressed his face to the door and then shook his head. Crossing the small room in two strides with Alexa in tow, he whipped open the window and they both gulped a lungful of fresh air. The window led to a back alley. Three feet or so to the right hung a fire escape. Hoisting his muscular frame over the edge, he reached and grasped the metal ladder. Pushing off with his feet, he pulled himself over. The fire escape held firm, and he turned to reach for her. She hung from the windowsill and held out her arms, grasping at his outstretched hands. As she pushed her torso over the sill, he pulled, and in one fluid movement dragged her into his expansive arms beside him.

"I'll go down first," he yelled as an explosion from below shook the fire escape. He turned to back down the metal stairs. Alexa followed. As they descended, red flames licked the outside of the first-story, and a window burst, spraying the alley with shattered glass.

When her feet hit solid ground, Alexa started for the front of the building. He tugged her arm to stop her and pointed down the back alley away from the hotel.

"What about your MG?"

"It's better this way. We need them to think we're still in the building."

They ran several blocks hand-in-hand through deserted back streets as the fire engines wailed in the distance, stopping when they came to the back of his bar. He pulled a key out of his pocket and let them in through the kitchen.

Standing hunched over in the dark kitchen panting, Alexa gradually regained her breath and swallowed to soothe the raw burn at the back of her throat. "You're probably thinking what I'm thinking," she said finally. "That fire was set."

"I'm 110 percent sure. I'll call a couple sources in the morning, though, and see what the word on the street is," he said.

"We left the MG so that everyone will think we didn't make it out alive. That's brilliant. Imelda and Roth won't know we're coming," she said, her eyes adjusting to the gloom as she began to make out the dish-washing sinks, commercial stove and countertops.

"Bingo," he replied.

"What now?" Alexa asked, taking the glass of water Macaw gave her and downing it all at once.

"We go to my room and if we're lucky get some shut-eye."

"I can't believe I've never asked this, but where is your room?"

"You mean you can't believe you don't know where I call home?"

Alexa felt surprised about not knowing this about him. "Something like that."

"It's upstairs. It's small. Don't expect much." He took her hand and pulled her with him around a corner which led to a steep, narrow flight of stairs. She followed him up, admiring how his muscular butt filled his jeans.

"They made this stairway for midgets or something. It's really a partial second story— just the one room and a bathroom. No one else comes up here, and it's hard to tell it exists from the street."

"Which is a good thing, I'm sure," said Alexa.

"Especially tonight."

They walked into a short hallway and Macaw unlocked the first door to the right, flipping on the light. He wasn't kidding about small. The room was about fifteen square feet. He had a double bed made up with a jungle theme comforter, a small chest of drawers and a painting on the wall of a tropical beach.

"Your room might be smaller, but your bed is a mansion compared to mine."

"You asking for an invitation?"

"Do I need one?"

He pulled her close. "You know you're always welcome."

"I probably smell like smoke," she said, nuzzling his neck with her mouth, running her hands along his strong back.

"I always wanted to sit in front of a campfire as a kid, but it was too damn hot in Panama for that kind of thing," Macaw said.

She giggled into his neck. "You bring up the strangest memories."

"Sorry. You bring up strange feelings."

"How strange?"

"I can give a demonstration, if you want."

"I want," she said, pressing her body to his, relishing his power and strength.

"Finally, we got a bed that fits us both," he said, pulling her with him to flip off the light and close the door, which creaked when he shut it.

Something about the creaking door sent a rush of panic through Alexa, and she froze.

"What's wrong?" he asked, flipping on the light again, concern in his eyes.

"I don't know. I feel. . . ." she stammered. Did she inhale too much smoke?

"Listen, it's been a rough night. I understand."

"No, it's not the fire. I don't know what it is."

"It's that again," he said, almost as if to himself.

"What again?"

Macaw searched her eyes. "You know I'll never hurt you, right? You trust me, don't you?"

"Of course, with my life," she replied without hesitation.

"I promise the sheets are clean. I've been spending a lot of time at my girlfriend's."

Alexa's heart clutched at his words. *My girlfriend's.*

"Turn off the light," she breathed.

"You sure?"

She nodded.

He flipped the switch and the room plummeted into darkness. Alexa sat on the bed and straddled him, taking possession of his mouth with hers and kissing him, slow and steady, exploring with her tongue. When she finished, she surprised herself by whispering, "Make love to me." Until then, the expression had always struck her as silly and embarrassing. But she couldn't have meant it more. She felt a new closeness between the two of them—an understanding that required no words.

His breath caressed her cheek when he whispered, "I've never met anyone like you. And that ain't no line."

In answer, Alexa grasped the hem of his T-shirt and pulled it up. Consumed by an even deeper desire and a faint glimmer of something she was afraid to name, she kissed every inch of his bare chest.

"It's my turn." Macaw unbuttoned her blouse. When he finished, she slid the shirt off her shoulders letting it fall behind her and then unclasped her bra and tossed it to the floor. She felt him lean forward, but she stopped him with her hand. A clock ticked somewhere in the dark room, and she thought—what if time could be suspended? What if they could sit here indefinitely, eye-to-eye, heart-to-heart? What if the bad things didn't really exist, like the girls, Roth, and her father's stroke? Or tonight's fire that could have taken their lives?

"Scary night, huh?" he said.

Alexa nodded, surprised as always at how he tuned into her thoughts. She cradled his hand in hers and kissed each finger, one at a time, then pressed his palm to her breast.

"You're trembling," he said, his voice tinged with concern. "We've been through a lot tonight. Let's just lay down."

She shook her head. "I meant it. I want you to make love to me. *Because* of tonight."

Macaw cradled her head in his hands and eased them both back onto the bed. Slowly, deliberately, he helped her slide out of her pants and panties. Then he removed his shorts and gently lowered himself on top of her. She lay still while he kissed her face and neck and arms, relishing the rush of security she felt as he guarded her with his body. When Macaw parted her legs and caressed her inner thighs, strumming her to a slow, steady state of desire, she heaved a contented moan, the sound mingling with the tears in her throat. As they united, she pressed herself close to his chest, wanting nothing more than to hold on forever.

Macaw entered Alexa, unable to restrain the desire he felt for this woman. He wanted to protect her soft vulnerability, take away the hidden pain he knew she sometimes felt, and wrap her in a blanket of safety. He let the fire inside him build, waiting, waiting, until their rhythm met each other's. When he sensed her pulling him down and then rising to meet him, he felt certain his heart would burst.

Afterward, he laid his head on her breasts and smiled while she stroked his hair, soon drifting off into a peaceful sleep.

They awoke intertwined in each other's arms, waking at the first rays of light streaming from the room's only window.

"Fun's over. Time to get to work," said Macaw, kissing her bare back. He jumped out of bed and went next door to take a quick shower.

Alexa smiled and stretched lazily as she listened to the water run, dozing off again until he returned to pull on a blue tank and jean shorts.

"I'm going down to my office to check on things," he said. "Find out what the word is. Feel free to use the bathroom while I'm gone."

"Wow, I get to take a real shower."

"It ain't the Ritz, but it definitely beats your place."

Alexa thought about the cantina and her little makeshift bathroom. "I wonder if they saved any of the building?"

"I'll know in a few minutes."

She slid out of bed and padded to the bathroom next door. Pulling out a clean towel from under the sink, she hung it next to the shower and then stepped into the small stall and turned on the water. After lathering up a bar of soap and rinsing off the smell of smoke and sex, she washed her hair with Macaw's shampoo. When she finished showering and toweling dry, she enveloped herself in his terrycloth robe that she found hanging on the back of the door. Breathing in his scent, she stood there for a minute and then frowned. What on earth was she doing? Out of all the stories she'd done and people she'd met. Why Macaw? But she knew why. He was the kindest, sexiest, strongest man she'd ever met. That's why. Any girl would go gah gah over him. Many probably had. Cocooned in his bathrobe and absently toweling her hair, she almost ran right into him in the hallway.

"Word is that the fire was set. The good news is they think we're dead. The bad news is Miguel didn't make it. Looks like he caught them, and they killed him for it. A hard knock on the head."

At the news, Alexa felt herself slipping forward. Macaw caught her, and helped her into his room, guiding her to the bed.

"This isn't worth it," she croaked. "Miguel's dead. They could come after you, Macaw."

"Hell it ain't worth it. We're gonna find Imelda and Roth and shut them down for good. You want Miguel's death to amount to nothing?"

Alexa shook her head. "No, but—"

"No buts. Since when do you back down?"

Macaw was right. "Since never. But I should go alone. You've done enough for me. I can't let you lose everything."

"They think I'm dead, remember? I'm going to hide out here and play ghost?"

"You've got a point. I guess we leave then. But where?"

He smiled. "That's better. I was getting worried about you. I'm thinking we head to the safe house Fernando told us about and locate Imelda. First, though, we stop at your Aunt Lupe's and take a day to regroup. I've scoped out where her place is located. It looks like a good hideout—pretty remote."

"It is nice and quiet," Alexa agreed, thinking of the hacienda her mother's sister called home. "But how do we get out of town without attracting attention?"

"We need some help with that, and I know just the person to call."

Forty minutes later, Ramona wiggled her voluptuous frame up the narrow steps, stopping in the doorway of Macaw's bedroom and shaking her head when her eyes fell on Alexa.

"I always dreamed you'd invite me to your bedroom, Macaw, but not like this."

"You're in my dreams always, pussycat," Macaw said. "Sorry to get you up so early."

"Anything for you, my love," she purred, clicking into the room in high heels, tight-fitting jeans and a hot red, silk blouse. Flourishing a black valise she carried under one arm, she unzipped it to expose several wigs.

"What about a redhead?" Macaw asked hopefully.

Ramona looked at him and tisked. "You are farther gone than I thought, *mi amor*. I've never seen you so out of your head." She extracted a shoulder-length auburn wig and held it up. "Will this do?"

"I like it," said Macaw.

"Seems fine to me."

"Fine? This is a $500 wig!"

"Sorry," Alexa apologized. "It looks just like real hair. Thanks." She reached for the wig, but Ramona ignored her outstretched hand.

"Before you try the wig, we choose a wardrobe. Ricardo!" she called to a man hovering in the hall. "Bring in the bag."

The six-foot-three, sober-faced bodyguard lugged in an oversized garment bag, flopped it onto the bed and retreated to the hall.

Unzipping it, Ramona extracted a variety of outfits, glancing at Alexa as she held each one up. She finally decided on a lime green halter top and a black mini skirt and handed them to Alexa. "I've got some large hoop earrings. That will be just the ticket. I put them in the skirt pocket," she instructed. "And here are your shoes." She held up black, three-inch stilettos.

Horrified at the garish ensemble, Alexa looked at Ramona in disbelief. "You've got to be kidding. I'll look like—"

"Baby, I'd be afraid to leave you on the street. You'd have the guys lining up at the curb," Macaw interjected, nodding in approval.

"I had a feeling you'd like it," Ramona said and sighed.

"So what am I? Her pimp?"

"Something like that." Ramona pulled out a sleek black suit and white tie.

"I thought we wanted to be inconspicuous," said Alexa. "Wearing this stuff, we'll be moving targets."

Ramona turned to Macaw and raised her eyebrows.

"It's called hiding in plain sight," he said. "You think they're going to be looking for a hooker and her pimp?"

"I guess not."

"I brought a fabulous silk shirt for you, *mi amor*," said Ramona as she took a deep blue shirt off a hanger and approached Macaw. When he whipped off his tank top and reached for the shirt, Ramona nearly clapped in approval at his sculpted chest. He slid it on, and she ran her fingers across his torso. "It seems to fit," she nodded in approval. "The suit should as well."

"What about wheels?" Macaw asked her.

"Hector has a nice black Cadillac CTS waiting for you out back. And I told him to keep your MG safe."

Macaw let out a low whistle. "Go, Ramona. I'm impressed."

"Hector is trying to make it up to me. He forgot our anniversary."

"When was your anniversary?"

"Six months ago."

Alexa couldn't help but laugh.

"Maybe after this one you'll forgive him?" asked Macaw.

"I haven't decided," she pouted. "A girl has her pride. Anyway, I must be off. The store opens in an hour, and I have some errands to run. Good luck, *mi amor*. Whenever you're done with whatever this is, come back to me. I can make you a happy man."

Macaw chuckled as she signaled for her bodyguard, who took the valise she shoved at him and picked up the garment bag with his other hand.

After they left, Alexa asked, "What is it with you and Ramona? I know it's not sex, but I can see there's something between you two."

"I helped her with someone near and dear to her heart—her sister. She was mixed up with the wrong crowd and got addicted to drugs a couple of years back, and Ramona didn't know what to do. Thought she'd be burying her before the year was out. I stepped in, took her in off the street and helped her sober up. She's been clean since and is expecting a baby soon."

"You're a miracle worker."

"That's what Ramona thought, too, but the truth is, her sister was ready to quit. I just happened to be there when she needed me, and I had the time and patience to help."

"It probably helped you too, considering what happened to Randy. How long did she stay with you?"

"Six months. But enough talk. Let's see it!"

"I really have to wear this get-up?"

"Damn straight you do."

"Right here? Right now?"

"Yeah, hurry up," he said, folding his arms across his chest impatiently.

Alexa slid out of the clothing she had worn escaping from the fire and put on the skirt and halter top, both of which were at least one size too small. Then she tugged on the wig, pushing stray hairs underneath.

"We're all set if we need a little spending money!" announced Macaw. "I like you as a redhead."

She screwed up her face at his remark. "So what next?"

"I say we wait until really late tonight. We'll do a little cruising first, so we don't attract attention. Then move out of town gradually. Your aunt's place is a little more than an hour south of here, right? We'll get there in the early morning. She an early bird?"

"Yes, up at first light."

"Perfect. In the meantime, let's do a test drive of that outfit."

15

They waited until after four am to slip into the Cadillac CTS behind Macaw's bar. As soon as she sat down, Alexa yanked the stilettos off, and Macaw chuckled.

"What's so funny?" She scowled as she rubbed her sore feet.

"All you did was walk down the stairs. Just wait until I have you working it on the streets."

"Hilarious. Just drive."

Macaw put the car in gear and eased out onto the street. "Man, I love my MG, but this beast drives nice. Still smells brand new, too." His demeanor seemed free and easy, but Alexa knew better. On high alert, his eyes swept the streets as he slowly joined the traffic.

"We'll cruise around for a while as we make our way to Highway 1, which turns into the 19. Barreling out of here will call too much attention to ourselves. Does your aunt's place overlook the ocean?"

"The hacienda sits in a little valley, but I think there are ocean views from some of the upstairs rooms."

"Sounds like a little piece of para—" Macaw stopped talking as he eyed a Chevy crawling by in the opposite direction.

"Someone we know?"

"Not sure. I think it might be our friends who tried to grab you the other day. Glad these windows are tinted. They're probably just checking out the new competition."

They cruised around for a while longer, weaving in and out of traffic, finally making it to the interstate, where they headed south. Once they were on the open road and moving at a good pace, Alexa breathed deeply.

"Looks like we're good so far," said Macaw, checking in the rearview mirror. "It'll be awhile before they figure out that our bodies aren't in the ashes. Gives us time to do what needs to be done. Put your seat back. Get some sleep."

"No, I'll stay awake and keep you company."

"Okay, suit yourself. So you spend much time at your aunt's hacienda?"

"Unfortunately, not too much. My mother brought me a few times when I was young, but once she died, the visits stopped. I did go back about five years ago on my own. And we've always kept in touch."

"Did your aunt come to visit you in Fallbrook?"

"A few times after my mother died, and I loved it, but then she never came back."

"You must really be looking forward to seeing her."

"I am," said Alexa, who didn't realize how much until then. How had *Tia* Lupe changed? She wondered. Older, of course. Not much chance she could be wiser—she was born that way.

"My aunt has run the hacienda and her business all by herself for thirty years. She was married a long time ago, but he died. Afterward, she decided to be totally in charge of her own destiny, so she has always kept the business separate from her personal life."

"Smart woman. How does she support herself? Did she turn it into a bed and breakfast?"

"No, she's too much of a loner for that. Believe it or not, she took over her father's business. Furniture making."

"No shit? I love a woman with a tool-belt."

"I'll keep that in mind."

"In your case, just the tool-belt."

"I guess we're not being followed?"

"No, why you guessing?"

"Because your mind is in the gutter again. The only time you take it out of the gutter is when we're in trouble."

"Another really good reason to keep us out of trouble."

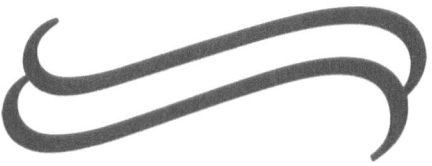

When Alexa dozed off, Macaw glanced over at her and smiled. She looked serene now, but damn, she was full of fire. Sure, he was helping her. A lot. But she could've and would've done all of this on her own. Fact was he wanted to help. Not only to stop Imelda and Roth's reign of terror, but the truth was, he couldn't get enough of Alexa. And that scared the shit out of him. Because soon enough, the ride would be over. He'd go back to his bar to rot, and Alexa would leave. Probably stepping up the rungs after this story. He certainly didn't have anything better to offer her. He just needed to play this out and thank his lucky stars he was with her now.

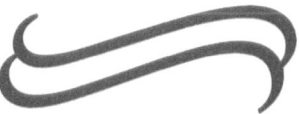

Alexa lifted her head forty-five minutes later and attempted to focus her eyes on him. Macaw asked, "How'd you sleep?"

"Really good. I hope I didn't snore."

"Yeah, but I just turned the radio up."

Alexa stuck out her tongue at him and then asked, "Where are we?"

"About fifteen minutes from your aunt's place."

"You okay?"

"Yeah, I'm fine. Still running on adrenaline. I have a tendency to do that."

"I'll say. Do you ever rest?"

"Yeah, sometimes. I'm gonna crash when we get to your aunt's place. She can take a chain saw to her furniture. I won't hear it."

"You must feel pretty comfortable that we're safe."

"For now."

A few minutes later, they pulled off the highway onto a narrow dirt road. The car bumped along as they descended into the small valley.

"Cell reception probably sucks here," said Macaw, who flipped open his phone and snorted. "Yeah, I barely have one bar."

"She's got a landline. We'll have to use that," said Alexa.

"My phone might not work, but do you wanna try calling?"

"It's probably not fair, but I'd love to surprise her. She's got a sturdy heart. She'll be okay."

Macaw chuckled and shook his head.

"What?"

"Your outfit might give her a heart attack."

"Shit!" Alexa exclaimed, covering cleavage with her hands. "What am I going to do? She'll think I've lost it."

"Tell her the truth—or at least part of it. You're undercover."

"I think that'll work."

A few minutes later, they pulled into the hacienda at daybreak, the sun peeking up over the hills behind them as they coasted into the driveway and shut off the engine.

"Damn, you undersold this place. What a beauty."

The hacienda sparkled in the early morning sunlight. Creeping fig covered much of the old stone building, except for the huge oval archway which had a family emblem of a lion and sword carved above the entrance.

"As you can see, Aunt Lupe married into money."

"I'll say. What'd her husband do?"

"His name was Emilio Sanchez, and he owned a fleet of fishing boats."

They climbed out of the car to the faint whisper of banana tree leaves shifting in the light morning breeze. After heading through the archway, thick with bright fuchsia bougainvillea, they entered a courtyard that displayed a large fountain with Saint Guadalupe in the center holding a bucket on her head from which water spewed. Spongy baby's tears outlined the stone pathway leading up to the fountain, and the jewel-toned leaves of croton and coleus sprang from pots surrounding the water feature at its base. Smaller archways framed the entire courtyard, leading to first-story rooms with their own shaded porticos. Above, potted burgundy geraniums lined the balcony of the second story.

Alexa and Macaw stood in the early morning stillness, admiring the scene.

"I forgot how incredible this courtyard is," said Alexa.

"Something smells just as incredible."

Alexa inhaled. "Orange blossoms, the sweetest scent ever." She pointed to a potted orange tree across the courtyard. "Those little white flowers on that tree over there. That's what you're smelling."

"Doesn't smell as good as you," said Macaw, putting his arm around her waist and pulling her close. "You think your aunt's up yet?"

At his words, the sound of running water erupted across the courtyard.

"I think so," said Alexa.

She and Macaw watched as a watering wand reached up to a potted fern and began dousing the plant. Alexa smiled as Tia Lupe emerged from behind a large split-leaf philodendron and began splashing water on surrounding plants.

"You gonna say something?" Macaw asked in a low voice.

"She'll see us soon enough," replied Alexa.

The second Alexa finished speaking, Aunt Lupe must have sensed their presence, because she spun around and shrieked, "*Ay, madre!* Alexa?"

"*Si, Tia,*" she said, walking across the courtyard to her aunt, who stood with a dumbfounded look on her face as the water continued to pour onto the cobblestone.

"I'm sorry to startle you."

"What on earth are you wearing, Alexa?"

"Forgive my clothing, Aunt Lupe. I'm on assignment."

"*Gracias a Dios!*" Her aunt let out a rich laugh, rolling her eyes heavenward. She shut off the hose and set it down, extending her arms in greeting.

Alexa embraced her aunt and then stepped back to meet her gaze, searching as always for a resemblance with her mother. It seemed as if Aunt Lupe did the same.

"You look more and more like Augustina every time I see you!" cried her aunt.

"I know it's been awhile since I visited, *Tia*," Alexa apologized, gazing into the kind face of her aunt, whose hair had turned a spun silver. Faint wrinkles etched the older woman's forehead, but her deepest lines by far were those around her mouth brought on by laughter, one of her greatest gifts.

"I have dreamed of this day, *mija*," she said to Alexa. "Even if work has brought you here, I have you now." Aunt Lupe raised an eyebrow at Macaw, who had walked up while they spoke.

"This is my friend, Macaw, *Tia*," said Alexa. "He has been helping me with the case."

"*Mucho gusto*," said Macaw, reaching out a hand and shaking Aunt Lupe's.

"Nice to meet you, as well," said Aunt Lupe, while her eyes studied Macaw's face. "Welcome to my hacienda."

"Thank you, *Señora* Sanchez."

"No formalities here. You may call me Lupe," said her aunt, who gestured toward the house. "I will put the two of you in the west wing. The light comes through in the evening, so the sun won't bother you in the morning, and it has a good view of the rose garden. Unless you require two separate rooms, and in that case, you will sleep in the east wing."

"The west wing is perfect," said Alexa.

They followed her aunt through the house, past mango-colored walls adorned with colorful local art. She wore a casual black skirt with a deep purple blouse and black ankle boots that clicked on the smooth stone floor as she walked.

"You both look like you could sleep all day. Please do. It's Sunday. Our only day of rest. You caught me before I left for early morning mass. Make yourselves comfortable. There are robes in the room, and I will get you both more appropriate clothing when I am in town."

"Thanks, Aunt Lupe, I wear a size—"

Lupe waved her hand in the air. "You wear a size seven, and your man wears an extra-large shirt and a size thirty-two, am I right? I will get you a selection of clothing to choose from."

"You're the best, *Tia.*"

"I know," said her aunt, stepping into a room with bright blue walls and a king-sized bed. In one corner of the room was a giant stuffed macaw hanging from the ceiling and in the other a lime-green armoire and dressing table. A terra-cotta-colored stone bar, complete with sink and refrigerator, ran the length of the other wall.

"There are some snacks and fruit in the kitchenette. Dinner is at seven sharp in the courtyard. Don't keep Saint Guadalupe waiting," she instructed, referring to her namesake statue in the fountain.

After her aunt had marched away, Alexa said, "She seems like a real task master, but she's actually a sweetheart."

"I can tell," said Macaw, putting his hands around her waist and drawing her close. "She sure has a soft spot for you. No kids of her own?"

Alexa shook her head. "My uncle couldn't have kids, but no one ever talked about it. I know it was really hard on my aunt, but she didn't complain. In many ways, I was the daughter she never had."

"She look like your mama?"

"A little. Mostly in the eyes. My mother was a lot more delicate. My aunt is strong from taking care of the hacienda and working with wood every day."

"Her niece is in great shape, too," Macaw said, kissing her neck. "Are you interested in a little *siesta?*"

"What about a little bath?" suggested Alexa.

"Bossy. Taking after your aunt, I see."

"I think you'll like the bathtub. We can take one together."

"Now I'm intrigued," said Macaw as he followed her out a set of

French doors into a small, sheltered courtyard. Stopping short in the doorway, he nodded in approval. "Now this is my kind of bathtub!"

Enclosed within the thick vegetation of elephant ear and bird of paradise intertwined with pothos, the small space featured a gray stone outdoor bathtub with silver faucets. Fresh emerald-green towels adorned with a sprig of purple bougainvillea lay next to the tub. Alexa leaned over and turned on the water.

"Damn, it's like she knew we were coming," marveled Macaw.

"It does seem that way, but I think she entertains quite a bit."

"She got a man?"

Alexa laughed as she adjusted the water. "Funny you should ask. I think she's got several."

Macaw chuckled. "Somehow that doesn't surprise me."

Satisfied at the temperature, Alexa reached behind her neck for the ties of the halter top and pulled. "I forgot how much I love it here. It's as if we're in some tropical paradise hidden away from the world," she said, peeling off the rest of her clothes and stepping slowly into the water.

As the stone bathtub steadily filled, Alexa sat on a ledge and let the splashing water caress the knots in her back brought on from sleeping in the car. The glow of early morning sun, lush surroundings and sight of Macaw's muscled body as he undressed, made her heave a contented sigh. Even better was the erection he brought with him as he eased himself into the water and waded her way. She smiled while he approached, thinking he'd take a cue from the lazy morning and let the water loosen his muscles, too, but he caught her off guard when he grabbed her and buried his face between her breasts, enjoying one, then the other. Breath raspy after his feast of her bosom, she sensed his impatience as he lifted her onto the edge of the tub and slid his hand between her thighs. At his touch, Alexa moaned and braced herself, arching her back and shifting her hips to invite him in. He took the invitation and entered quickly, slamming into her hard and fast, no doubt bruising her bottom. Surprised and delighted at his sponta-neous animal energy, she cried out his name several times as she came.

Afterward, he stood leaning over her. "Shit, sorry," he said, when he finally caught his breath. "It's your fault, though. You had to take off the top."

"You can repay me by soaping up my back," said Alexa, handing him a lavender-scented bar of soap and soft washcloth.

After lathering each other up and soaking until their eyelids drooped, they got out and toweled off, climbing into the bed under silky smooth sheets.

"This is the best bed we've slept in together, but I don't have the energy to do anything."

"Me neither," said Alexa, lying quietly beside him and watching him drift off to sleep.

Alexa woke at twilight, the air thick with humidity and Macaw so close he felt like a second skin.

"Good evening, sleepy head," he said and ran his hand along her flat stomach.

"Sorry, but this is going to have to wait."

"What am I supposed to do with this boner?" He looked down.

Alexa laughed. "I would tell you to take a cold shower. But seriously, my aunt meant it when she said to be on time for dinner."

"Damn," said Macaw, rolling onto his back to look up at the plaster ceiling and slowly circling ceiling fan. "I take back every good thing I said about her."

Alexa reached for her cell phone and checked the time. "It's a quarter to seven. We need to get up and get dressed."

"In what?"

"My aunt probably left our clothing outside the room." Alexa hopped out of bed and padded to the door. Opening it a crack, she saw a large bag, quickly snatched it and re-shut the door.

"I guess you know your aunt pretty well," said Macaw, who had raised himself up on one elbow. "What'd she get us?"

"It looks like a few different outfits." Alexa lifted up a jade silk shirt

Macaw's size and black trouser shorts. Then another shirt with a jungle print and khakis.

"Looks good," he nodded. "I'll take the silk for tonight. What'd she get you?"

Alexa pulled out a buttercup yellow silk halter dress and gasped, "Oh, my. It's beautiful. And so is this one!" she said, holding up a shimmery deep blue number with spaghetti straps.

"I like them both but do the yellow tonight."

Alexa nodded in agreement and took one last look in the bag. Several pairs of black jeans and blue T-shirts remained. Apparently, her aunt hadn't liked their other disguises.

"Man, I smell something amazing," said Macaw, jumping up to put on his clothes and gesturing for her to hurry.

"Hold on. I've got to brush my hair." Alexa sat down at the dressing table, and Macaw came over and took the brush from her hand. He brushed her long, black hair for several minutes, a look on his face she had never seen before. When he finished, she pinned her mane back with a barrette decorated with daisies that she found on the dressing table.

In the courtyard, the crickets warmed up for their nightly serenade as the hush of dusk settled into the garden. Flames from tiki torches moved in the breeze, and the heady scent of night jasmine mingled with the aroma of what could only be Aunt Lupe's famous *arroz con pollo*. Next to the fountain sat a teak table and three chairs. On the table was a carafe of what looked like sangria and two glasses.

"I guess your aunt's not joining us for a drink?" said Macaw, pulling out a chair for Alexa.

"Doesn't look that way," she said, sitting down.

Macaw poured them both a glass and took a sip. "This is fabulous."

"I love a man with good taste," said her aunt, who appeared with a bowl of tortilla strips and fresh salsa. "Forgive me for not joining you, but a friend stopped by earlier. He was hungry, so we ate, and I had my share of sangria."

Macaw raised his eyebrows in the direction of Alexa when her aunt mentioned her "friend." To stop herself from laughing at his expression, she stuck a tortilla strip in her mouth.

Once she swallowed, she said, "It smells like your delicious *arroz con pollo, Tia.*"

"Of course, I only make your favorite for such a special occasion." Aunt Lupe sat down in the third chair and crossed her legs. She wore an ankle-length slinky, brown dress and burnt orange lipstick, her hair smoothed back with a leather headband.

"Your friend left so soon?" asked Alexa.

"Yes, other commitments, but that is just as well. I have more time to visit with you. I see you are wearing your mother's barrette."

Alexa's hand flew to the barrette in her hair. "This was my mother's?"

"Yes, daisies were her favorite flower. You may keep it, if you wish."

"I will cherish it," said Alexa. "Thanks."

"So, tell me. What are you up to? And where did you meet this handsome man?"

"To answer your second question first, Macaw and I met in La Paz a few weeks ago when I was right in the middle of this story. What I'm up to now is that I'm supposed to be on vacation visiting you."

Aunt Lupe raised one eyebrow. "But you are visiting me, are you not?"

"Exactly. That's the official story, anyway. The truth is, even though my employer thinks the last story is finished, I don't agree. Too many rough edges."

"And rough edges cause splinters and pain," said Aunt Lupe, running her hand along the wooden tabletop.

"Did you make this table, *Tia*? It's beautiful."

Her aunt nodded. "It's part of my outdoor line."

"How's business?"

"Wonderful. My pieces are gaining recognition in the international circuit. I've had to hire more people to keep up on the basic pieces in the line, because I spend most of my time on commissioned work."

"I've seen some of your recent furniture on your website, *Tia*. It's fantastic."

"Thank you, *mi amor*. Now for the main course." Her aunt left and returned with two steaming bowls of the savory chicken and rice dish Alexa associated with her mother. Inhaling deeply, Alexa took a big mouthful of the rich broth. "Mmm, yummy, *Tia*. Just like I remember."

Her aunt smiled.

They chatted the evening away, discussing Alexa's work, Macaw's childhood in Panama and how her aunt met her husband. Finally, *Tia* rose and stretched. "It is past my bedtime, but please stay and enjoy the evening. I will see you in the morning. Leticia comes in at six and will prepare whatever you like when you awake. I will probably be in my studio by then, but you are welcome to visit."

Macaw rose and kissed Lupe's hand, thanking her for her hospitality and remarking on her wonderful food.

"This man has lips like fire," she said approvingly to Alexa.

Alexa smiled. "Goodnight *Tia*."

"*Buenas noches, mi amor.*"

Macaw and Alexa finished another glass of sangria and talked until they both began to yawn.

"I'm still lagging from too little sleep the last couple of days," he said, getting up and extinguishing the tiki torches.

"Me, too. Let's go to bed. Oh, darn."

"What?"

"I forgot to ask my aunt if I can get onto her computer and pick up my email. I'd also like to check the news and see if there's anything about the fire. I guess I'll have to do that tomorrow."

"Tomorrow's another day," agreed Macaw. He put his arm around her as they walked back to the room.

16

Alexa woke in the early morning, glancing over at Macaw, who still slept deeply. She slid out of bed and reached for her robe but changed her mind and pulled on Macaw's instead. Inhaling the scent of his maleness soothed the apprehension thrumming at the back of her consciousness. While a huge part of her wanted to end this nightmare and bring in Roth and Imelda, another part of her ached at what the end meant. Saying goodbye to Macaw.

Padding barefoot into the courtyard, she walked over the spongy groundcover and approached the fountain. A bee buzzed around the water, then zoomed down to a dandelion that had transplanted itself in a pot of croton. When it finished rummaging around in the bright yellow flower and flew off, she reached down and picked it, inhaling its slightly acrid scent, then froze. Anxiety slithered around her neck, tightened its noose, and then the memory hit her.

Alexa had been picking dandelions in the sunshine—making a necklace, looping the green ends to the flower heads—when a shadow engulfed her. She knew who towered over her without looking up.

"Well, there's my little missy. Come and play with Uncle Freddy."

"Leave me alone," Alexa yelled.

"What's going on out there?" Alexa's father came from inside the house and stood on the front porch.

"Nothing, Tom. Alexa's just being a girl." Uncle Freddy swayed slightly.

"Have you been drinking again, Fred?"

"No."

"I have to go down and check on the trees," her father called over.

"Must be nice to have a job," Freddy replied. "I lost mine, remember?"

"So go out and find another one, Fred, instead of wallowing and drinking. Alexa, come with me." She sprang up and gladly ran to the safety of her father's warm hand.

Lowering herself onto her aunt's wooden bench next to the fountain, Alexa burrowed into Macaw's warm robe and waited for the unease brought on by the memory to loosen its grip on her stomach. Running water had a way of doing that—calming and steadying her. But the question continued to nag and run around in her head. Why did her mother come to Mexico? Why wasn't Alexa with her?

"You are awake early, *mija*," said her aunt, appearing next to Alexa. "I'm surprised you're not with that hunk of a man."

"I couldn't sleep," she said. "Please join me, *Tia*."

Her aunt sat down next to her and adjusted the furniture-making smock she wore.

"Too many thoughts about your story? It sounds like something that would keep me awake as well."

"Yes, that of course. But there's more, and it all seems to have been brought on by this investigation. Ever since I started with this story, I've had dreams and memories, and it's so hard to sort out what is real."

"Memories of what?"

"My mother, my father, my uncle."

"Are they good or bad dreams and memories?"

"Both."

"Tell me about them, and I will do my best to help untangle them if I can."

Where to start? thought Alexa. Her mother, of course.

"Why did Mama leave Papa and come here? He says to visit you, but was there more?"

Her aunt was silent for a moment.

"Please, *Tia*, tell me. Was it because of my uncle?"

"How did you know?"

"I told you, I've been remembering things. He hurt my mother, didn't he? That's why she came here? To get away from him?"

Lupe nodded and seemed to choose her words carefully. "Yes, your uncle—that no good viper—was the reason Augustina left. Your father is a good man, but he had a stupid spot for his younger brother. Your mother couldn't muster up the courage to tell your father the truth. I offered to talk to Tom for her, but she forbade it. I had to follow the wishes of my sister."

"That must have been difficult for you," said Alexa.

"Not as difficult as burying her and knowing that she had left you behind," said Lupe, putting her hand on Alexa's. "All of it—everything— was Frederico's fault. He deserved every day he spent in prison."

Alexa's eyes widened. "He went to prison?"

"You didn't know?"

"No, I just thought Papa finally had enough of him."

"Ah, what a relief it was for me when I heard they locked your uncle up. Finally, away from you. I could sleep again."

"Away from me?" Alexa asked, the familiar anxiety catching in her throat.

Lupe quickly searched Alexa's eyes with her own, then looked away.

"What *Tia*? What aren't you telling me?" Alexa grabbed her aunt's hands. "Please, I must know."

"Your mother wasn't sure, but she was afraid, that's why she came here with you."

"My mother brought me here?" Alexa was stunned. All these years she'd thought her mother had left her at the ranch when she came to Mexico!

"*Si, mi amor*, to protect you," said her aunt, brushing Alexa's hair out of her face.

"Protect me? Protect me from what?"

"Your uncle, she was afraid that—"

And then it hit Alexa, like a wave knocking her down and pummeling her in the sand so hard she couldn't get back up. "That he would molest me," finished Alexa.

Her aunt sucked in her breath. "*Ay, Dios mío,* yes, and I have prayed over the years that it didn't happen. Your mother went to her grave hoping." She looked at Alexa with questions in her eyes.

Alexa moaned and fell to her knees in front of her aunt, laying her head in her lap. "Oh, Aunt Lupe, the memories, they haunt me. I was so young. The thoughts, they come to me like bad dreams, always unclear. But yes, I remember, I do." Alexa hesitated, the sobs shaking her body. "It's just that I wanted so much to forget."

"*Mija*, I am so, so sorry," her aunt soothed as she stroked Alexa's hair. "I did not tell you, because I hoped that it wasn't true. You were so young, and your mother and I thought that if we told you, it might have put ideas in your head. I did come and visit for a time after your mother died to check up on you, but your uncle knew the right people and got my passport revoked. I nearly went *loco* with panic, until I heard that he had been put in prison. Then I could sleep again—especially when he died. Please forgive my silence all of these years."

Alexa raised her head and gazed at her aunt through teary eyes. "It's not your fault. You didn't know."

"Listen to me carefully," her aunt said, taking Alexa's face in her hands and looking steadily into her eyes. "You must remember this. Nothing that happened, nothing, was ever your fault. You are no longer that defenseless little girl. It is very important you understand that. Look at the life you've made for yourself. Look at the brave things you have done. I am so proud of you."

Alexa nodded as tears slipped down her cheeks. "Thank you, *Tia*."

"I have never spoken about this with your father," added her aunt. "But I can tell you I know for sure that he never intentionally hurt you. His error was falling under his brother's spell. I think he could never have imagined such a thing. That's why Augustina brought you to Mexico with her. But even here she couldn't get away."

"What do you mean, she couldn't get away?"

"Freddy. He found you both—"

Aunt Lupe was cut off when one of her workers bolted into the court-yard panting. "It is Samuel, *Señora* Lupe. He has cut himself with the band saw. Bad."

Her aunt jumped to her feet. "I'm so sorry, *mi amor*! We will finish when I have dealt with this emergency."

"Go, *Tia*. I'm fine." Alexa waved her on. And in many ways, she told the truth. Though she had just remembered that her uncle violated her, she also discovered that her mother had not left Fallbrook for Mexico without her.

A few minutes later, she felt Macaw's hand on her shoulder. "Now's the time to nab Imelda. I have reception if I walk out to the back of the property, and I just listened to a voicemail. Word is she's at the *Cabo* property."

"Macaw," she reached and touched his arm. "For the first time in my life, I'm hearing from my aunt important things about myself and my mother that I never knew. I need to know the truth. Lupe went to take care of an injured worker, but she'll be back."

"The family reunion's gonna have to wait if you want a shot at Imelda."

Macaw was right. It had waited more than two decades. What was another day or two? Getting Imelda and Roth was top priority.

"I'll tell my aunt and grab my stuff."

"Okay, hurry."

When Alexa arrived in the furniture shop, she found her aunt shouting orders to another worker to bring the car around as she held a blood-soaked rag against a distraught man's hand.

"I know you can't talk now. I just wanted to tell you that Macaw and I have a lead, and we're leaving. We'll be back in a few days. Before we go, do you need help?"

"No, child, I have plenty of help. *Vaya con Dios.*"

"You go with God as well," Alexa answered, then ran back to the bedroom to throw a few things in a bag she found in the closet. Macaw had already changed into the jeans and T-shirt Lupe had provided. Alexa flung off the robe, threw her clothes on, and they hopped in the Cadillac. As they pulled away from the hacienda, Alexa remembered that she never checked her email or voicemail. No time now.

After they drove for a while, Macaw finally broke the silence. "Want to tell me what's up? It sounds like you and Lupe had a pretty heavy-duty conversation."

Alexa remained silent.

"If you don't want to tell me, it's okay."

"I want to tell you. So here goes. The good news is that my mother never left me. She brought me here to Mexico when she came. The bad news is that my uncle molested me." She said the last words quietly, cautiously.

"I had a feeling."

"You had a feeling? Why?" She turned to look at him.

"Your dreams. You talk, you know."

"Why didn't you say something?"

"You didn't say anything specific." Macaw let go of the steering wheel and threw up his hands. "And besides, what was I gonna say?"

Alexa shrugged and gazed out the window as the Mexican countryside slipped by.

"You okay?"

"I'm not going to freak, if that's what you mean. Ever since I started on this story, I've known something was off. I've had dreams over the years that didn't make much sense, but they've been really persistent since Rodolfo and I saw those little girls in the warehouse. I guess it's better to face it. Don't they say that? So you can get past it?"

"They say that. You sure you're up to the task of hunting down Imelda after the news you just got? She's tough to handle on a good day."

"Are you kidding me? Knowing what happened to me when I was a defenseless little girl makes me more positive than ever that I want to stop them. Maybe that's why, deep down, this story matters so much to me. The injustice of it all. The damage to those girls. I won't rest until they prosecute Imelda and Roth."

As they drove on in silence, Macaw thought about Alexa as a little girl being violated by her scumbag uncle and felt the familiar bone-sucking rage that plagued him whenever he saw someone weak and powerless get swallowed up. He almost wished that the bastard was alive, because then he could take his time killing him. The fury always blindsided him like this. And scared him. Mostly because he didn't recognize himself. Was this the way it was with his old man when he hit his mama? Maybe, he thought, but Macaw knew that he could never strike a woman or a child. Truth was, though his old man suffered from a perpetual case of nastiness, there were some good memories, too. They snuck in now and then like slivers of light making their way into a closet. In a way, the good memories were harder to deal with than the bad ones. He could think about the crappy times with disgust and discard them. The good memories of his father hoisting him on his shoulders at the fair and holding his hand when they stepped into the ocean brought up soft feelings that threatened to smother him if he didn't harden up against them. The irony was, Alexa stirred up those same yielding feelings, and that shocked the shit out of him. How had he let this happen? Since when did he let a broad in this far? Since never. Glancing at her now, he laughed to himself and thought—hell, she can come in even deeper. She could frigging take over, and he'd just lay back and smile.

When they approached Cabo San Lucas midmorning, Alexa exclaimed, "I hear Cabo is fun. Too bad we're not here on vacation."

"You're on vacation, remember? Once we finish with Imelda and Roth, we'll go out clubbing."

"It's a deal," said Alexa. "How far to Imelda's compound?"

Macaw removed the map he had tucked in the visor and took a quick glance. "Looks like it's a little ways out of downtown. Another twenty minutes and we should be there. We're going to want to wait for night-time, though. Imelda is no night owl—she gets sloppy when the sun sets. Want to stop for a bite and then maybe find a nice beach?"

"All sounds perfect," said Alexa.

They stopped at the Hard Rock Café in town for lunch. Alexa chose an enchilada plate with beans and rice and Macaw a steaming plate of *chiles rellanos*. As they ate surrounded by walls sporting hard rock memorabilia, the band in the next room played a Van Halen song, and Alexa tapped her foot to the beat.

"Randy would have loved this place," mused Macaw. "Van Halen was one of his favorites. He always said he wanted to play the bongos. Too bad he took up drugs instead."

Macaw's voice was light, but Alexa could hear the pain underneath his words.

She put her hand on his. "What happened to him isn't your fault, you know. Nothing you could have done would have saved him."

"You don't know that for sure."

"You're right. But what I do know for sure is that you tried hard to turn him around. He meant the world to you, and he knew it. You're punishing yourself for something that happened years ago. You have to stop."

Macaw gave Alexa a hot look and then melted when he met her gaze. She was right. He had to stop flogging himself about Randy.

"Looks like we both have some issues to deal with," he replied. "First, though, we gotta get Imelda and Roth."

After lunch, they found a fairly deserted section on Punta Palmilla beach, where they sat on a blanket they found in the trunk of the Cadillac and talked for a time; then lay back and dozed in each other's arms. When the sun started to set, Macaw's phone rang, and he answered.

"Tatiana, you got my message. Yeah, I had pretty bad cell reception for a while there. It's better now."

He listened for a moment as they got up and knocked the sand off of their legs. "Our friend's definitely slippery. Last seen in Cabo? Really. That may be good news. Thanks. Keep me posted." He flipped his phone closed.

"Good friend of mine, Tatiana Romero. She's a border patrol agent," said Macaw as Alexa shook the sand off the blanket and folded it. "Looks like Roth might be in this neck of the woods. What are the odds?"

"That's great. You've got friends everywhere. Another person you helped?"

"No, actually, she helps me get in and out of Mexico when I need to."

"Nice to know people in the right places."

"Yep, that's for sure." He took Alexa's hand. "We have to come up with a backup plan for tonight. If something happens to me. I get hurt, or worse, you take care of yourself and run."

Alexa shook her head.

Macaw sighed. "I had a feeling you wouldn't cooperate."

"You shouldn't even be in this mess," said Alexa. "The only reason you are is because of me. The least I can do is stick with you."

"Alexa promise me if things get rough and you have an out that you'll take it."

"All I can say is I'll try," she said.

They walked back to the car and got in, and Macaw started the vehicle up and headed for Imelda's safe house. A few minutes later, he pulled over on the side of the road. "I'm pretty sure this is it. We'll walk up," he said, patting his gun holster. "You ready?"

"As I'll ever be," said Alexa as they got out of the car. While they crept up the long main drive, she strained to hear, finally making out faint traces of a woman's voice. The light had vanished from the sky, and the moon was nearly nonexistent, which was good for what Alexa and Macaw had in mind.

"I have the security code, but we still have to get in under the radar," he whispered. "Stay low and keep to the shadows as much as possible."

"Do you think she's alone?"

"Not sure about that one. Will Roth be there? I don't know. We get a hold of her, though, we can force her to spill where he is."

Alexa shuddered when she thought about seeing Imelda again. Reaching into her pocket to check for her cell phone, her fingers touched on her rosary beads. A peaceful feeling radiated from them, soothing her. Not exactly sure how it was done, she grasped the beads and said a short prayer for herself and Macaw.

When they came to the hulking mansion, Macaw turned down a pathway that seemed to lead to the back. They came to a gate and the security box Fernando had described, and Macaw punched in the code. As the gate clicked and he pushed it open, she once again felt overwhelming gratitude for his help.

"We're in," Macaw said, as he walked through the gate, Alexa following close to him. Ears hyper-tuned, she heard voices. How far were they? She wondered. It was so hard to tell. Treading cautiously over the rocky terrain, she strained to see what lay ahead, trying to imagine what Imelda could have in store for them if they were caught. There was a good probability she had posted armed guards throughout the area, which could mean that she and Macaw were walking directly into a snare. Alexa stumbled over a large rock, and Macaw reached out and grabbed her arm to steady her. When they arrived at a thicket, he stopped and released the safety on his gun. Then with the weapon raised, he led them around the thicket slowly, stopping right under a lighted window. Alexa looked up into the window at the same time Imelda gazed out. "Macaw, Imelda," she hissed.

As Macaw raised the gun toward the window, Alexa heard the whine of a nearby gate. In the next instant, snarls erupted from all sides.

"Shit! Dogs!" Macaw cursed. He grabbed Alexa and pulled her close, shooting at the first snarling Rottweiler that came at them. That dog fell to its side, only to be replaced by several more. "Back through the gate!" he yelled, pushing her in the direction where they had come from and shooting at another dog.

They ran toward the gate with the dogs at their heels. Macaw managed to turn and shoot several, but three replacements came out of the darkness. When they were just a few feet from the gate, Alexa heard a particularly nasty snarl as a dog bit down, catching her pant leg. She screeched and pulled her leg away, relief washing through her when she managed to get her leg free and slip through the still open gate to safety.

Right behind Alexa, Macaw reached for the gate just as one of the dogs sprang from the side, jumping up and sinking its teeth into the flesh of his forearm. Pain seared all the way up to his shoulder as he tried to shake off the beast. Finally a hard knee to the dog's side caused him to let loose and yelp. He gripped the knob to the gate—locked. The security backup system had already been re-armed.

With his good arm, he scaled the fence, pulling himself up and over, landing on the other side next to Alexa. Once his feet hit the pavement, they sprinted down the driveway and hopped into the car on the side of the road. Macaw turned over the engine and hit the gas as Alexa pulled her door closed.

"Where are we going?" Alexa cried as Macaw accelerated. Then she saw his arm. "You're bleeding."

"My arm's okay," he gritted his teeth. "We're going to a buddy's house in *Todos Santos*. He'll put us up." Truth was, his armed throbbed. The dog had done a number on him. Poor mutt didn't know any better. But that bitch knew better, and he still didn't have her.

Alexa turned to peer back at the road they left behind and relief rushed through her. "It doesn't look like anyone is following us."

"Good," said Macaw. "Hopefully they're heading south back into *Cabo*."

After what seemed like an eternity to Alexa, Macaw pulled off the road and they bumped along a dirt path until the car lights illuminated a shack that appeared to be sitting in the middle of nowhere.

"Doesn't seem like Ron's around, but that's okay. It's usually not locked," Macaw said as he stopped the car and they got out.

He was right. The door opened.

"Looks like it's been ransacked, I know," said Macaw of the messy, one-room shack. Dishes were stacked in the sink and take-out containers littered the kitchen countertops. Macaw went to the refrigerator and pulled out two beers, handing one to Alexa.

"Calm your nerves," he said, walking back outside.

Maybe it was the adrenaline from the run. She didn't know. But Alexa, who usually sipped her drinks, stood there in Ron's kitchen and guzzled half her beer down and then finished the rest. When she was done, her hands still shook, so she opened the refrigerator and pulled out another one, pulling the tab and drinking half of that.

Outside, she found Macaw leaning against a retaining wall cradling his arm. "The stars don't quit out here," he said as she came to stand next to him. "It's amazing what you can see when there's no light pollution."

Alexa looked at his torn flesh. "You don't quit. You're incredible!"

"Yeah?" Macaw turned to her and grinned. "I like this. Go on."

"Sorry, that was really crazy back there. Right now, I'm a ball of nerves, and I don't know what I'm saying."

"What do you mean you don't know what you're saying? I saved your ass."

I know, and I'm grateful, but—"

"But what? Would it hurt that bad to thank me? Admit that you needed my help?"

"No, I can say thank you," she sputtered. "Thank you. There, I said it."

Macaw laughed. "I can tell that was really hard for you."

"I said it, didn't I?"

"Yeah, you said it. What else you have to say?"

What else did she have to say? Oh, hell, thought Alexa, why not? The beer and adrenaline combined had given her a pretty good buzz. "I've never felt this way before," she admitted.

"What way?"

"I think I—" Alexa felt as if she was on a precipice of some sort. One quick shove and she'd fall without stopping. She had to get a grip on herself.

Macaw moved in close. "What way?"

Scooting away a few inches, she countered, "You're so damned sure of yourself. It's annoying."

"And you aren't?"

"Me?" Alexa was stunned, never having thought of herself as self-assured. Obstinate, yes, but sure of herself?

"What were you about to say?" he insisted.

Breathing in the crisp night air, Alexa looked up at the riot of stars in the sky and suddenly felt reckless—like plunging into the deep end and only coming up when her air was completely gone—then gasping and feeling her lungs heave—feeling out of control and truly alive.

"You're completely wrong for me. But I'm in—in—love with you." There. She'd said it. It was done.

He smiled.

"Are you going to say something or just stand there with that goofy grin?"

"I take offense to that. What's wrong with my grin?" Macaw asked.

She gripped the stone ledge where she sat, mad at herself that she'd let the alcohol loosen her tongue. Maybe he didn't love her after all.

Macaw leaned in and put his lips to her ear. "I've loved you since the second time I saw you."

"Why the second time?"

"The first time I thought that you were completely wrong for me. That a better answer?"

Alexa smiled.

17

As Macaw kissed her neck, Alexa felt him wince. She pulled back and noticed a slight bead of sweat covering his brow.

"Let me see your arm!"

"I tell you I love you and you want to play nurse?"

The bite was deep and had torn sideways. Blood pooled in the wound and had trickled down his arm. His T-shirt was sticky with blood.

"We have to clean this right away."

"I've always heard dog mouths are clean?"

"Old wives' tale," said Alexa. She went back into the shack and rummaged around in Ron's bathroom. Typical icky bachelor pad, she noted. Filthy toilet bowl, inch-thick dust and badly stocked medicine cabinet—antacid, pain reliever and a prescription for antibiotics that had expired three years before.

"No antiseptic or bandages," she called out to Macaw.

"Of course not. He's a guy. We never get hurt."

"I have to clean that somehow."

"Look for vodka or something. I think he keeps his hard stuff under the sink."

"Will Jack Daniel's work?"

"I'm sure it'll do the trick, but what a waste."

"There will be enough if you want a shot first," said Alexa. "I need you inside where I can see."

Macaw came in the shack and pushed a stack of newspapers off a chair with his good hand. Then he sat down and took the shot of whiskey Alexa had poured into a tumbler she'd found at the back of the kitchen cupboard.

"Can't believe you found a clean glass," he said, handing it back to her after he downed the amber liquid.

"Me neither. Your arm, please."

Macaw sighed and held out his arm.

Using a whiskey-soaked napkin, Alexa cautiously dabbed the tear, which was only about two inches long, but deep. "This really needs to be stitched up."

"So, stitch it up," said Macaw, jerking when the alcohol hit the wound.

"I'm a writer, not a nurse!"

"I shot the dogs. You're on your own with this one."

"Why don't we go into town and try to find a doctor? We could be careful."

"No doctor. Imelda's arm is far-reaching. She has connections everywhere."

Macaw was right. Alexa peered around the little shack. "Any chance your friend has a needle and thread?"

Macaw snorted. "Yeah, he sews in his spare time. He's a fisherman, though. His fishing stuff should be around here somewhere."

"Fishing line would make great sutures," said Alexa. She searched for his gear, finally finding a tackle box on top of the refrigerator. Inside she located a thin-gauge fishing line, but there was only one needle in the box, and it was four inches long.

When Macaw saw her proposed operating tool, he shook his head vigorously. "What the hell are you going to do with *that?*"

"I'm going to stitch you up. It's the only needle he has. I just have to do a few stitches." She threaded the needle and doused it with whiskey.

Her bravado was an act, she knew, as she grasped his arm and felt his body stiffen. Dreading hurting him further, she wished she could just bandage the wound with an old shirt, but even her meager medical knowledge told her that it couldn't stay open for much longer. She'd do as few stitches as she could—just enough to keep the skin together until they could get some real help. Holding her breath to steady herself, Alexa stuck the needle through the skin near one end of the bite, brought it over and carefully pushed it through the other side of the wound. She stopped with the needle in midair and asked, "You okay?"

He grimaced and nodded, beads of sweat now standing out on his forehead.

Then she looped the thread back over and pierced the skin again, this time tightening the thread slightly before repeating the process.

When she finished with the stitching, she knotted the fishing line several times and cut it close.

"It's not pretty, but it should do the trick," she said, admiring her handiwork.

"Stick to writing."

"That's the thanks I get?" She got up and pulled open a chest of drawers, removing an old shirt, which she tore into strips and then tied around the wound. "You need antibiotic cream at the very least. Oral medicine would be best. This could get septic fast. Your buddy has a prescription in there, but it's three years old."

"Have you no faith in Jack Daniel's? Is there anymore left? I'd like another shot."

"Just enough for both of us to have a little," said Alexa, who emptied the contents of the whiskey into the tumbler and handed it to him along with two pain relievers she'd found in the medicine cabinet.

Macaw downed half of it along with the pills and handed it back to her.

"To surviving a dog attack," she said as she finished off the whiskey, coughing after she swallowed. Then she added, "I saw her. She was there."

"I know. I saw the viper, too. Not sure if she saw us, but it's just like that sick wack job to have attack dogs come out if the security system is breached."

"I'm sure she left the safe house," said Alexa.

"Definitely. Where she'll head next is anybody's guess. We'll find her, though." Macaw yawned.

"Do you think your buddy will be back tonight?"

"Hard to say. He's been known to go out drinking and stay at a girl-friend's house. We might have the place to ourselves. Why?"

"We'll be lucky to fit two of us in his bed, let alone three."

"There's always the couch."

"There's a couch?"

"Yeah, that mound over there covered in clothing."

"This place is disgusting."

"I agree. Even for me, and I'm a guy."

After they both cleaned up in the bathroom, they lay down in Ron's bed. Alexa was careful not to press against his arm as she settled down to a restless sleep.

Alexa woke in the early morning hours. From her vantage point in the narrow bed, she could see the sunrise through the front window—pink, purple, then golden hues coming up over the horizon. She lay in awe watching the show when Macaw said quietly, "It's amazing what Mother Nature can create."

"I didn't know you were awake."

"Just woke up a minute ago. Pain's kinda bad right now."

Alexa shifted to inspect his arm. Touching the area tentatively, she frowned.

"I was worried about this. It's really hot. That means it's infected." She sat up in bed and felt his forehead. Also, hot.

"You're not going anywhere until I can get you some antibiotics."

"How do you propose to do that?"

"I can make it into town. I'm sure there's a pharmacy. You don't want to mess around with an animal bite infection."

"You sure about going out on your own?"

"I worked on my own before I met you, remember?"

Macaw awoke to Imelda's black widow eyes.

"Fuck me."

"No time for that *pendejo*. We're going on a trip. Get him up," she shouted to the two goons with her. When they yanked him from Ron's bed and pulled him to his feet, Macaw yelled.

"Dramatic as usual, Macaw?" Imelda snarled. Her eyes dropped to his arm. "My *perros* have a snack? Good—serves you right. Maybe next time you'll think before double-crossing me. I thought you learned the first time. Where's the *puta*?"

Dizzy and lightheaded, Macaw tried to focus on Imelda's nasty face. Hard considering the grip her boy had on his arm, which hurt like a mother fucker. "She's gone," he tried not to let her know the depths of his pain.

Imelda raised her eyebrows. "Gone? Just like that?"

"Yeah, after the dogs, she couldn't take the heat anymore, so she packed up and left me hanging."

Imelda ordered one of her men to search the premises. He went out back and came in the front door with someone—but it wasn't Alexa.

"Hey, watch it," Ron cried. He saw Macaw and asked, "Who the hell is this freak?" For his comment, Imelda's man hit him on the side of the head with the butt of his gun.

"*Estúpido*," Imelda yelled and rushed at her man, kicking him in the shins. "You knock this *pendejo* out, how am I going to get information from him?" She turned her attention to Ron, scowling into his face. "Where's the bitch?"

"What bitch?" Ron looked genuinely confused.

"Macaw's bitch."

"Macaw doesn't have a girl, as far as I know, man."

"I know she's here."

"Seriously, I have no idea what you're talking about."

Imelda stood there for a few seconds, as if weighing her options. "I was supposed to bring *la princesa* back with us," she said to no one in particular. "The boss isn't going to be happy at all. I can't go back empty-handed, so you'll have to do for now, Macaw."

"Look, lady, there's no one here," exclaimed Ron.

Imelda turned to the man holding him. "Knock him out." At that the goon twisted Macaw's friend around and cracked him on the back of the head with his gun, dumping his limp body on the floor.

"Shit, you didn't have to do that," said Macaw.

"Shit, you didn't have to do that," mimicked Imelda. "Since when you so sentimental, *puto?*" She gestured to the front door. "We've got some-place a lot better to go. When we get where we're going, I'm sure with a little persuasion on that arm, you can help us find her."

Macaw stood pinned between the two men, panting. "Yeah, and we can have a tea party," he said.

"Get him in the car," she ordered. "We need to get back. A hurricane is supposed to hit within the next hour."

"But it looks pretty clear right now, boss," said the goon who had hit Ron.

"It's always calm before the storm, moron," snapped Imelda.

Before they threw him in the back of the waiting van, Macaw glanced to the south and saw some nasty black clouds gathering.

When Alexa pulled up in front of the shack, she congratulated herself on a successful trip into town. She managed to get Macaw plenty of antibiotics, pain reliever and breakfast burritos without anyone questioning her. The only bad news was that it looked like a storm might be coming in. That would slow them down, but maybe it was just as well. Macaw definitely needed some rest.

Alarm bells sounded in her head the second she saw the front door of the shack gaping open. Inside, she found a short American guy leaning against the couch, rubbing the back of his head.

"They took Macaw," he said, when he saw her.

Alexa dropped the package of medicine and breakfast burritos on the floor. A dark dread oozed throughout her insides, and those three words reverberated in her head. Ron appeared to be saying other things, but his words sounded like muffled background noise—a television turned on low—traffic outside a four-story window. When she finally heard him, he stood in front of her, a concerned look on his face.

"Look, man. You must be Macaw's old lady. You okay?" His tattooed arms gripped her shoulders as if to steady her, but they shook more than Alexa. "I'm Ron Turk. This is my place."

"It's my fault," she croaked, her throat tight. "I shouldn't have left him."

"Believe me, there was nothing you could have done. They had guns, and that bitch was dead serious. They're looking for you, too. She was talking about some boss man who wants you."

Roth, thought Alexa. She heard something ringing. Her cell phone? Pulling it out of her front pocket, she looked at it, surprised.

"Great reception, huh? I have no idea why, and I don't ask," said Ron.

Alexa recognized the number. *Esperanza.*

"Hello, Essie?"

"Lexie? I can tell by the tone of your voice—something's not right. Did you hear about your father—is that it?"

"My father? What about my father?"

"I thought you knew. He had some complications."

"What kind of complications?"

"I'm not sure. Violet just said it was a setback and asked me to find you, which I've been trying to do for days."

"Is Papa okay?"

"She said to tell you that he's okay, but there was some sort of relapse. It didn't sound like life or death, if that's what you mean."

"Oh, okay, good."

"But I think you should at least call."

"I will," said Alexa.

"What's going on, Lexie? Talk to me."

"They got Macaw."

"Macaw? I'm confused. Who's Macaw? Is he that guy you told me about when you were here last?"

Alexa nodded.

"Lexie, say something. What the hell is going on?"

"I'm sorry. I just. I went out for medicine. He was bitten by a dog, and they took him while I was gone."

"Who took him?"

"I don't know. Imelda Gomez or Senator Roth's men."

"Roth is the other reason why I called you. I guess you didn't get my emails?"

"No. I haven't had email or cell phone reception until now."

"I found some really interesting things about Roth."

"Tell me."

"You sitting down?"

"Go ahead," said Alexa.

"Roth has a connection to someone you knew well."

"Who?"

"Your Uncle Freddy."

"What?"

"I did a little research, and it turns out that your uncle did some time for child porn. Roth spearheaded the investigation that brought your uncle down. Freddy was sentenced to ten years. Did you know your uncle served some time?"

"I just found out about that yesterday."

"Didn't you tell me he died from lung cancer?"

"That's what my father said."

"Maybe he had lung cancer, but the truth is they killed him in prison about eight months after he went in. Child molesters don't do too well inside."

There was a time when Alexa would have cheered at the news she had just received. Today she could only think of Macaw and her father.

"Alexa, you don't sound good. I saw your article. It looks like you've wrapped things up. Your dad really needs you. Come home."

"I have to find Macaw."

"No, Alexa. Get out of there. Let the professionals take care of things."

"I've got to find him."

"Alexa! Now? You pick now to fall in love. It could get you killed!"

"I need your help."

"I don't have anything else for you, except sound advice."

"I need the number of a San Diego border patrol agent."

"I might be able to find him. What's his name?"

"It's a she. Her name is Tatiana Romero."

"I should be able to get her number pretty quickly. Give me a little time. I'll get back to you as soon as I can."

Alexa stood with the phone in her hand looking out the open door at the trees whipping in the steadily worsening wind. Papa had a setback? Was he in the hospital again? She should be there with him. What if he didn't make it? She'd never be able to live with herself. On the other hand, how could she leave Macaw? Especially in the hands of Imelda and Roth. She loved her father. But she loved Macaw, as well. And Papa was surrounded by excellent care. Macaw was on his own.

I'm sorry, Papa, she thought. I've got to get to Macaw. I can't abandon him. I know you'd understand after what happened with Mama. I've heard you say you would have done anything to get her back. I have that chance, and I'm taking it.

When Esperanza called a couple of minutes later, Alexa jotted Tatiana's number on the side of a take-out bag.

"Lexie," pleaded Esperanza. "Call her and let the authorities take care of this."

"I'm going to get him."

"You're being an idiot, and hard-headed. If you won't listen to reason, at least be careful."

"I will. I promise. But if something does happen to me—"

"Don't say that."

"Take care of my dad."

"You know I will. I hope this guy is worth it, Lexie," said her friend as rolls of thunder sounded in the distance.

"He's definitely worth it, Essie."

When she hung up with her old friend, Alexa's mind worked hot and clear. She dialed Tatiana's number and was lucky to get her on the first ring.

"My name is Alexa Kent. I'm Macaw's friend."

"Oh, hi, yes. I talked to Macaw yesterday, and I was just getting ready to call him."

"Unfortunately, something has happened. It looks like Roth's men got Macaw. I have to find Roth."

"I just got Roth's address," said Tatiana. "It's a mansion on *Puente* Hills Road. 5510 West. You think he's there?"

"It's the only thing that makes sense at this point."

"You've got backup?"

Alexa remained silent.

"Listen, Macaw may have told you that we're friends. I can send some people to help you. Where are you?"

"I'm too far from Roth's. Tell them to meet me there."

"It'd be better if you waited."

"Macaw is sick; his arm is infected, and he has a high fever. Imelda has hurt him before, and this time she's going to kill him."

"Shit," said Tatiana. "With this storm coming in, it's going to take the backup I'm sending in a while to get to Roth's. It looks like you're the only hope he has right now. Be careful. I could tell by the tone in Macaw's voice that he wouldn't want anything to happen to you."

"Thanks, Tatiana," said Alexa, who flipped her phone shut.

Lightning illuminated the shack as Alexa prepared to leave.

"Whoa, you can't go out in that," Ron warned, lowering the volume on his shortwave radio. "They say it's going to be a big hurricane."

She barely heard him. Instead, the hottest fury she had ever known propelled her. No one was going to take another person she loved. She had been a child, a victim, all those years ago. But that was then. Now she would be the one in control or die trying.

"You obviously aren't going to listen to reason," Ron said as she went for the door a few minutes later. "Listen, I snagged Macaw's gun. Here it is. It's fully loaded. The safety's on. And just in case, I've got this fishing knife, too."

"Thanks," said Alexa, taking the weapons. "I'll get him. Don't worry."

"I want to believe you. I'm going with you."

Alexa didn't want anyone to slow her down or get in the way of finding Macaw. She smiled faintly. "I'll be in the car."

"Great, I'll be right out."

Alexa left the shack and hopped into the car, carefully placing the gun and sheathed knife on the passenger seat. She then locked the doors. Turning the motor over and throwing the car into reverse, she backed out of the dirt driveway onto the street. When she pulled out onto the road, she saw Ron running after her. She threw the Cadillac into gear and accelerated in the direction of Land's End and Macaw.

18

As Alexa drove away from the shack, mist coated the car windshield, but she knew a downpour would begin before her journey finished. Reports from Ron's shortwave radio had warned that within the next hour, Hurricane Marisol would slam the west coast of Baja, down near Cabo, right where she was headed. The windshield wipers started with a spasm when she flipped them on, and worry threaded its way through her stomach when she thought of Macaw—weakened and at the mercy of Imelda. They hadn't killed him, she was sure. If they'd wanted him dead, they would have finished the job at Ron's. No, they took him for something. Perhaps to lure her? Well, she was on her way.

The route was treacherous in spots, but a direct one. She just needed to stay on Highway 19 and weave her way along the coast. Hands welded to the steering wheel, she drove on as the black storm clouds huddled ahead soon approached, blocking the sun's rays until it appeared to be dusk rather than midday. She turned on the car lights to announce her presence but doubted that few people would be brave enough to venture out in an impending hurricane. When a bolt of lightning illuminated the far-off hills, Alexa suddenly realized how utterly alone she really was. No Macaw or Aunt Lupe, Papa so far away and ill, and her mother gone. As the angry black storm clouds gathered in the sky in front of her, the buried memories started flying at her like fat bugs splattering on the windshield. Uncle Freddy. Mama crying. Tears erupted from her eyes as rain started pelting the car.

Awhile later, the rain pounded down harder, and gusts of wind began buffeting the Cadillac, forcing her to slow the vehicle to a crawl. She looked out at the treacherous drop off the side of the road. Slow and steady was what she'd do. She'd reach Macaw, even if she had to get out and run.

Continuing on, Alexa recalled Tatiana's directions. She needed to take a left onto a dirt road before she got to Land's End. The turn-off was supposed to be easy to spot because of a nearby lighthouse. Seeing the lighthouse in the distance and the way the lights swept across the thunderhead of clouds stirred an ominous feeling in Alexa. The memory crept into her mind like the shroud of suffocating darkness now closing in around her. She remembered those lights. She remembered herself as a child, arms outstretched, screaming for her mother. Shocked by the confusing vision, she didn't see the tree until she hit it. Although she'd been going slowly, the impact snapped her head back on the seat.

"Shit, shit, shit, shit!" Alexa yelled, pounding the steering wheel and ramming the car into reverse. She attempted to back up, but felt the tires slip and spin. Now what? She had no idea how far to Roth's house. She threw the car keys under the seat and reached for Macaw's gun and Ron's knife, which she strapped to her leg. Alexa exited the car gun in hand and slammed the door against the driving rain. She'd find Macaw at Roth's, she just knew it. First, she'd distract Roth and Imelda and then shoot to wound both of them. If that didn't work, she wouldn't hesitate at killing them. Then she'd get Macaw out of there and to a hospital.

Pausing mid-step, she worked her fingers into her pocket and grasped the rosary beads. "I've never needed you more than I do tonight, Mama," she shouted into the wind. "Please help me." At her words, it started to rain harder. Head down, she continued her journey, raindrops needling into her cheeks. The lighthouse loomed larger as she came to a dirt road. This must be it, she thought, turning to the left and soldiering on. By now her clothes were soaked and clinging to her. How she would stealthily enter Roth's house and get to Macaw was beyond her, but she had to try. Finally, a large structure appeared up ahead, and she searched it for light, spying some on the northeast corner of the building. She wondered what she'd soon be up against. How many men did Roth have working for him? Where was Imelda?

When Imelda's van finally jerked to a stop, Macaw grunted.

"That all you have to say?" Imelda shot back. "Not thanks for the ride?" Macaw didn't reply.

"Take him to a back room in the house while I talk to the boss," she ordered her men, one of whom yanked the van's door open and grabbed him by his bad arm, sending bolts of pain straight to his head. Macaw considered trying to run, but the wind and rain whipping his face told him this wasn't the time or place. Best to conserve his energy and let the goons drag him into the mansion they now headed toward. Once inside the large marble entryway, Imelda's man pressed a gun into his ribs and Macaw kept moving toward the back of the house.

"This one okay?" asked the goon leading the way as he threw open a door.

"As long as the door locks."

They pushed him in and slammed the door. As he landed on the floor, Macaw grabbed hold of his injured arm.

Now what? He must be at Roth's house in his spa room. Lying on the cool tile floor, he wondered what the fuck was wrong with him. He didn't think he'd ever felt this weak or dizzy. And where the hell was Alexa? Hopefully she hadn't gotten caught in any crossfire but stayed at Ron's to wait out the storm. Fat chance, he thought. Knowing her, she was out in the hurricane trying to find him. Macaw dropped off as he awaited his fate, waking to a blonde head peering down at him. "Hi, I'm Shannon," the girl whispered.

"Water," croaked Macaw.

"I'll be back," she said and disappeared.

Had he imagined her? Macaw thought as he drifted off again.

"Well, well, well. Macaw is down." This time Imelda's ugly face filled his vision. "What am I going to do with you, *cholo*?"

"Fuck you," said Macaw.

Imelda kicked his side, and he yelled.

"You think you're such a big *hombre* now, huh?"

One of Imelda's guards put his head in the door and asked, "You need any help, boss?"

"No, I want this fun all to myself. You and Jorge go check the grounds."

"Get up before I kick you again!" she screeched at Macaw when the guard left. "Fight me like a real man."

Macaw pushed himself up on his good arm and stood.

"That's better." She grinned, then pulled some steel nun chucks from her pocket and smacked him against the head with them.

"You're fucking nuts!" he cried, struggling to stop the blinding pain and dizziness that threatened to overtake him.

"You're the one who's nuts," said Imelda. "You screwed up a great moneymaker for me, and you're going to pay big. So is that bitch girl-friend of yours."

At the mention of Alexa, rage ignited in Macaw's chest. "You're the worst kind of slime," he growled, yanking the nun chucks from her grasp and knocking her feet from under her with his foot, which sent her crashing onto the tile floor. As she lay there unmoving, Macaw slowly approached. He couldn't be this lucky. When he nudged her with his foot, she sat up and sank her teeth into his shin.

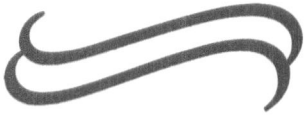

Alexa was surprised to find the massive gate that enclosed the property ajar when she reached it. Slipping inside, she wondered, was this a trap? If so, they hadn't stopped her yet. When she stood just beneath the windows of a lighted room, Alexa stopped and peered in, thankful for the cover of night. For several long minutes, she strained to see if there was anyone in the room. Finally, she spotted a figure sitting in a chair. Was that Roth?

Sneaking around to the back of the building, she snuck up a short flight of stairs to a door, which she was shocked to find opened when she tried it. Entering as quietly as possible with the gun drawn, she gasped when she came face-to-face with a man. As he moved to reach for something, Alexa released the safety on her gun.

"Stop!" she said. "Put your hands in the air."

"That's no way to say hello, Alexa," said the man, who appeared to be her age. Too young for Roth, she calculated. And his voice sounded familiar. She detected the smell of menthol cigarettes on his sour breath. The assailant in her room that night! Probably the person who killed Miguel. A new wave of fury broke in Alexa.

"I've come for Macaw. Where is he?"

"That's no way to greet a host. Didn't your mother ever teach you manners? Oh, that's right, your mother is dead."

"You know nothing about my mother. Shut up."

"I know a lot more than you think," he said and laughed.

"I know you've got Macaw. Take me to him now."

"Do we have a visitor, Paul?" called a voice from the other room. "Show her in."

Alexa motioned Paul into the room. "Keep your hands up, and back in slowly."

Paul moved into the dimly lit room. In an overstuffed armchair sat a man of about sixty. He had a glass of what looked like a brandy in one hand and a cigar in the other.

"You must be Roth," she said, remembering the cigars that Fernando said Imelda got for an important client.

He smiled. "Alexa, you've finally come. I've been waiting for you."

"Where's Macaw?"

"You look just like her."

"Who?"

"Augustina, of course."

Taking advantage of her lapse in attention, Paul started to reach for her gun, but she stepped back, the gun still on him. Aiming the weapon at his head, she said to Roth, "Tell your man to put his hands up or someone is going to feel a bullet."

Roth brought the glass to his mouth and sipped. "You have the same fire and determination that was so uniquely Augustina. How I miss that."

"What in the hell are you talking about? Why should I even think you knew my mother?"

"Because we were much more than friends."

Roth's words distracted Alexa just enough to give Paul a second opening. He grabbed the gun and pulled her to him, making her cry out at his vice grip.

"Don't hurt her Paul."

"Where's Macaw?"

"You disappoint me, Alexa. I want to talk about your mother, and all you do is worry about that Third World thug. I wouldn't even have bothered with him, but Imelda insisted. She had plans for him, and I thought you might come after him, and then I'd finally have Augustina back."

"What do you want with me?" Alexa demanded as she struggled under Paul's grip.

"For you to take over where your mother left off."

"My mother never had anything to do with you. She was happily married to my father."

"That farmer? I could give her a much better life, and she knew it. When she came here to visit your aunt, and I saw her in town, I watched her every chance I got until I finally arranged to meet her. Then I told her my wife had died of cancer and asked her advice to help a struggling single father with two children. Women can't resist that."

"I know my mother would never willingly stay with you."

"Oh, she stayed all right, once she understood I would kill your aunt and father if you both didn't remain with me. She knew I would carry out my threats."

"Both of us?"

"You came with her. Don't you remember?"

Images of the lighthouse flashed into Alexa's mind again.

"But the accident. I was at home. How did my mother die?"

With a clenched fist, Roth struck the end table next to his chair, and his brandy sloshed over. "Your no-good uncle is the reason your mother died. Freddy ruined everything. He wanted more money after losing his job with the Secret Service. When I told him I wasn't going to give him a bigger cut of the business, he took you, because he knew your mother would go after you! Jumped right on a plane in La Paz and flew you straight to your father to win points with him. It was storming like tonight when Augustina took my car and ran off the road near Land's End. I have a monument there—in her honor. A *descanso*, I believe is what the Mexican people call it." Lightning struck outside the window behind where Roth sat, lighting up his white hair. "I made Freddy pay, though. The FBI started snooping around the operation—wanted to bring in someone—so I gave them your uncle."

"And you kept selling children!" exploded Alexa.

"The children we find in those dirty little villages would be dead in a year or two of malnutrition anyway. We're actually doing their parents a favor. Many families are able to survive for years on the money I pay them. So, you see, we all win."

"You speak of them as if they are animals," said Alexa. "They're human beings."

"Children are animals! Just ask my own mother. All I ever did was try to please her, and she treated me worse than garbage. Even after I became a senator and bought her everything she ever wanted. It was never enough."

Alexa struggled again, and Paul shook her, yelling, "Stop it bitch!"

"I taught you better manners than that, son," said Roth. "Let her go. She's not going anywhere without Macaw."

"Son?" asked Alexa as Paul pushed her into the center of the room and kept the gun trained on her.

"Oh, yes, you didn't know? Paul's my son," said Roth. "I taught him all I know about the business."

"You're the one who visited me in my room. You set that fire!" Alexa yelled at Paul.

"Your evasion skills are especially impressive, Alexa," Roth said and nodded. "You managed to evade my buddies at the INS a few times—even in San Diego, and then those poor excuses for hired guns in Mexico couldn't even get to you!"

"You should have listened when you had the chance," Paul sneered. "If you had just shut your trap and gone home to Fallbrook, none of this would have happened."

"Oh, but that's not true," said Roth. "This was preordained. Don't you see, son? Augustina has come back to me—through Alexa."

"Dad, she's a reporter! Use your head. They're going to notice she's missing."

"Be quiet, Paul. Everything will be fine. No one noticed when Shannon disappeared, remember?"

"Where's Shannon?" Alexa was almost afraid to find out.

"We're holding her here."

"You took her from *Diablo* Street?"

"Of course, I couldn't have her running her trap to everyone."

When Alexa's hand grazed her pocket and she felt her mother's rosary beads, it gave her an idea. "My mother loved to sing," she said.

"Ah, yes. I heard her singing to you once when she thought no one could hear. The voice of a nightingale."

"I like to sing, too."

"You do! That's splendid. Sing for me, Augustina," Roth said, smiling at her.

"I don't like an audience."

"Of course. Go check on our other guests, Paul."

"Dad, that's not a good idea—"

"Go!"

Paul skulked from the room, and Alexa began singing the Spanish nursery rhyme her mother used to sing, then she started on other nursery rhyme favorites. After a few minutes, Roth closed his eyes and smiled. This was Alexa's chance! Still singing, she reached down and pulled the knife from the sheath on her leg and slipped out the door. Just as she dashed down the hall toward where Paul had gone, she heard Roth cry, "Don't stop singing, Augustina. It's so beautiful."

She managed to run several yards before she felt Paul grab her from behind. With one quick backward thrust, she stabbed him in the stomach with the knife and his hands loosened their hold. Swinging around, she watched the surprise on his face turn to horror as he collapsed to his knees. That's for Miguel, she thought as she wrenched the gun from his grasp and demanded, "Where's Macaw?"

"I'll never tell you, bitch."

"I've got reinforcements coming—including the paramedics. You tell me where he is, I tell them where you are."

He held his stomach and looked down to see that his hands were covered with blood. "Swear it?" he pleaded.

Alexa nodded.

"Back of the house in the spa room," he sputtered. "Arched door on the right."

Alexa sprinted down the hallway. Just as she reached the door, she heard Roth bellow his son's name. She cursed when she found the door locked.

"Stand back!" she yelled, waiting for a brief moment before firing a shot at the doorknob and watching it buck loose to dangle against the door. One swift kick and she was in, almost crying out at the sight of Macaw, splayed out in the center of the room. She rushed to his side and checked his pulse. Burning up, but still alive.

Sensing someone behind her, Alexa swung around to see Shannon holding a glass of water.

"I think she's dead," said the girl, pointing to Imelda's lifeless body floating face-first in the Jacuzzi. "After she bit him, he was so mad, he pushed her into the water. He just passed out a little while ago. I've been trying to bring him to."

"Macaw! Wake up, damn it! You can't leave me," Alexa cried as she set the gun down and stroked his face. "Please, please, wake up!"

"There you are, Augustina," said Roth's voice from the open doorway.

Before Alexa knew what had happened, Shannon grabbed Macaw's gun and pointed it at her father.

"Shannon, baby, put that down," he soothed. "You're upset. Why don't we get you some medicine?"

"Like the medicine you gave me to shut me up about what you did to me and all of those little girls? That medicine, Daddy?"

"C'mon, Shannon, you want drugs? I'll give you all you want. Drop the gun. You're just confused right now," demanded Roth as sirens wailed in the distance. Tatiana's reinforcements finally arriving.

"No, Daddy, you're confused if you think I'm going to let you hurt any more little girls."

Alexa sat by Macaw's side transfixed as Shannon pulled the trigger three times, hitting her father in the face and chest and splattering blood all over the doorway. With a look of disbelief, Roth swayed for a few seconds before falling backward into the hallway.

So intent was she on the sight in the doorway that Alexa jumped when Macaw said in a husky voice, "Damn, you're finally here. My hero."

"There you go again, being sweet," said Alexa.

"How many times I have to tell you, I'm not even close to swee—"

Alexa cut him off with a kiss on the mouth.

2 MONTHS LATER

The hurricane season had passed by the time Macaw was strong enough for an extended car ride. This special day had dawned clear and cloudless. Fitting, Alexa thought as they wound their way down the coast toward Land's End.

The last several weeks at Aunt Lupe's had been idyllic. Lazy days spent enjoying the garden, taking baths together, fattening up on delicious food. After that night at Roth's, Macaw spent two weeks in the hospital. He had become dangerously septic from the dog bite and suffered a concussion and three broken ribs. Once she got him settled at Aunt Lupe's, Alexa pampered him. He made a poor patient at first, but finally became accustomed to two women fussing over him as if he were the only man within 100 miles.

"Rodolfo's wife called. She's ecstatic," said Alexa. "Wants to thank you for giving him the job managing your bar. Except for an occasional drunken fight, he is away from the violence, and she's thrilled."

"No problem, I was happy to do it. He's thorough and level-headed. And I'm going to need someone like that, especially next week."

"Yeah, why?" Alexa smiled.

"You change your mind?"

"Never, but I'm not changing my last name."

"What's wrong with Elvia?"

"Nothing, but everyone knows me by my writing name."

Macaw nodded. "Ramona has some killer tuxes ready for the big day. She even talked Ron into wearing one."

"She certainly has a way with men. You should have seen her fawning all over my dad. He lapped it up, and boy was Violet pissed!"

Macaw laughed. "I saw. I think Violet asked him out that night, didn't she?"

"Yes, she did. Finally. Maybe I should thank Ramona."

"Your aunt and Violet make quite a pair in the kitchen. The food at the reception is going to be fantastic."

Alexa looked out the window and smiled. Life was good. Esperanza was coming the next day to help her pick out a dress. Thrilled over what he and the publisher considered her best story ever about Roth's trafficking empire and its welcome downfall, Peter was surprised about the wedding, but planned to attend. They were holding the ceremony at Aunt Lupe's hacienda, followed by a smaller event a few days later at the ranch.

"You sure you're okay with starting a story in Peru for our honeymoon?" asked Alexa. "It'll be far from relaxing."

"We've taken it easy for more than two months. I'm getting antsy, and I don't want you to lose your job. They'll only wait so long. Besides, those Peruvians make some killer *empanadas*."

"You're going as my bodyguard?"

"Hell, I thought you were my bodyguard. While I love covering you and all, I think after our trip I'm going to enroll at the police academy in San Diego."

"Police academy!"

"Don't sound so shocked. I'm thinking after I pay my dues, I can become a sketch artist. Hell, I could even work for the FBI—maybe follow you around."

"Your mama will be excited. I know you told me she has never been thrilled with you owning a bar."

"She's more excited about me marrying you. I've had to sit on the phone and listen to her yack and yack about her dress and shoes. And she has made me promise a million times that I'll rush her from the airport to the hair stylist Aunt Lupe recommended."

Macaw shifted in his seat and peered up ahead. "Is that the rock outcropping Shannon told you about?"

"I think that's the spot."

"How's Shannon doing, anyway?"

"Great. She has been clean for two months now. She didn't say it, but I think she was relieved that Paul pulled through. He'll be spending many years in prison, though."

The impressive stone outcropping on the beach below at Land's End rose into view as they pulled over and hopped out of the car.

"Shannon said that the *descanso* is right next to the road," said Alexa, searching the highway's shoulder for the flat headstone that marked the spot where her mother's car ran off the road. It didn't take long to find the intricately engraved marble stone. She knelt down and wiped the highway dust off, revealing the inscription, *Beloved Augustina*. Next to it she set the vase of daisies she had brought. *Dia de los muertos.* All her life, Alexa heard about this Latin holiday that honored the lives of those who had passed away. Today she celebrated it.

"I hate to give Roth any credit," she said, "but my mother's headstone is beautiful. I know her remains are in the cemetery back in Fallbrook, but I feel a connection with her here, where she spent her final seconds of life." Alexa reached into her pant pocket and removed her mother's rosary beads.

"I finally understand, Mama. You never left me," she said aloud. "I'm sure you already know this, but Papa had no idea about Freddy. He thought his brother was a hero to bring me home. I know that all you and Papa ever wanted was for me to be happy, and I can honestly say that I am."

From the *descanso*, Alexa walked into the middle of the road and looked out at the ocean.

"What are you doing?" Macaw called out. "There's a truck coming."

"They say that on a clear day if you look through the arches made by the outcropping down there on the beach you can see Mazatlan." Alexa searched the horizon.

"You can find what you're looking for without standing in oncoming traffic."

Macaw was right. Alexa turned and walked out of the road right into his waiting arms.

EPILOGUE

Ramona Valdez looked at herself in the mirror in the restaurant's opulent lady's room. She needed a fresh coat of lipstick. Opening her shiny, gold evening bag, she extracted a tube of maroon lipstick and painted her lips, her brown eyes flashing back at her, wary, alert.

She knew. She always did. Right before anything happened. It was the sixth sense she relied on to survive in the underworld she'd been navigating for the past several years.

Hector's time was just about up. She could feel and see it. The furtive glances cast his way. The tension in his enforcer's jaw. The whispers that stopped when he walked into a meeting or restaurant, like tonight. They'd be disposing of him soon. She just had no idea when or how.

Admiring herself in the tight-fitting, gold evening gown covered in black sequins that accented her many curves, she considered again asking Macaw to keep an ear open for chatter, but she didn't want to put him in danger. He'd helped her so much with her sister already. Besides, he had his own life to live now with Alexa. She'd never seen him so happy.

Fluffing her black, lustrous hair with her hands, Ramona noted how good she looked tonight. Definitely the part of a first-class mistress. Just a hint of cleavage showing at the top of the scooped neck of her dress. The rest of her bosom reserved for Hector's private viewing pleasure later.

Ramona took a deep breath and crossed herself before exiting the bathroom. Once back in the restaurant's dining room, she stiffened at the sight of the table she'd been sitting at with Hector. It was empty. He and his bodyguard always waited for her. As she considered her next move, a large hand gripped her upper arm and began guiding her to the front door.

No point in protesting. There was nowhere to run. The elimination had obviously begun.

See what happens with Ramona in *Discovered Indiscretions*.

A NOTE FOR YOU

Dear Reading Gem,

Thanks for spending time with me, Alexa and Macaw! While each of the books in the Discovered Truth Series can be read as a standalone, it's fun to experience the progression and get to know the characters. The series progresses as minor characters introduced in each book become main characters in subsequent books. It's exciting to see what they'll do next!

The Discovered Truth series features complex, gutsy women and equally complicated, charismatic men who find themselves immersed in dangerous and intriguing modern-day challenges, such as human trafficking, drug smuggling, national security threats, and identity theft. When the heroine and hero meet, worlds collide and sparks fly, kindling unforgettable romance and intrigue.

If you like the series, please leave a review and comment. Your opinion matters and is incredibly powerful.

Thanks again and talk soon!

STAY ENLIGHTENED

Thanks for reading! Let's stay in touch. In appreciation of you, I post updates, insider information, and sneak peeks of upcoming books on my website at https://www.juliebawdendavis.com/fiction. You can also email me at Julie@JulieBawdenDavis.com, follow me on Facebook, and find me on Amazon.

Even better, you can join my VIP Reading Gems mailing list here. I also created a Facebook group especially for you! Join Julie's Reading Gems to get the inside scoop on what's going on with the Discovered Truth Series. Find out how characters are created, and what they might do next. I also ask for Reading Gem opinions on upcoming covers and even plot twists. And there are contests and giveaways!

Escape to Unforgettable Romance and Intrigue...

BOOKS IN THE DISCOVERED TRUTH SERIES

Discovered Beginnings:
(FREE at https://www.juliebawdendavis.com/fiction)
Discovered Secrets
Discovered Memories
Discovered Indiscretions
Discovered Liaisons
Discovered Betrayal
Discovered Denial
Discovered Distractions
Discovered Deception
Discovered Lies
Discovered Vengeance
Discovered Redemption
Discovered Obsession
Discovered Transgressions
Discovered Suspicion
Discovered Escape
Discovered Promises
Discovered Cover-up
Discovered Intentions

Box Sets

The Discovered Truth Series Box Set Books 1-4

The Discovered Truth Series Box Set Books 5-8

The Discovered Truth Series Box Set Books 9-12

The Discovered Truth Series Box Set Books 13-16